CREEK

D0149323

OLD DEPOT

FALCON/MAIN

SWALLOW

WAXWING

YELLOW LEGS

ROOKSVILLE

SANTA MARIA PUBLIC LIBRARY

N

A. Isaac & David Lawson's house
B. Rooksville Presbyterian Church
C. Fire Station
D. Post Office
E. Courthouse
F. Fountain Park

G. Pearson's Bakery
H. Gas-N-Go
I. Railroad spur
J. Duck Blind Restaurant
K. Chum's Hardware

Mercy Creek

Mercy Creek

Matt Matthews

Hub City Press
Spartanburg, SC

First printing, May 2011
Second printing, May 2011
Cover design: Emily Louise Smith
Interior design: JoAnn Mitchell Brasington
Proofreaders: Megan DeMoss, Jan Scalisi
Author photo: Randy Tyner
Front map: Harold Tarleton
Printed in Saline, MI by McNaughton & Gunn Inc.
Cover image: Marsh Blush © Michel McNinch, oil, 16x20, michelmcninch.com

Library of Congress Cataloging-in-Publication Data

Matthews, Matt, 1964-
      Mercy Creek / Matt Matthews. -- 1st ed.
      p. cm.
      ISBN 978-1-891885-77-8 (hardcover : alk. paper)
      1. Teenage boys—Fiction. 2. City and town life—Virginia—Fiction.
      3. Secrecy—Fiction. 4. Vandalism—Fiction. 5. Eccentrics and eccentricities—
      Fiction. I. Title.
PS3613.A849M47 2011
813'.6—dc22   2010041416

This project is made possible by a Library Services and Technology Act grant from the Institute of Museum
and Library Services administered by the South Carolina State Library and by the South Carolina Arts
Commission and Humanities Council SC.

186 West Main Street
Spartanburg SC 29306
864-577-9349 www.hubcity.org

For all the Saints:

▶ ■ ❤ ● ◀

❤ Rachel, comrade, *te entrego esta centuria*; ● Joseph, Benjamin, and John Mark, entrusted to our care; ▶ Mom and Pops, to whom I was entrusted; ■ Janet Peery, who read a flawed early draft of these pages but said "keep writing this"; ● Tom Hester, patron, critic, friend.

1

Isaac pulled the covers up to his chin and laced his fingers over his chest, pretending he was lying in state at the baseball hall of fame where hordes of fans had lined up for one last glimpse of their favorite first baseman. That felt good—pretending he was the one who had gone away and that everyone else was left behind missing him.

Hanging just below his ceiling were the balloons that his girlfriend Jenny had tied to his 16th birthday present—a potted geranium. It was the best she could do, she said, before she left town right after final exams for her summer job. Her mother owned Always In Bloom out on the highway. A plant was convenient.

This was the first Friday of summer vacation. But Jenny was gone, and she couldn't hide her enthusiasm about leaving. And though Isaac was glad Mr. Chum had hired him at 50 cents above minimum wage at the hardware store, it was just sinking in that he would spend most of his daylight hours working in that warehouse with the likes of Crazy Eddie giving him a hard time.

The phone had rung at six o'clock and awakened him. His father, David, stumbled out of bed in the next bedroom and practiced saying hello with impossible enthusiasm like an announcer on a late-night infomercial selling knives.

"Hello," Isaac's dad said. "No, no. I was awake."

It was a lie. His preacher father was never awake at six a.m. It was Isaac's mother who had been the early riser. She, not his father, had handled the home front, answered the phone, took the lead in family decisions.

"Yes, well, Ina, the waiting is the hardest part. Yes, yes."

Isaac's mother had always said that, that the waiting was the hardest part. She had a hundred zingers like that. Every black cloud has a silver lining. You can't know about someone else unless you walk a mile in their shoes. She'd been dead less than a year, and though they had annoyed him when she was alive, whenever these little sayings popped into his head it was like a part of her had never left. He hated it when somebody stole her words, like his father was doing now.

Isaac was tired of pretending to be a corpse, so he punched his pillow and stuck his feet out from underneath his quilt. The balloons, only a weekend old, were running out of air. The plant looked sick. Five birthday cards sat on his dresser next to his blue lava lamp. He squeezed his eyes shut and thought about Jenny in Virginia Beach working at her aunt's bed and breakfast. She got to swim in the ocean anytime she wanted, got to cruise the strip with her cousin, got to hear the bands on the boardwalk. He wondered how she was doing. Maybe he'd send her a potted plant.

Like it or not, he was the one left behind, stuck and restless in Rooksville. He got up and checked his cell phone on the bedside table. No message. No missed calls. No surprise.

He grabbed his chin-up bar in the doorjamb and pulled himself up. Blisters on his hands from work had popped and were covering over with calluses but were still tender. His shoulders ached from all the hauling he'd done at the warehouse, but he pulled anyway, and he pulled hard. One. He gritted his teeth. Two. By the end of the summer, he wanted to get to fifty. He could only do twelve, on a good day.

He watched the blue globs of wax in his lava lamp change from one surreal shape to another. And he listened to his dad on the phone.

Knowing it was Ina Greer made it easier for Isaac to piece things together. Mrs. Greer was in charge of the church prayer chain, and six a.m. wasn't too early for these eight or ten church ladies to begin calling each other if they thought somebody or something needed praying over.

Isaac knew by his father's tone that this was no emergency. Always an expert at sounding interested, he was humming little yeses between Ina's words. Isaac had had whole conversations with him that he'd have to repeat because his dad was more interested in *Newsweek*. His father sounded perfectly tuned in with Ina Greer, which meant it was possible that, after her first few lines, he hadn't heard a thing.

"Kerry is with him," his dad said. "He's got the support he needs. Uh-huh. And the kids? Yes. Too young to know. Right."

Mystery solved. Ina was calling about Kerry Lange's grown son, Albert, who was having surgery on his testicles. It had been on the prayer chain for weeks and was announced during the concerns in worship for the last two Sundays. They found a lump and suspected cancer. The most dramatic words on the prayer chain were they and lump. They almost always meant doctors. And talk of lumps made everyone whisper.

Isaac had seen the ladies huddle between Sunday school and worship to discuss prayer concerns. Sometimes he'd sit on the steps leading to the children's classrooms and eavesdrop. And he couldn't help but to listen to his mother when she had gotten calls. Marie Lawson had loved the prayer chain because it was a great way to keep in touch with the natives, as she put it. Many times her dinner grew cold as Isaac and his dad ate silently, listening to Marie ask questions about somebody's mother-in-law's gallbladder.

The first five pull-ups were the easiest, but the least efficient. His body didn't want to go up, and his thin, protesting arms didn't want to do all the work. By number six, he found a better rhythm. Like lava, his body became fluid, all the muscles working together, every ounce of energy harnessed to get his 155 pounds up to that silver bar. He could hardly feel six and seven. No pain, only the trickles of sweat and the pounding of his pulse in his ears. Eight. Isaac tried not to think of poor Albert Lange losing his balls. Nine.

Isaac's dad spoke to Ina Greer with his characteristic soothing voice, steady and deep. Everything his dad said seemed to come out slick. Isaac wasn't good with words. Two weeks before, his coach had tapped him to give a speech at the team's year-end banquet. Isaac didn't want to, but the coach said the guy with the best batting average had to give a speech. It went with the territory. So Isaac did, reluctantly. He read every typed word without once looking up. He quoted Jefferson, Vince Lombardi, and Archibald Norman, who had founded the town when the railroad put in a spur through the middle of the potato fields. Isaac talked about hard work and never giving up. When he finished, he was so glad it was over it took him a moment to realize the applause was for him. The coach called it a home run.

Isaac tried not to think of Jenny. But he missed the feel of her long hair when he held her and the heat of her breath when they kissed.

Ten. He was slowing down. His strength was evaporating.

He tried to think of the Jenny that got him mad, the Jenny that was smiling when she waved goodbye. That was what might get him over the hump. That was what might get him a few more. Eleven.

He thought about the car insurance (twelve), and the things he couldn't afford (thirteen), and the things he couldn't change (fourteen). Almost every cent of his first four paychecks was going towards his car insurance. No insurance, no license is what his dad said. The toll across the Chesapeake Bay Bridge Tunnel was ten dollars each way. There was gas to buy and the cost of dates. And time. With traffic, it was a two-hour drive.

His pulse was pounding now, and his eyes stung with sweat. He caught a glimpse of the cottonwoods shedding their blossoms into the brightening sky like wisps of snow. Halfway to fifteen. Snow in the middle of June was about as likely as him having a good summer in this nowhere hick town. Fifteen.

Halfway to sixteen was as far as Isaac could go. His feet ached as he dropped to the floor. Gathering his rubbery, numb arms to his chest, he fell face first into his cool pillow. He could hear the annoying drone of his dad's electric razor, and he felt lightheaded, splotches of black floating across his field of vision.

Isaac had spent past summers playing baseball. This summer he wanted to make money, and Chum's Hardware was as good a place as any to do it. He couldn't fit both a job and the select team in, so baseball got the ax. His school coach didn't like it, but Isaac told him he'd come back for his junior year stronger and mentally ready. That's where the pull-ups came in. Most of Isaac's friends were playing, though, and judging from the schedule posted at the American Legion he'd never see them. They had games all over the state.

His friends would be traveling. His Jenny would be gone until Labor Day. And his mother wasn't around to do whatever it was she did that made him know everything was going to be all right. He was not only stranded in Rooksville, he was stranded alone.

A miniature crime spree had spiced things up, however, which made for interesting gossip and flashy headlines in the weekly newspaper. There had been two break-ins in town since May. Two homes had been vandalized, and P.O.T.S.—People of the Shore—was offering a $5,000 reward for information leading to a conviction. Though he didn't think the crime spree had made it on the prayer chain, it was big news.

Five thousand dollars would perk up Isaac's summer prospects. He had no idea how he could ever catch whoever was responsible for the break-ins, but that didn't stop him from thinking about the reward. He curled up into a ball on top of his covers, listing all the things he could do with that kind of cash.

Season tickets to Oriole games. A new first baseman's glove. Speakers for the car. A letter jacket for the fall. Cable TV—which was another thing his dad didn't like. "We've got enough drama in our lives without watching other people's on cable TV," he had said. Besides, on his pastor's salary, he not only couldn't afford it, but didn't want to pay for it. But if Isaac had the money, he could pay the bill. He'd take that rusted antenna on the roof and chuck it into the flowerbed.

His father didn't want Isaac messing around with the break-ins. They had talked about it one day over dinner at the Duck Blind. It was dangerous was all he would say. And couldn't Isaac think of better things to do than start sniffing at the trail of a local criminal? Isaac figured his dad didn't think he was old enough or smart enough to do it, which is why, of course, he vowed he would.

✟ ✟ ✟

"What are you going to do, sleep all day?" His father leaned against the frame of Isaac's open door. He had a clean-shaved, damp face. His tie dangled around his neck, untied. His suspenders hung like lassos from his waist. "It's almost 7:15," he said, holding out a box of frozen waffles. "You want some breakfast?"

"I must have dozed off," Isaac said. "I heard you talking to Ina Greer this morning."

"Yes, yes. The ladies are praying for Albert Lange. Thought I needed to be kept in the loop." He looked at his wristwatch. "He's having surgery right now. They found a lump—"

"I know," Isaac said. "I know."

"You're looking a little blue," David Lawson said. He had a folded newspaper in his other hand.

Isaac slipped out of bed, covering his pillow and smoothing the quilt with heavy arms, then sat lightly on the edge of the made bed and looked down at his toenails.

"Have you had time to look at the vacation brochures I gave you?"

Isaac shook his head.

"Lily at the travel agency has a bunch of them, from everywhere."

Isaac said uh-huh and nodded.

"Or we could stay here on the Shore," his dad said. "Go up to Chincoteague like last year. The Watsons still say it's not too late to use their house. The pony penning is always pretty neat."

"We do that every year."

"That's because we like it," his dad said. "Don't we?"

Virginia's Eastern Shore was all Isaac had known. Rooksville was a sleepy small town nestled on the sandy bay side of the Shore. That's how the chamber of commerce website described it. Aerial photos of the town showed it laid out in a near perfect grid of short streets fronted by the Chesapeake Bay and bounded on two sides by the swooping loop of the southern branch of Norman Creek.

From the air, the water and land of his hometown fit together like a puzzle. He'd traipsed through those marshes and creeks and fished on the bay. He'd hit his first homerun in Little League at Norman Park, and he'd learned to drive on the less traveled part of Kingfisher Street that led over Norman Creek, past the new high school, and out of town.

But on the ground, Rooksville was boring. There was no mall and only one place to get french fries after nine o'clock at night. By sunset, everybody either was going to sleep or had gone somewhere else.

Chincoteague to the north was much the same, except in the summer when it became a tourist trap. And home to wild ponies during the annual penning. Isaac liked the crowds and the ponies and the fact that I Scream!, an ice cream parlor, kept late hours.

"Maybe it would be good to get off the Shore this year," Isaac heard himself saying. "I only have a week off, though. That's not much time."

"A road trip, maybe," his father said excitedly. "Father and son on the open highway."

"I only have a week," Isaac said again.

His father seemed to droop, then stepped into the room and sat down in the desk chair, opening *The Shore News*.

If his mother were alive they'd not be having this conversation. His mom would be the go-between. She'd have a sense of direction of what the family wanted and needed, of the best place to go. She'd take a poll. Plant ideas. They'd probably go to Chincoteague for a week of swimming and poking around in the small shops. Isaac and his dad would scout out a good place on the east side of the island from which to watch the ponies being swum across the sound from Assateague, then they'd make the rounds to the pens to see the ponies huddling together before they were separated from their mothers and sold off. They had to thin the herd annually because Assateague couldn't sustain them, but it seemed crueler to Isaac this year.

"I feel like I should be happy," Isaac said. He wasn't sure he wanted to share his misgivings about the summer with his dad, but who else was there? "I mean, I've got the whole summer in front of me. But there's nothing to do."

"Right," his father said, holding the front page at arm's length. He wasn't wearing his reading glasses.

"It's different for you," Isaac said quietly.

"Sure it is," his dad said. He looked over the paper.

"I mean, you're content. You visit old folks all day long and they tell you things they've told you before. They give you homemade jelly."

"Yes, yes." His dad nodded, then looked up, startled. "What did you say?"

"And your girlfriend's not so far away," Isaac continued.

"I don't have a girlfriend, son." His father was blushing.

But it was true. Clara Edwards, the church treasurer, liked his company as much as he liked hers. She was pretty. Her little Tom, who had just finished kindergarten, was the only thing good that had come from a brief marriage to her ex, who would be in the state pen until Tom got to college.

"You and Miss Edwards having dinner. You and Miss Edwards having budget meetings. It might make it to the prayer chain pretty soon."

"Maybe you should try breaking into houses," his father said at last, irritably handing Isaac the paper.

Vandals Strike Again
by Ronnie Greene

Rooksville—Another vandalized house has been ruined by what Police Chief Reginald Williams thinks might be an "expensive prank."

Nathan G. Parramore's Cowry Street home was discovered flooded Thursday, June 8, by a neighbor who called police.

Williams said someone entered the house, stopped up the sink and bathtub drains, and left all indoor water faucets running. Flames were painted on the wall in an upstairs bedroom, Williams said.

He said the water had been left running for as long as four days when the neighbor last visited the house, ironically, to water the indoor plants as a favor to Parramore, who is in a Norfolk hospital recovering from surgery.

Two other houses were vandalized similarly last month.

"2002 is turning out to be quite the year for property damage and frayed nerves," Williams said. "I'm puzzled, because in each case there is no sign of a break-in. No broken glass, no obviously picked locks. Nothing."

Williams reports no suspects. He confirmed that People of the Shore (P.O.T.S.), a local civic group, is offering a $5,000 reward to anyone who provides information leading to the arrest and conviction of those responsible. However, Williams said the P.O.T.S. reward is not linked to his department's ongoing investigation.

"Same story," his dad said, as Isaac finished reading and handed the paper back. "Flames painted on the walls. All the drains stopped up and the faucets left running. Hit Nathan Parramore's house this time. Swamped it pretty good." His father was humming. "Old Nathan's in Norfolk getting his knee replaced. He's a member of our church, you know. Seldom comes."

"If I got that reward money, maybe things would look up," Isaac said sullenly. "I'll buy us cable TV, for starters. Orioles' season tickets. And Baltimore hotels for night games." He straightened the *Sports Illustrateds* on his bedside table. "I wouldn't be so strapped for money," he said. "Buy some stuff. That might be nice. For a change."

"Like I told you before," his dad said into the paper, "I think that's a really bad idea. Think your summer's bad now, try getting mixed up with the pushers at the bottom of these break-ins."

"I'm not getting mixed up with anybody," Isaac said. "And how do you know it's pushers?"

"It fits."

Isaac got up, pulled his cut-offs on, then stood by the window. The antique glass had bubbles in it, which his mother had said was one of the things that had attracted them to buy this house. The sun had climbed just above the cedar hedgerow on the tomato field across the street. Yellow light filled the room. Mr. Whitcomb lurched past in his green pickup, tired gears shifting. The cottonwood blossoms drifted across the road into the cedars. It was hard to see the world through rippled glass.

David Lawson flipped through the pages, stopping in the middle section. "Our vacation bible school ad made it in," he said, "and with only one typo. They left the second 'a' out of vacation." His father said the word aloud a few times and laughed to himself. Vaction Bible School. "VBS'll give you something to do this summer," his dad said. "It's only two weeks away. Every little kid in town is looking forward to the puppet show you do every year. My famous son."

"I never officially told Mrs. Greer that I would do it," Isaac said. Ina Greer did a little of everything at their church. "I'm getting a little old for puppet shows, don't you think?"

"Tell that to the people at Sesame Street. Big Bird is big business. Besides, Ina Greer is counting on you."

"So?"

His dad crumpled the paper in his lap. For once his father seemed at a momentary loss for words, a moment Isaac knew would not last. "When you were a kid, everybody gave to you. So, now's your chance to give something back."

Isaac could feel a sermon coming on.

"All winter long people have been giving things to us. It's right for us, for you, to give back. People have been making us meals. Taking us out. Inviting us over to their family gatherings because they thought that without your mother we didn't have a family. But we do."

"I know," Isaac said. "I know."

But his dad wasn't listening. "You and I are a family, and we are part of a bigger family, this church, for one thing, and this community, this boring community which has been very good to us, for another. I just think it's worth giving back to. We're not supposed to be selfish with our time and gifts. We're supposed to share." His father was standing now with his frozen waffles and the newspaper.

"Is the sermon over?" Isaac asked.

"Yes," his father said, looking suddenly embarrassed. "Everything but the closing hymn."

That caught Isaac off guard. "That's funny," Isaac chuckled softly. "Everything but the closing hymn."

"Yeah," his father said, slowly exhaling. "I'm sorry. It's just that in a small church everybody's got to chip in to make it work. Seems like I preach that to everybody, even you. Sorry. I'm paid to do church work, of course, and you're not. I understand. Guess I'd play hooky some too, if I could get by with it. I'd start by getting them to take me off that stupid prayer chain, for one thing." His father looked at his wrist watch. "It can't still be 7:15," he said, tapping the glass of his Timex with the corner of the waffle box.

Isaac looked at his alarm clock. It glowed 7:45. He stepped into his Nikes and started tying them fast.

"I'll drive you," his dad said.

"I could drive myself," Isaac said, lacing the other shoe.

"I keep forgetting we have two cars. Fewer drivers. Right," his father said. "Well, don't speed."

"I'll walk," Isaac said, putting on a belt and slipping his keys in his front pocket. He imagined fingering $5,000 in crisp one hundred dollar bills. Do rich people worry about being late? Surely their lives were easier. Had to be. Isaac glanced in his mirror and ran his fingers through his hair. He turned for his bedroom door and his dad awkwardly stepped out of his way. They looked into each other's faces, and Isaac was shocked that he was a tad taller than his father.

"Here," his dad said, ceremoniously presenting the box of frozen waffles. "This is my body given for you. Do this in remembrance of me."

It was what his dad said at communion in church. These were words he had committed to memory, words that sounded good whether he meant them or not, words he could say without thinking. They were like the little yeses he had said to Mrs. Greer that morning, like all the distracted uh-huhs and rights he had offered up automatically when Isaac was trying to say something, was trying to be heard.

"It'll thaw before you get there."

Isaac took a waffle out of the box and stepped past his father for the stairs. "Thanks for the balanced breakfast," Isaac said, taking the steps by twos. He thought of Albert Lange under the knife that very moment and wondered if Albert knew that every Presbyterian on the Eastern Shore was praying for his testicles. The world must be filled with people like Albert, uncertain and afraid of the future. He hit the front door running, bound for Chum's.

2

The warehouse behind the hardware store was dark and cool. Bulbs hung from the bare wooden rafters. Eddie was opening the big, sliding doors onto the fenced lumberyard. Light flooded in, and that, with the movement of work, would warm the place.

Isaac stood panting before the bulletin board where his timecard was thumb-tacked. It was 7:59, according to the dusty wall clock. He had run the several blocks over, cutting through Miss Thomson's backyard from the alley.

He had gotten a postcard from Jenny and thumb-tacked it next to his timecard. She'd only been gone four days when the card had arrived. He had stood at the mailbox and smelled it and imagined her fingers touching it, touching him, his face. He had pressed his lips onto her cursive words and had been embarrassed when Mr. Whitcomb had hollered out from next door, "You're supposed to read the mail, not eat it!"

It was a picture of the Cavalier Hotel at the north end of the public beach, sitting grandly atop the terraced hill overlooking Pacific Avenue. The bed and breakfast Jenny's aunt owned was nearby. This was Jenny's backyard, her playground. A world of touristy fun and excitement. Wax museums. Mini golf. Live music. He pictured himself there. With Jenny.

"You work here or just stand around?" It was Eddie, holding a glass coffeepot of water.

Last Halloween, on a dare, Isaac went with school friends out to Eddie's farm. Some boys kept running up to the porch ringing the doorbell. Isaac sat in the bed of Jim Freeman's pickup out on the road with Jenny, watching. They were wrapped up in a blanket. Jenny was laughing. Isaac's heart began to sink each time Eddie opened the door and hollered out into the darkness. The last time they rang the bell, Eddie bounded onto the porch and fired a shotgun into the air, blowing the gutter off the porch.

"Stupid kids!" he yelled out, loading.

They tore out, running the gravel road without headlights, laughing too hard the whole way. Isaac, though, didn't think it was funny, and had a hard time pretending, wrapped up in a blanket with someone who did. Isaac's friends had called him Crazy Eddie ever since.

Eddie did have a way of looking at you like you'd done something wrong. He was looking at Isaac that way now.

"Well?"

"I work here, Eddie. Chill out. I'm just checking in."

"Can't you figure the technology?" Eddie snatched the timecard from Isaac. He looked at it and said seven-fifty-nine quietly to himself. He looked at Isaac, poking the card back towards his face. "You take your pencil," Eddie said, "and you write down the time you get in."

"Right," Isaac said. "Can't you see that that's what I did?"

"You forgot one thing. The work part. Once you check in, you're supposed to get to work."

Though Mr. Chum was his boss, not Eddie, Isaac felt intimidated by Eddie. It took some effort standing up to his growling, however harmless it was.

"Eddie, did you have gasoline for breakfast?"

"What I had for breakfast is none of your dang business." Eddie poured the pot of water into the coffeemaker on the workbench under the cluttered bulletin board. Isaac pulled himself onto the narrow workbench that ran along the wall and sat with his legs dangling. He tried to look relaxed, though Eddie made him edgy. Better to make friends than enemies, his mother used to say.

He looked out over the half-lit warehouse. It was his job to clean and organize the whole place during the summer, a job seemingly not done since Chum's opened in 1922. The founding Mr. Chum was dead. His son, Billy, had continued the business, and his son, William, ran things now.

Billy dropped in a couple of times a week to chat with the regulars who sat around the potbellied stove near the center of the store. People always came in to shoot the breeze. William ran the store with his wife, Susan, who did the books. Their son, Will, ran the lumberyard out back. They were all named William Ball Chum, but numbered differently. It was a small-town dynasty.

Eddie wore denim overalls on his scarecrow frame and a freshly ironed, white, short-sleeved shirt. He looked as if he shaved every other day, and his stubble had some red left in it around his chin. The thick hair on his head looked like a whitecap in the bay. At nearly six-and-a-half feet, he was wiry with an enormous strike zone. On some days he looked to be nearly a hundred, but he worked like a younger man. He covered lots of ground in those long strides and could handle awkward pieces of lumber with an ease Isaac could not match.

Everybody in town knew Eddie. Eddie worked in the lumberyard some, did all the carpentry work and painting and small repairs to the buildings, and made deliveries each afternoon. Mostly he stayed out of everyone's way, and they stayed out of his. As far as Isaac knew, Eddie had worked here his whole life.

Eddie was standoffish, but that didn't stop Isaac from trying to hook him into conversation. Trying to get him to talk was a game.

"Eddie, ever dream of getting out of this town?"

"Nope," he said, as he busied himself putting the lid back onto the coffee tin.

"Don't you have any ambition?" Isaac winced. "Sorry, that came out wrong. But you've lived here all your life. I can't believe you never wanted to leave."

"Who said I never wanted to leave? There was a time when I wanted to, and I did. Just like that."

"You did?"

"Why, of course. A man's got to do what a man's got to do. And there was a time when I had to leave. Wanted to."

"What happened?"

"What do you mean, what happened? I left, that's what happened."

"Where'd you go?"

"College," Eddie said, "as if it's any of your business."

"You? You went to college?" Isaac felt himself blush. "Sorry, again."

"Yes, I went to college. Before that I was in the war. Came to Chum's in the fall of '52."

"Wow," Isaac said. "You got to see the world!"

"Don't be silly, boy. We were at war, for Pete's sake. It wasn't a vacation. Don't you know anything?" Eddie scowled.

"Where'd you go?"

"Navy, technically. I was really in the Coast Guard, but the Navy called the shots during the war. Stationed at Norfolk my whole hitch. Patrolled this very coast. I've seen the islands on both sides of the shore, the creeks and bays. Used to know my way around these marshes as well as a blue heron. What else you want to know? My social security number?"

"Where did you go to college?"

"RPI in Richmond. Didn't finish, though."

"Why not?"

"My daddy needed help with the farm, that's why. So, I came back."

"And you've been here ever since?"

Eddie grunted. He had begun absently putting tools in their places on the pegboard that hung next to the bulletin board. They were cheap tools: a hammer missing part of its claw, wooden-handled screwdrivers.

"You've been here ever since," Isaac said to the ceiling. "I don't see how you've stood it."

"You make do." Eddie let a piece of knotted pine drop onto the floor. He aimed it with the toe of his boot, then kicked it sliding towards the scrap pile by the door, a rooster tail of dust arching behind it.

"There's nothing to do here," Isaac said. "No wonder everybody moves away as soon as they get the chance."

"Good riddance to them," Eddie said. He was leaning against the counter now, holding his whiskered chin in one hand and idly working the joints of the fingers of his other.

"My dad says there's plenty to do, but what does he know?"

Eddie turned to the coffee maker and poured himself a cup. "I'd offer you some," he said, "but it'll stunt your growth, and you're short enough as it is."

Eddie stepped into a patch of sunlight. Isaac watched him look around the room, taking in its dark corners and high, sagging roof undergirded by sagging, crisscrossed rafters. Slats and beams of light found entry through cracks in the board walls and nail holes in the corrugated roof.

"You'd be wise to get to work, boy. Chum says he wants this place cleaner than clean, and it'll take every bit of the summer to do it."

Isaac hopped off the bench and swatted the seat of his pants with his palms; he studied the sawdust as it writhed up like tiny silkworms into the lit air.

"There's another thing," Eddie said. "You'd be wise to pay attention to your old man. He knows more than you think he does."

"Right," Isaac said with a groan. "Everybody thinks my dad is so wonderful." He made himself look right into Eddie's eyes. "That's getting real old."

"I didn't say nothing about wonderful," Eddie said. "I just said he was smarter than you, which isn't hard."

"Whatever," Isaac said, shaking his head.

Eddie was quiet for a second. "Look," he said, "some people respect your father because he's done things. You know?"

"No," Isaac said. "I have no idea what you're talking about."

"He's done things," Eddie said. "Proven himself."

"What's that got to do with anything?"

"In this town? Everything," Eddie said, turning to look out the open warehouse doorway into the lumberyard filling with light. "Believe you me, son, it means everything."

Isaac headed for the store up front. He knew that one day he'd come back to this town having proven himself, whatever that meant. He'd come back having done something important. Invented something. Pinch hit in the World Series. Something. People who had never left the Shore would gather to ask him about his successes in the world. He'd try not to brag or talk down to them, and they would know him for himself, not as his father's son. Even Eddie would be surprised.

But for now, there was nothing to do. There was nothing on the Shore but this endless job with Crazy Eddie. Nothing exciting but an elusive $5,000 reward that he'd probably never touch. But in Virginia Beach there was Jenny. She was real.

And he could touch her.

3

There were baseball games that Isaac knew were lost by the end of the first inning. At the state high school tournament in Roanoke last spring, they had played a team that looked like weightlifters with beards and had started a pitcher who could make a fastball look like an aspirin.

The second Isaac looked at Jenny at her doorstep in Virginia Beach, he felt he was up against the same impossible odds. Maybe it was the way she awkwardly drummed her fingers on her thigh, but he knew something was up. And he knew it wasn't good.

Billy Birdsong was the biggest problem. Every part of his muscular body rippled beneath an even tan. He had a gold hoop earring and a small tattoo of flames at the base of his spine like his butt was on fire. He had a perfect chip in his front tooth. Jenny practically floated when she looked at Billy. It made Isaac sick.

They had decided to rollerblade to Rudy's on Friday evening after Isaac got there from the Shore after work. Jenny, her cousin Libby, Billy, and Billy's sidekick named "Tube" apparently went everywhere on rollerblades. Billy had an extra pair for Isaac. They were a half-size too small. When Billy strapped him in, he looked at Isaac sitting on the front steps of the Wild Flower and asked, "How's that?" Isaac said they were perfect. Isaac had never worn rollerblades and didn't know how they were supposed to feel. Jenny and her friends flitted around the driveway; it looked easy. When Isaac tried to stand, the plates of the earth's crust shifted and he landed on his butt, hitting his elbow going down. His right arm tingled for the next thirty hours. Jenny and her friends couldn't stop laughing. Libby said Isaac's clumsiness was cute. Billy helped Isaac up and helped break his frequent falls every block or so, all the way to Rudy's, which was nineteen blocks away. Isaac resented the charity.

After an expensive dinner that included three-dollar iced tea, they wove towards home on their rollerblades, making lazy circles around Isaac, who walked in his sock feet the whole way, one heavy skate in each hand, his feet raw with blisters.

They stopped at the Tastee Freeze. Isaac got a mint chocolate chip waffle cone. Jenny didn't want to share, and she had a new favorite, coffee bean. She wanted a cup—and only one scoop—because she was watching her weight. Isaac wanted to know since when she needed to watch her weight. She looked perfect.

Moonlight and a cool breeze played on the water. An orchestra generated applause and heat on the 35th Street stage on the boardwalk; people his grandparents' age danced to horn solos and the slapping of a spirited bass. Slower numbers were lifted on serene violins, which made the air tremble and caused goose bumps to rise on Isaac's forearms. This was exactly like he had imagined it would be. A lazy, moonlit night watching couples stroll down the boardwalk, hearing the heavy beat of cars cruising down Atlantic with open windows and radios throbbing. This is exactly what he wanted, except for one thing: Jenny didn't want him to be there.

Isaac watched Jenny watch the ocean. Her shoulder-length hair was pulled back in a wild ponytail. Wisps had come out and framed her brown face. She was wearing a yellow, clingy dress with a profusion of sunflowers blooming around her breasts. Billy Birdsong was trying to juggle balled-up napkins with a plastic spoon stuck on his nose. Isaac watched them all laugh. Jenny laughed the hardest, waving her palm lightly in front of her nose and delicious lips. Her tanned legs looked awkward manacled to clumsy rollerblades, but she was still gorgeous, still perfect. Every inch of her. She glimpsed Isaac watching her and she looked away, towards Billy. She immediately brightened. Isaac looked back out over the ocean.

They left for the Wild Flower just before midnight. Isaac took off his socks and walked alone on the wet sand. The refreshing water bore shards of moonlight weightlessly to the shore. The others skated lazily along the boardwalk. Billy Birdsong and Jenny drifted side by side.

Isaac slept on a couch in the laundry room. It was a soft nest out of the way of guests. With the kind of peck you'd give a puppy, Jenny kissed him on the forehead before trotting off to the attic room she and Libby shared. After what only seemed a nanosecond of sleep, it was time to wake up. Jenny's Aunt Frances had begun getting breakfast ready before five o'clock. Isaac stumbled into the bright kitchen to help.

Cinnamon rolls were on cookie sheets ready to go into the oven. A juicer sat on one side of the counter. Bags of English muffins and a tub of cream cheese, sticks of butter in oblong cut-glass dishes, and plastic canisters of granola cluttered the other side. Two big coffeepots gurgled, beginning to create morning smells that reminded him of the coffeepots in the store tended by Susan and William Chum, and the one in the warehouse kept by Eddie.

Limping, Isaac helped Frances to set the dining room table and beat two dozen eggs. "Does Jenny help you with breakfast?" Isaac asked as he beat the eggs.

"Usually, yes. Saturday is a big cleaning day, so I let the girls sleep in." Frances smiled as she sliced thin sausage patties. She was friendly in an efficient way.

"You're good at this," Isaac said, watching Frances move from one project to the next at the counter.

"Thanks," she said. "This was my aunt's place before it was mine. Except for changing the name to the Wild Flower, I do everything the way she did. She was a good teacher."

"Does Jenny like it here?"

"I think so," Frances said. "Libby sure likes the company. They hit it off real well; it's nice to get to know your cousin."

"We sure miss her back at home. Everybody in the church says hello." Isaac was putting slices of bread in the eight-slot toaster. "Does she miss home?" he asked.

"Have you asked her that question?"

"No, ma'am," Isaac said. "Not directly."

She smiled wistfully. "It took me years to miss my home on the Eastern Shore. But like everybody else, I had left. By the time I knew I missed it, I was too rooted here to go back. And, of course, I was another person." Frances winked and started grating a stick of cinnamon into the scrambled eggs.

↯ ↯ ↯

They swam in the ocean before lunch. They ate burgers at the Tastee Freeze. Billy Birdsong suggested an early movie. Jenny and Libby had to be back by three to begin stripping beds, washing sheets, and vacuuming for Sunday's arrivals. Jenny agreed to let Isaac help.

"A movie sounds great," Jenny said.

"That's not what you said this morning," Libby said.

Jenny cut her a sharp glance.

"A movie it is," said Billy.

Isaac barely had enough money for the bridge tunnel toll on the way home. He hadn't known how easy it was to blow a hundred bucks in less than twenty-four hours. Dinner had cost fifty bucks.

"I've got another idea," Isaac said. Everyone looked at him. He felt their collective gaze. Billy and Tube wore disinterested smirks. Libby seemed curious. Jenny looked embarrassed.

"I've never seen the Cavalier Hotel and I'd like to," Isaac said. "Could we go there?"

Jenny lightly shook her head no. Libby seemed open to the idea.

"I hear they have an indoor pool in the basement," Tube said. "The people who stay at the hotel don't even bother to go down there in the summer, is what I've heard. It's too hot."

"Let's go find out," Billy Birdsong said. "We can sneak in. We can skinny-dip."

Isaac noticed that Jenny blushed. And she smiled.

↯ ↯ ↯

Isaac came home early because it was pointless to stay. Jenny was as elusive as some pie-in-the-sky $5,000 reward. He helped Jenny and Libby clean. He worked furiously with the vacuum. He did the whole house, all three floors, in forty minutes. He thought alternately of Billy Birdsong and the sunflowers on the front of Jenny's gauzy, yellow dress. When the dryer was full, he emptied the washer and, as instructed, dutifully hung a load of thick towels neatly on the back line. The sun would bake them dry before dinner. Isaac cleaned three toilets and three bathtubs. Unlike the warehouse back home, the Wild Flower was so clean to begin with, he hardly could tell where they had cleaned and where they hadn't.

Libby and Jenny restocked the bathrooms and helped Frances get the grocery list together. When Libby and Frances went to the store together, Isaac felt awkward being alone in the house with Jenny. He sensed she felt it too.

They both were tired. The clothes on the line were almost dry. The bathrooms in the guest rooms gleamed. Isaac and Jenny sat in the living room and dozed. This was the first time he actually felt he was with her, that she was actually present. It would be his last, he figured too. He didn't know why that was true, only that it was. One more disappointment. One more loss.

When he woke up, he watched Jenny sleep. Then he got his backpack and set it by the door. He touched her arm.

She stirred awake and looked into his eyes. For a split second, it was the old Jenny. He was on his knees. She was draped across the couch. She looked like the John Singer Sargent painting of the woman on a couch he'd seen in one of his mom's art history books.

When his mother became less able to venture out of the house except for visits to doctors, she loved looking at art books. A year ago, his father picked Isaac up on the last day of school and drove him to the big bookstores in Virginia Beach. They bought as many oversized art books as they could find—all intense inks and glossy pages. Pissarro. Picasso. Monet. Degas. Studies in Cubism and Post Impressionism and Expressionism and Renaissance. Byzantine mosaics and Russian icons and African madonnas. Landscape artists like Cole and his friends in the Hudson River School. Mary Cassatt, Van Gogh, Hopper. Isaac liked the Winslow Homer pictures of the Bahamas and Modigliani's female nudes the best.

Isaac got the sense that his father hoped that if they could just buy enough art books, his mother wouldn't die. Whether David Lawson thought that or not, Isaac did by the time they got home. Isaac read the introductions to those books and looked at every single picture. If he could learn enough about the art his mother loved, she would have another reason to live. His devotion might somehow bend the will of her tiring body towards health, break the building momentum of cancer cells devouring her liver and ovaries and stomach.

The buying spree was a waste. His mother liked looking at the same pictures in the books she already owned. She told Isaac that the old pictures, like the one of the young woman reclining on that couch, were part of her world. And now that her days were short, her world needed to get smaller, not bigger. She didn't have the energy to add new things or to get to know new friends. "Friends" is what she called the artists and their subjects. She added one more thing: buying all those books wasn't a waste. It was an extravagant gesture. People who love each other, she said, do things like that, generous things, things that don't always seem to make sense.

With or without the gesture, she was dead by the middle of August.

Isaac looked at Jenny on that couch, her hair undone, and the warm sheet from the dryer layered in folds across her shoulders and lap.

"I think it's time for me to go."

She seemed momentarily surprised. "It's early," she said, sitting up.

"Shhh," he said, rubbing her arm. He held both of her hands. She sank back into the cushions and closed her eyes, sighing weakly. Tears arose from beneath each brown eyelash and tracked down her smooth cheeks. He kissed her folded hands.

He stood up and she did too. And without opening her eyes, she hugged him around his waist, resting the side of her face on his chest. He could feel her shape pressed against his, the slight jerking her body made as she cried. His sunburned chest stung. He didn't know what to say, and he didn't know what to do, so he kissed the top of her head where her hair was neatly parted in a straight line. And he said goodbye.

On his way over the seventeen-mile bridge tunnel, he set his mother's Honda's cruise control on fifty-seven and turned up his iPod. Queen and Barenaked Ladies couldn't compete with the roar of wind whipping through his open windows, so he turned them off and drove across that vast expanse of open water without music. If he collected the reward, he could tuck a Bazooka bass in the trunk. Then, he could hear the radio with the windows down even if he drove two hundred miles per hour.

When he got home, his father would know the weekend didn't go well. He would ask questions, and Isaac began practicing answers aloud. The weekend wasn't what he'd hoped, Isaac said. It felt weird and uncomfortable to be with Jenny. The harder he tried, the further away she felt. Nothing he imagined saying sounded right.

His mother would understand. She would ask a few deep questions, but mainly she'd listen and nod like a true mourner. He wanted to sit at the kitchen table while she made a late dinner just for him.

Who would sit with him now? Who cared? Isaac's baseball buddies would howl with laughter and pretend to cry if he spilled his guts. His father would be more than willing to talk about it; he had the perfect sermon for anything. Eddie might get a monumental kick out of this—and Isaac wasn't sure why he thought of sharing it with Eddie, anyway.

Here he was on the middle of a bridge, a desert of water all around. He was racing away from the excitement and pain of the city—the Cavalier Hotel, the blue neon, and three-dollar iced tea. As he got closer to home, he felt halfway to nowhere.

Isaac pulled into his driveway just before nine. Miss Edwards' station wagon was parked out front. Great, he thought.

When Isaac opened the garage door into the kitchen, his dad and Miss Edwards were sitting at the kitchen table. They had had dinner. She must have cooked because the kitchen was immaculate. There were candles. They looked so happy. His heart sank, but he tried not to let it show.

"You're home early," his dad said, pushing away from the table. "Can I get you some grub?"

"No, thanks," Isaac grunted, head down. There wasn't room at the table for him anyway. He looked at Miss Edwards, who glowed with smiling eyes, and he managed to say hello as politely as he could, then walked towards his room. His father patted him firmly on his sunburned back as he shuffled past. Isaac winced.

"Tommy's out in the backyard," his dad said. "Sure would be easier to play catch with two people."

Isaac didn't want Miss Edwards to see him like this. He didn't want her to care about him. He didn't want another woman in his house who wasn't his own mother.

So he went outside.

Tom's face broadened into a giddy smile when he saw Isaac. He had been throwing a scuffed-up baseball against the brick wall at the back of the house. He was wearing Isaac's good glove. His mother had given Isaac that glove when he was in the sixth grade. His father had said it was too expensive and that it was too big for his small hand. "He'll grow into it," his mother had said. Isaac snatched his glove from Tom and gave him an old plastic one instead.

It was almost dark. The full moon and backyard floodlights stretched the lingering twilight. They started playing catch, but Tom was pitifully afraid of the ball.

Isaac threw the ball hard at Tom's glove. Tom would close his eyes and bend away, trying to keep his glove up. The ball would ricochet off the glove, and, seemingly relieved it wasn't airborne anymore, Tom would smile and chase after it.

His throws were irritatingly wild. The off-target throws, an off-target summer, a rotten weekend. Isaac tried to contain the simmering he felt inside with a put-on smile, but there was no joy, only teeth.

"Into the glove, Tom. Throw it right into my glove."

"My daddy would probably say the same thing, Isaac. I'll do better!"

Tom didn't know about his dad. And Isaac wanted to tell him, to spill the poison beans. If your daddy's such a good man, he wanted to say, why's he in jail? Your daddy's a drug addict. Born into a good family, had it all, and threw it all away, a thief who stole his own parents' silverware to pay for his habit. He stayed drunk and ran drugs and had arms that looked like railroad tracks, he wanted to say. Time you learned the truth.

Isaac shuddered at the thought of saying such cruel words. He zinged a ball hard at Tom's glove.

"Oww," Tom said, then scurried after it into the azaleas by the garage. He'd overthrow Isaac, and Isaac would snap at him, "Into the glove." Tom began throwing underhanded, aiming gentle arcs into Isaac's glove.

"Not like a girl," Isaac said, trying to stifle his dark anger. "Throw it hard, like a baseball player."

Isaac burned one into Tom's glove. It bounced out. Tom opened his eyes, took off his glove, and shook his hand. "Ouch," he said. "That really hurts." Tom shook the sting out of his hand, glaring at Isaac, eyes filling with tears.

Isaac could feel the good part of him rise up out of his body. He felt like he was floating, looking down on a strange body that resembled his in the backyard, looking down on little Tom holding his stung hand, trying hard to cover his quiet crying, trying hard to be a big boy, a baseball player, like Isaac. All that was left of Isaac in the yard was the sunburned part, the angry part, the crazy part.

A firefly distracted Tom, and he began jumping after it.

Isaac picked up the ball and tossed it into his glove a few times. "Better scoot out of the way, Tom," Isaac warned, mustering all the gentleness he could. He drew a bead onto the garage. Eyes trained on Isaac, Tom moved obediently out of the way towards the backdoor of the house.

While Isaac wasn't a pitcher, he took his stance and sighted a strike zone inches above the azaleas asleep in their bed. He wound up, and with all his might hurled a fastball into the wall of the garage. The ball popped into the siding. The wall seemed to wail, old aluminum siding letting out a terrible shriek. The ball rebounded past Isaac like a crisp line drive, scudding across the slick grass into the dark yard.

Tom's face blanched white.

The neighbor's porch light snapped on. Mr. Whitcomb stormed out onto the stoop in his bathrobe and, to Isaac's amusement, clutching a base-ball bat.

Reverend Lawson and Miss Edwards raced through the backdoor, grinding to a halt on the patio like two cartoon characters. Without taking his eyes off of Isaac, Tom backed into his mother's arms as she stood on the patio. The three of them huddled like a refugee family, two parents rising up to protect their little boy against a force over which they had absolutely no control.

Isaac just stood there alone in the damp grass, a thousand miles away.

4

Isaac was leaning against the corrugated metal door of the warehouse at quarter to seven when Eddie drove up in the store's beat-up GMC pickup. A cursive "You're a friend at Chum's" was painted on the muddy tailgate.

"Being late is one thing," Eddie said. He looked at his wrist watch. "Being an hour and a quarter early is another. You bucking for a raise, or just want to be president of the company?"

"Cut me some slack, Eddie."

Eddie gave Isaac a sideways glance while rattling the locked door open. Isaac followed him in, went to his timecard over the work bench, and stared at the Cavalier Hotel. He thought of all the other hotels on the wave-combed strip of sand standing like a ludicrous, high-rise wall against the sea.

"How was your weekend? You two lovebirds have a nice time?"

"Lovebird, Eddie. Singular."

Isaac felt numb about losing his cool with Tom Edwards, numb about Jenny, numb about the weekend. He was polite to Jenny, who had dumped him, and scathing with Tom, who had just wanted to play some catch. He had skipped church the next day because he couldn't bear facing Tom and his mom.

Eddie bumped Isaac roughly when he reached for the coffeepot. He bumped him again on his way to the water fountain. He said over his shoulder, "A man's got to do what a man's got to do. Maybe she'll understand one day why you had to break things off." Eddie leaned against the fountain as the slow trickle of water filled the pot. "Yes, sir," Eddie quipped, "a leader's got to lead, I've been told."

"Then maybe she should be president."

Eddie said, "Oh," quietly to himself. He poured the water into the coffee maker and slid the pot onto its burner. He reached up to the shelf above the bench and got down the tin of coffee and a filter. "Technically speaking," Eddie said as he inserted the paper filter, "I believe you'll find that a lovebird is a variety of parrot. You can buy them in pet stores. They tolerate cages, but they can't survive in the wild." Eddie measured the coffee and poured it in the waiting filter. He turned the machine on and looked at Isaac. "But you aren't interested in technicalities, are you, son?"

"My love life is the least of my troubles, Eddie. And I'm sure enough not interested in parrots." Isaac unpinned the picture of the Cavalier Hotel. "You know," he said, leaning the postcard so that Eddie could get a good look, "this hotel is bigger in the picture than in real life." He resisted the urge to drop it into the trash, pinning it back onto the board instead. "Enjoy your caffeine fix," he said, heading into the store.

"Good to the last drop," Eddie mumbled.

On the wall next to the door into the store was a poster that took Isaac's mind off of his failing love life. In four-inch block letters it read REWARD. It said that information leading to a conviction in the recent vandalisms would be rewarded with $5,000 from P.O.T.S.

Before the break-ins, People of the Shore—P.O.T.S.—was interested in getting the grass cut in neglected front yards and suggesting fines for people who refused to haul away the rusted Cameros they kept on concrete blocks on the weedy sides of their houses. The group didn't want their town going to pot, which, apparently had nothing to do with its acronym. They had also devoted themselves to getting town buildings onto the National Register of Historic Places.

Mr. Wilson required Isaac's U.S. History class to write a paper about community action. Isaac and several classmates wrote about P.O.T.S. and their efforts to get laws passed prohibiting the use of vinyl siding on houses within town limits, and lowering the height one's grass could grow before it violated town code from ten inches to five. P.O.T.S. even tried to get Archibald Norman's birthday declared a town holiday. Only the holiday proposal passed. Mr. Taylor, president of the bank, welcomed the chance to be closed on his wedding anniversary.

Rufus Greer, Ina's husband, had confided to Isaac that P.O.T.S.—which had only about twenty members—was filled with a bunch of "retired fanatics who didn't have anything better to do." He had also said that Reginald Williams, the police chief, avoided the P.O.T.S. crowd because they were always nagging him to enforce some arcane law that he didn't even know existed. The chief was old enough for retirement, but he hoped to keep drawing a paycheck to help his grandkids through school. He was rethinking his vocation, Rufus had said.

Rufus urged Isaac to read about McCarthyism and to put something about that in his report by way of comparison. Isaac did, and Mr. Wilson loved his paper, especially the part where Isaac suggested that P.O.T.S. was going too far and its founder and president, Hank Grady, was a Lawn Nazi.

In a lapse of judgment, Mr. Wilson gave P.O.T.S. a copy of all the class reports after midterms. A few days later, Isaac got a handwritten letter on official P.O.T.S. stationery. At first Isaac thought the letter was a joke because it was covered in what looked like claw marks made with a red, felt tip pen. As he studied it, actual words began to emerge from the scars. He could decipher only one full sentence: "Since when is it heavy handed to fight against those forces that would allow the land you love to go to the dogs?!!!" Mr. Wilson helped translate the signature. It was signed by Hank Grady.

Mr. Wilson privately told Isaac that he never imagined a grown man would send a high school sophomore hate mail. Isaac was just glad he got an "A" on the report and that his path would never cross with Hank Grady's.

The rusting cars and tall grass did not inflame P.O.T.S. nearly as much as the break-ins. After the second break-in on May 28th, they called special meetings, pressured Police Chief Williams for an arrest, and, to speed things along, offered the $5,000 reward to catch the culprit, whom Hank Grady had called Dead Meat. That's what it said in the *News*.

Overnight, P.O.T.S. had gone from lawn police to vigilantes. Isaac liked the stir it caused. A little excitement in town never hurt anyone. But what Isaac decidedly did not like was bumping into Hank Grady first thing every morning at Chum's.

↓ ↓ ↓

Isaac clocked in every day out back in the warehouse. He'd look at the Cavalier Hotel postcard, and set his bag lunch next to Eddie's in the small, dented refrigerator under the counter. Before he began his endless cleaning chores in the warehouse, he'd go up front to the store to oil-mop the hardwood floor and straighten the shelves.

Every day he'd have to mop around the regulars—old men who dribbled chewing tobacco into empty Dr Pepper bottles and talked all morning around the stove in the middle of the store. Sometimes the group would swell to twelve men, including the postman. Mr. Chum would occasionally lean against a metal shelf, and when his father, Billy, made his rounds, he'd always pull up a chair. But usually there were five guys. Hank Grady was almost always one of them.

They sat in wooden rockers with cane seats, droning on about how things weren't like they used to be. "Ain't it awful" is what his mom had called that kind of talking. The chairs were for sale, but Isaac didn't see how anyone could ever buy one since they were usually occupied. Hank Grady sat motionless like a mountain in his chair, and it seemed to Isaac the others were oriented in such a way as to give him prominence. Every morning when Isaac came into the store, Hank Grady would give him a hard look from beneath bushy, black eyebrows.

Today they were gumming the scuttlebutt about the latest break-in. Two of the men had the newspaper draped over their laps. If Isaac couldn't get clues listening in while he swept, then he figured he'd at least get opinions. He might get both. And either would be a help.

Harvey Norris said that it was a shame. Everyone nodded. Mr. Peake muttered yep, yep, yep like a schnauzer grousing in its sleep. His rocking picked up speed. Isaac had noticed Mr. Peake's black, plastic glasses would slide down his nose like he'd washed his face with butter every morning. He had a nervous habit of pushing them up with his pinky, the only full finger remaining on his left hand after he had lopped off the others with a table saw.

"Kids are at the bottom of this," Grady said.

Isaac mopped the side aisles and listened.

"They don't know what to do with themselves nowadays," Grady pontificated. "Damn teenagers. And teachers aren't allowed to spank them anymore in school. Every kid needs his hide tanned ever so often. That's what an ass is for, ain't it?"

The men grunted in unison. Mr. Peake nodded so hard his glasses slipped off onto the sports page.

Isaac kept his head down. He kept working. His pattern was the same each day. When he'd finished the side aisles, he'd tear off the previous day's date from the calendar that was glued to the back of the National cash register. Isaac tore off Saturday and Sunday, leaving Monday, and nodded at Mr. Chum perched on a torn vinyl stool, figuring the daily crossword.

High on the back wall hung a yellowed poster of all the presidents in little ovals up to Eisenhower, with an eagle and American flag in the center. A large Standard clock that shone like a full moon hung below the poster. It was almost nine.

"Says here," Mr. Peake said, rapping the front page, "that it'll take over $50,000 to fix Parramore's place up."

"That eyesore had needed fixing up for a long time," Lester Mellande said.

Isaac heard the gurgly slop of someone squirting a stream of tobacco into a bottle. Mr. Peake's rocking kept time like the choir director's metronome. Harvey Norris squeaked when he laughed.

The narrow, rectangular store had floor-to-ceiling windows at the front door, and, on the other end, the checkout counter ran the width of the back wall. The store felt smaller than it was because it was so tightly packed.

Chum's carried acetone in cans of every size. The store had a rack with spools of colored rope, poly rope, cotton braided rope, hemp, and chains. A whole aisle was lined with metal bins in the shape of bailing scoops filled with lock nuts and washers. Bolts and nails filled another aisle. Scales hung from the ceiling because they sold by weight, and if a customer didn't watch his head he was liable to crack it. Out back, they sold kerosene and propane.

"World's going to hell in a hand basket," Grady intoned. "That's all there is to it, what with these kids raging with hormones and idleness. When we were kids, we showed respect and worked for everything we got."

The men nodded again like they had elastic necks.

Isaac silently glided from the back of the store to the front with his mop. He hadn't heard anything from his buddies about the break-ins. Since he was just finishing tenth grade, though, he was out of touch with the middle school crowd and not yet fully in-the-know with the kids in upper grades.

Except for when Hank Grady glared at him, Isaac liked mopping in the mornings. He'd stretch this part of the job out, taking his time dusting and making sure items on the shelves were in perfect rows. He sometimes let this take up to forty-five minutes. When it broiled outside, the air conditioning was a bonus.

Chum's sold kite string, shotgun shells locked in a glass cabinet, and hunting vests in camouflage and hunter orange. They sold rods and reels, torches, and galvanized pails. They sold tools. One section along the wall had countless brands and sizes of hammers, from twenty-five pound malls to tack hammers. They sold air hammers and ratchet sets and air compressors. They sold reciprocating saws and jigsaws and circular saws and grinders and band saws. What they didn't have in stock, like table saws, which were too big to display, Mr. Chum could order from one of the eight big catalogs that sat open on the checkout counter, like handyman Bibles on the world's widest pulpit.

Isaac delighted in straightening those items that people had poked through the day before. To him, they were like ancient bones sprawled about an extinct watering hole, and he was the archeologist responsible for laying them out in the shape of the dinosaur.

The wooden floor was rutted and scarred, faded in some spots and dark with unknown spills in others. Rusted lines marred the boards where shelves had once stood. Chinks, gouges, and stains marked a half century of hard use.

"Why do you suppose they're doing it?" Harvey asked. He wore a pink shirt and enormous green Bermuda shorts. He was the only one who never chewed, and he looked more like a retired golfer than a man who worked with his hands. "Nothing's stolen. Painted flames above the bed each time. Clogged drains and all the faucets left running. Water damage, sure, but nothing stolen."

Mike Lindvall said, "It's kind of like arson, without the actual fire. I mean, the painted flames."

"The moral of the story is don't go out of town," Mr. Jackson said. "That's when they hit. When you're out of town. Or, in the case of Nathan Parramore, in the hospital."

Isaac had made his way to the middle aisle and tried his best to mop around the men. Harvey smiled and lifted his short legs like a kindergartner showing off that he could lift both feet at once. Grady glared at Harvey, then Isaac.

"Isn't Isaac a nigger name?" Grady said.

"Grady!" Harvey said in his high voice. "Don't be rude."

"He doesn't know any other way," Mr. Jackson said.

The men laughed but looked away.

Isaac scanned their faces for an idea of whether or not it was a serious question. Harvey's face turned pink. He leaned into the cane poked into the floor like a mast between his knees, adjusting himself awkwardly in his rocker, shaking his head.

Grady, whose eyebrows sat like tree branches above black eyes, hadn't flinched. "When I was still farming," Grady said, not taking his eyes off Isaac, "half the colored boys who worked for me were named Isaac and Ezekiel. I had a Jeremiah or two who worked for me, and a bunch of women whose names sounded made up. So, I'm just wondering where'd you get Isaac from."

"You had a field full of prophets," Lindvall said, snickering.

Isaac looked around the circle. All of the men looked away. They seemed afraid or embarrassed, somehow, but nobody said so, and nobody got up to leave.

"Well?" Grady grunted impatiently. "Your name. Where does it come from?"

"It's Hebrew," Isaac heard himself say. He eyed the head of his dusty mop as he tapped it lightly to the floor. He cleared his throat and tried not to let his voice waver. He felt trapped in the silence. "Means laughter," he said.

Grady said, "Speak up."

"You heard me," Isaac snapped, surprised by how the words spurted out.

Grady's rocker creaked. Harvey blew his nose.

"Ain't Hebrew the language of the Indians?" Mr. Lindvall asked.

"Dad-burn-it, Mike, you don't know squat," Mr. Mellande said. Lester Mellande cut the grass at the Methodist church every Saturday. "If you knew your Old Testament, you'd know there was a book in it called Hebrews. You'd also know it was the language of angels." He folded up his newspaper, then rolled it tightly in his left hand. "Biblical literacy ain't what it used to be," he said, standing up. "Gotta go, boys. Grandkids are coming over this morning, and my wife and I have this arrangement that makes it easier: She's the good cop, I'm the bad."

Isaac was furious, but relieved to disappear into the last of the mopping. Half of the guys on his school baseball team were black; they were strong players, whom he called many names: pin-heads, slackers, and momma's boys. And they dished it right back; cutting each other down was what the whole team did, and they did it outrageously. But one word nobody used was nigger. It demeaned everybody.

As Lester Mellande took his leave, the men turned to the subject of Indians, language, and how the Chesapeake blue crab was doing. By his final pass with the mop, they were back on the break-ins.

"I say it's kids," Hank Grady said again. "And I think they need to be rounded up and taught a lesson."

Somebody mumbled an "Amen."

Isaac's dad had carted him along to Chum's Hardware since he was a kid. He had rocked in the chairs by that stove in the afternoons when the regulars weren't there, had wandered the aisles waiting for his dad. Had he encountered Hank Grady he might have thought differently, but Isaac had always liked Chum's.

There was a lot to like, besides the rows and rows of stuff. No matter what time it was, the store smelled like coffee. Susan Chum kept two pots going until closing time. The slow-motion propellers of three ceiling fans stirred in other fragrances: sawdust from the lumberyard out back, paint, a customer's pipe smoke. When the front door was propped open, Isaac could smell bread from Pearson's Bakery across the street and the sewer smell of nearby Norman Creek at low tide.

As he shook the mop out on the front sidewalk, a woman asked Isaac about having a key made. He pointed his mop handle to the back. "Mr. Chum'll help you, ma'am."

He stood on the sidewalk watching the cloud of dust he had just shaken out of his mop drift past the barbershop. The sun glinted off the pin oak leaves across the street at the city fountain. It was going to be hot.

"Isaac," Mr. Chum called out from the back.

Isaac walked quickly to the back counter.

"I'm out of blanks. Can you go out back and get some for me?"

Isaac turned his back to the men at the stove and quietly admitted that he didn't know what blanks were or where they were kept.

"Come on, son," Mr. Chum said quietly, winking. "I'll show you." Mr. Chum led Isaac through the back door, across the loading dock of the lumberyard, and into the warehouse. The blanks—uncut keys—were hanging on a board about eight feet wide and half as tall on a wall that Isaac doubted he'd ever get to in his cleaning mission. Cobwebs clotted with dust looped from hook to hook.

Above the three rows of blanks were other cut keys, hanging on brass cup hooks under numbers handwritten with an ink pen. There were hundreds of hooks, most of which were filled with keys of many shapes. Some were silver or bronze but many were black with age and grime.

"What are these?" Isaac asked, pointing to the keys above the blanks.

"We used to keep a copy of every key we made," Mr. Chum said as he strolled back to the store. "We kept a book of what key belonged to what customer. That way, if somebody ever lost a key, we'd match it up, and make a replacement."

"Did people like you keeping copies of their keys? Did they even know about it?"

"They did when they'd lose one."

"No offense, but who wants you to have a key to their house?" Isaac tried not to look astonished.

Mr. Chum settled his TruValue Hardware hat on his head as he stepped toward the door. He looked out over the lumberyard and the houses beyond the fence. He jingled the key blanks in his open palm. He had gray eyes and big, white eyebrows and smelled faintly of coffee, newsprint, and turpentine. "Isaac, when we did this it was in the day that people didn't lock their houses, before your time. Most of these keys belong to doors that don't even exist anymore: to boat trailers rusting in the dump, to frozen-up tractors and old pickups and dog cages, things like that. We don't do it anymore. We'd have a hundred thousand keys, if we did. And God only knows where that old ledger is. I look at that old board and can't tell what's what, as if it mattered anymore. But back in the day people trusted one another, and it was as right as rain for the local locksmith to have a copy of everybody's keys."

He smiled at Isaac and took a long look around the warehouse. "We'd have a neater shop if my father and grandfather weren't such pack rats."

Back in the store, Mr. Chum asked the woman where she was from as he ground the key.

"Norfolk," she said. "We bought a little place near Evidence Gap. A fixer-upper for the weekends."

The regulars had stopped rocking and were staring. Isaac thought they might be making her nervous. Isaac tried, with difficulty, not to add to her agony. She was voluptuously sexy, and Isaac felt himself blushing, felt his mouth going dry. She wore a light blue tank top beneath her buttoned blouse. Her nails were done, and she absently tapped them on the counter.

Isaac focused on Mr. Chum instead of her. He watched him grind the key, hold it against the wire buffer brush, blow it off, and hold it up to the light—the clone against the original. Mr. Chum wiped both keys on his shirt, then slipped them into the woman's open hand.

"Thanks," she said, digging through her small purse.

Isaac watched Mr. Chum punch buttons on the cash register. The drawer rang open, and he took the woman's new fifty and made change. They all watched her disappear across Main Street.

"The Shore is changing, Isaac," Mr. Chum said, looking out the front windows. "Used to know everybody here. Now we've got come-heres from everywhere, buying land, building houses. Tourists. You name it."

"We used to have poachers and moonshiners," Mr. Peake chortled. He had resumed his rocking and was going so fast, Isaac thought the momentum might fling him to the floor.

"And women wearing pants now," Hank Grady said, struggling up from his rocking chair. His overalls, in a former life, could have been a trampoline. "Whatever happened to dresses? We've got it all now. Faggots too. Pretty soon it'll be as crowded as the city."

Isaac liked the idea of crowds. Maybe then this town wouldn't be so boring.

↓ ↓ ↓

Isaac stepped into the warehouse like he used to step into the batter's box: a final sweeping look around the place, then settling deliberately into a stance, and boring a hole in the pitcher's eyes with as mean a grimace as he could muster. This was his way of slowing things down, shucking off the distractions, focusing on the pitcher's every movement so as not to get put into a wheelchair with a wild fastball. He looked at the back corner of the warehouse where he had left off Friday. The space in his head filled only with the corner of that room, the task at hand, the darkness, the dust. He cleared his throat and set out digging through the piles of junk.

Behind a teetering pile of pallets were half-crushed cardboard boxes filled with junk: rusted S-hooks in one, razor blades in another, rusted screws that had never made it into the store in yet another. Along the wall were sacks of concrete, the ones on top sagging open, the ones on the bottom hardened by the rain that splashed in from knot holes and gaps in the wall.

He felt the sweat beginning to run down his back, and thought about Jenny and her big-city friends. Isaac had Eddie, Hank Grady, and his pastor-father. He'd been dealt such a rotten hand. His friends were playing summer ball. Jenny was living it up in Virginia Beach. His father was dating the church treasurer not even a year after his mom had died, and he was a glorified maid at a hardware store.

Isaac worked through lunch, lifting, hauling, shoving. Thinking of Grady's foul mouth sparked a blaze. He fumed. He tore twisted nails out of reusable four-by-fours.

He felt stuck. Looking around the warehouse didn't help. The clutter was so profound, the stacks so high, the piles so dense that he could hardly tell he'd done any work. The dumpster outside was full, and the warehouse no less so.

He dragged old tractor attachments into the lumberyard for Will to look at and decide what to do with. Three attachments made in Suffolk for digging peanuts lay in the dim light like a train wreck. They were heavy and their wheels were gone, but he dragged them out anyway, gouging white streaks in the concrete floor. A yellow plow implement had a row of tines that looked like teeth. A green one said John Deere.

He stacked. He swept. He manhandled. He shoveled.

He thought about the break-ins and imagined spending the reward money. It was a lot easier spending imaginary money than it was to go about earning the real thing at $5.65 an hour. Isaac had no list of suspects. The Jordan twins were always getting into trouble, but they would have broken in with crowbars. Or explosives.

Maybe it was drug dealers, like his father said. But nothing was stolen, so that didn't make sense. He hated to admit that Hank Grady and the regulars were right. Somebody was doing this just for kicks. It was the sort of thing kids might do. But what kids?

He thought of the pretty woman who had bought the key that morning. He couldn't imagine anyone choosing to move to the Shore. Her new key cost $1.59. If the vandals had keys to the houses they hit, there'd be no signs of breaking and entering. Even the Jordan boys might be able to pull off something like that if they had a key.

Lots of things would be possible if only you had the key.

5

The infielders were testing their luck by inching in. They were inside the baselines, dangerously close to home, prowling like nimble tigers, and yelling.

"Come on, Isaac," Andy Andrews hollered. "Punch it through! Get it past us!"

Isaac was known for being able to control his bat. And it was squirting grounders in every direction, finding the hole, which earned him a .306 last season—Ty Cobb's minor league average. This time he was going to fool them all by swinging for the fence. It felt good to be back in the box.

Outfielders were waving their arms distractingly, hooting. "Who do you love, Isaac Lawson? Who do you love?"

Andy's pickup truck was just behind the fence on the third base line, windows and doors wide open. The Chevy was old, but it ran, and the red paint was so chalky and the road cancer had pocked the body with so many rust spots that it looked almost orange. But the hubcaps were domes of shiny silver. Even in the last of the twilight sun, they looked like chrome planets. And the stereo was tricked out. Bo Diddley was blaring, I walk 47 miles of barbed wire, I use a cobra-snake for a necktie . . .

"Come on, Isaac," Lee Stewart yelled from first. "Let's see what you got."

Alvis Mann stood like a statue on the mound, honing in on the quarter-inch of the strike zone that he was going to obliterate. He wore a t-shirt with a picture of Bob Marley on it, Originale printed in block letters. Isaac pumped his grip and exhaled steadily through pursed lips.

Somebody yelled, "Batter, batter, batter. Swing batter, batter."

Isaac had never batted against his old teammate Alvis. He was a pretty good pitcher, sometimes wild, not much finesse, but lots of speed. During training last winter, at not even 150 pounds, he was benching 310. The guy was a beast. He was fast, a pretty good hitter, and despite his compact size, he had strength, and instinct. When he was on, he was on. His nostrils flared as he launched into his wind up and his teeth flashed when he hurled a rocket low and inside. It was a thing of beauty, an achingly perfect pitch.

The ball popped into Matt Costello's glove and everybody howled.

"STRI—KE!"

"Made you back up, didn't he," Matt said as he lobbed the ball back to Alvis. "He's gotten better since spring ball."

Isaac eased off his tiptoes. He shook his head and tapped his cleats lightly with his bat. "Sure has," Isaac said. "Steroids?"

"Practice, practice, practice," Matt said, squatting again, fingering a sign between his legs to Alvis, who was watching like a hawk from the mound. Isaac took his place again, this time a little more cautiously.

Even though this was a pick-up game, and even though there were only three girls in the stands, the players were dialed in. Only chumps ever just played baseball.

And Isaac was rusty.

Music throbbed through Andy's new speakers: Tell me, who do you love? Who do you love?

"Who do you love, Isaac?" The girls mimicked from the stands. "Who do you love?" Andy shouted from third. "Whooo do you love?"

While the girls were yelling, "batter, batter, batter," Isaac tipped back Alvin's nuclear fastball into the metal stands. The ball spanked around the bleachers, evoking a thousand irritated metal echoes. The girls in the bleachers covered their heads and shrieked with laughter.

"Better watch it," Andy threatened, puffed up, protective, pretending.

Helen, who was sitting in the bleachers, was Andy's girlfriend. Very sweet. Very tight t-shirt. She was with Lee Stewart's twin sisters, just hanging out. Nothing better to do on a Thursday evening than paint your nails at Norman Field while a few professional wannabes ran their paces.

Isaac was glad to be there. The guys didn't have a game this week, so they had a little extra energy after practice for hitting a few more. Isaac had caught them winding down in the dugout and dared them to give him an up at the plate. He had taken a few cracks at the warm-up pitches and the fielders, caught the flies, easily covering the freshly mown distances like antelope. Such grace, such unhurried speed. Isaac glowed.

Andy had said, let's play, and everybody started whooping it up and talking trash.

Now it was one-and-one and Alvis looked like a statue again, gleaming with sweat. Alvis uncoiled a curve ball that missed wide. Then he threw a strike Isaac hardly even saw, but he swung anyway to hails and hails of laughter.

Isaac tried to shake it off. He yelled at Lee on first. "You're playing too close. If coach were here he'd tell you to back it up."

"I'm the quarterback of the infield," Lee boasted. "And you, Little Isaac, are the quarterback of my mama's quilting club."

"That hurt," Matt said, squatting for the pitch. "How's that for close?"

Alvis threw a high fastball that Isaac let go. Matt practically stood to catch it. "Cool it down," he said. "Full count, Mr. Lawson." Isaac cut his eyes to Matt, who said, "No pressure. It's just that the stands are going crazy and it's all up to you." Matt threw the ball back to Alvis.

The stands were empty. The girls were sitting in Andy's truck.

"It's okay if you've spent the summer getting soft," Matt said behind his mask, faking a wheezy laugh. "QB of Mrs. Stewart's quilting club."

Isaac pulled one wide, precariously close to Andy's truck blaring a strange mix of retro rock and Dixie Chicks. I'm up on the tight wire, one side's ice and one is fire. He pulled the next change-up wide again, closer to Andy's truck. I'm up on the tightrope, one side's hate and one is hope.

"You got a problem with me," Andy hollered, "take it up with me, not my truck."

Somebody said, "It's your dad's truck."

"Yeah," somebody else said, "and it's your old man's music."

But Isaac was only halfway listening. He and Alvis Mann were looking into each other's eyes. Isaac pumped his grip and met Alvis' fastball with a check swing. The ball arched lamely just over Lee's head. His hands stung. It was an awful-looking hit, but no one caught it, and Isaac sprinted to first with Matt Costello yelling after him. "You hit like a girl, Isaac. What happened to you?!"

Everyone was laughing. Isaac felt stronger in his upper body, but his legs were shaky and he was out of breath. It was probably nervous jitters, given that he didn't really want to look like a girl in front of the guys. But he was also out of shape. He'd been doing pull-ups, but he hadn't been doing any running. Mental note: start jogging and running wind sprints.

"That was one shitty hit," Lee said.

"But, hey," Isaac said, panting and pointing to the bag, "I'm here. And I'm safe."

"And you're right," Lee said. "I probably was playing too close. Just wanted you to feel the pressure."

"It worked," Isaac said. "I was scared to death."

Steve Pincus jogged in from center field to take the next at bat. The guys on the bench were busy bagging up bats and practice balls. They were barefoot, done with baseball for the day. Steve was the retired fire chief's grandson, a lean athlete who ripped a single down third base. Andy Andrews kicked the dirt and made like he was mad for letting it squeak by. But it was a good hit. As it was getting past dinnertime, everybody was getting a little punchy. Isaac took second.

The second baseman was Mike Pearson, related, but not directly, to Pearson's Bakery. Everybody who grew up on the Shore was related to each other somehow. "How's your summer going?" he asked Isaac. "You making any money?"

"Millions," Isaac said, "but I miss you guys."

"Man, all we do is play baseball and sign autographs." Mike was impossibly tall and thin, like the rest of his body had not yet caught up with his upward growth spurt.

"After the game," Isaac said, "maybe you could sign my buttocks."

"No need to be so jealous," Mike said, sauntering back to his position. "Not everyone can be famous and good looking," he said over his shoulder.

Alvis struck two guys out in six pitches.

Steve, who was on first, went back to the plate for another go. "I need the practice, guys," he said.

The outfield was empty by now; the fielders were rinsing out the big orange water jug and gathering with the girls at Andy's truck. The girls were sitting on the tailgate swinging their legs, "Life in the Fast Lane" blaring.

Steve crushed a grounder down third on the first pitch. But Andy, in one fluid, cat-like swoop, trapped it in a stutter-stepped dive, rolled, and sprung up ball-in-hand ready to throw. Isaac hovered near second, waiting to take off for third, but Andy eyed second menacingly enough that Isaac did a little slide to keep his foot on the bag. Without warning, Andy threw it on a string to first, the ball snapping into Lee Stewart's glove a full stride before Steve tagged the bag and coasted down the foul line into right field. Lee zipped it to Mike just as fast, and the gloved ball was on Isaac's chest in an instant. Mike looked down to make sure Isaac's foot was firmly on the bag. Isaac was leaning away, but was safe.

"I'm just toying with you children," Andy yelled, grinning.

Mike flipped his glove lightly into Isaac's face and pushed him off second, wrestling him to the dirt. "It's not baseball if you don't have dirt in your face."

Isaac shoved Mike off and they both lay on their backs for a moment admiring the sky. Songbirds flitted from treetops. Higher up, gulls practiced their acrobatics.

Andy walked over to Isaac and offered him a hand up. "Watch me, child," Andy said. "And learn from me. I will teach you to play baseball like a man."

Alvis Mann looked at Andy and shook his head. "You have a future in used car sales," he said, stepping off the mound to the dugout. "I'm going home for my mama's cooking."

"And a shower," Mike said, pulling second base out of the ground and putting it under his arm. "Please get a shower. And, this time, use soap."

"I've got your soap," Alvis said, grandly flipping them off.

Isaac squirted ketchup on his pile of fries. Andy said that wasn't how you did it. He snatched the bottle away and squirted his ketchup in a gory puddle next to his fries. He explained that ketchup was for dipping, one fry at a time. Andy was like that.

Lee passed on the ketchup but asked for salt and began shaking furiously. When the waitress walked up, he stopped, looked around the booth, and then looked back at her like a puppy that had just gotten the brownies off the counter.

She was gorgeous. She put her hands on her full hips, and slowly shook her head. "Fellas," she said, "if you keep eating like this you won't be able to fit into this booth by winter."

"Baby, baby," Andy quipped back, "we work out." He held up his arm and flexed his bicep.

"Yeah," she said, "tell that to your arteries."

Kate Bradshaw would be a senior in the fall. Isaac knew her because everybody knew everybody, but he didn't run in the same circles with her. And he had never noticed her like he noticed her now. Her apron was tied tightly around her small waist. She wore a tight, short-sleeved t-shirt. She had blue eyes, an easy smile that showed off a dimple in her left cheek. A thin gold chain hung around her neck and disappeared between her ample breasts. She leaned over and with a long, bare arm slapped down the bill. She smelled of flowers and spearmint gum.

"I'm not letting you order anything else, except a side of string beans," she said, looking at Andy. "They're fresh, like you."

Andy, Lee, and Isaac watched her without speaking as she walked towards the kitchen. "Damn," Andy said. "She's so hot."

Kate was smart, had some paintings in a student exhibit at city hall, and was really good looking. "Everybody likes Kate," Andy said more soberly. "But nobody dates her."

"That's because she's out of everybody's league," Lee said, resuming the spirited shaking of salt on his fries. "And she scored higher on her SAT's than Einstein. Her tits, relatively speaking, are infinitely better than Einstein's." Isaac laughed, momentarily forgetting how miserable his summer was shaping up to be.

They had left the field, showered at home, and devoured their mother's cooking on the run. Isaac had eaten a frozen waffle in the dark of his empty kitchen. Now Andy and Lee sat together on one side of the booth and Isaac sat on the other for a second round of eating. They looked different clean, Andy with gel in his hair and a green Izod, Lee in a white T. Between the three of them, the table was cluttered with three large shakes, three extra large fries, and one Coke each.

Andy was a rising senior and Lee would be a junior like Isaac. This summer, the two of them played baseball and had little time to do anything else. But last summer, Andy had worked at Chum's. That's why Isaac wanted to talk with him. He wanted to know what Andy knew about the key board. When Isaac brought it up, it took him a while to jog Andy's memory. Even though Andy had worked mainly with Will in the lumberyard out back, and not in the warehouse or store, everyone who worked at Chum's and many who did not passed through the warehouse to get to the store. How can you miss a key board practically as big as a wall? But Andy, apparently, had. Lee, who had been going in and out of Chum's his whole life with his dad, remembered the board, which made Isaac feel a little better. Finally, Andy remembered, but it was still fuzzy and what did it matter?

"There was no sign of forced entry," Isaac said about the break-ins. "So how'd they get in? If they had a key it would be easy, right?" Isaac told them about Hank Grady's theory that teenagers were doing it.

"I've heard about the houses getting flooded, who hasn't?" Andy said dismissively. "But I haven't paid attention to details. And I don't have a clue who could be doing this."

Lee nodded his head thoughtfully. "Why would you break into a place and not steal stuff? Why would you break into the homes of old people? This is freaking my grandmother out," he said, stuffing the last of his fries in his mouth. "She's even locking her doors at night. She checks them before she goes to bed. She checks them in the middle of the night when she gets up to pee. My dad took her shotgun away last week. He though she might accidentally shoot one of my little cousins."

"So how are the people doing this getting in?" Isaac asked.

The boys shrugged.

"What if the people doing this had a key?" Isaac asked.

He asked Lee and Andy if they knew what was on that key board. They were as surprised as Isaac had been to find that the cut keys were copies of people's orders. Tractor keys. Barn keys. Front door keys. The thing that identified those numbered keys with actual properties was a ledger that was, according to Mr. Chum, long lost. "Since you hardly remembered that there was a key board," Isaac said to Andy, "there's no chance you know anything about a ledger. Like, where it is. Do you?"

"As a matter of fact," Andy said, whispering, "I do know where the ledger is."

Isaac looked around, then slowly leaned forward. Lee leaned forward too. "Where?" they both said at once.

"I keep the ledger in my basement behind the skeletons of all of my pirate ancestors . . . "

"You're an asshole," Lee said, motioning for the waitress.

Andy leered at them. "I've been breaking into those houses," he said in a criminal voice. "I'm your man."

Isaac was shaking his head, taking the last slurps from his milkshake. "And what, pray tell, do the flames on the walls mean?" Isaac asked. "And the stopped-up sinks? What's that all about?"

Andy lifted his arms and stretched his strong frame in the booth. "I honestly don't have a clue what it means," Andy said. "I hope they catch the bastards."

The smell of ketchup made Isaac's nostrils twitch. Harsh fluorescent light filled the diner, along with the odor of burgers and fish from the grill, sautéed onions, lime, coffee, pickles, pepper, flat soda. Faintly, he smelled flowers.

As Kate approached the table, Andy leaned forward. "And you're right, Isaac," he said. "I have no clue about any ledger or where it is. Chum doesn't lie, and if Chum doesn't know, I imagine nobody does. However the crooks got into and wrecked those houses, the keys, if they even had keys, couldn't have come from Chum's Hardware."

"In your opinion," Isaac said.

"In my professional opinion," Andy said.

"Deep thoughts, fellas?" The boys looked up at Kate, who stood over them, feigning impatience.

"Give me two fried eggs, Kate," Lee said, expansively. "Over easy, please, ma'am. And one slice of whole-wheat toast with butter."

"You make me sick," she said, glaring at their dirty plates crowded on the small table. "I just can't believe any of you."

"It's whole wheat," Lee said.

She took the bill off the table and pulled out a pen from behind her ear. Her sandy hair was piled on top of her head. She stood poised to write. "I suppose all of you heart attacks want fried eggs?"

"With bacon," Andy chimed in. "And Cokes all around."

"And you?" She looked at Isaac with eyebrows raised.

"String beans?" Isaac asked, smiling sheepishly.

"You're a suck up!" Andy yelled. Lee leaned over the table and punched Isaac in the arm, hard.

"You are a suck up," Kate said. "But the beans are in season. And good for you." She glared at the other boys, turned smartly, and walked away. Andy and Lee eyeballed her tight jeans. She yelled the order through the pass-through window into the kitchen.

Isaac gazed outside at the streetlight shining above the asphalt parking lot. It was hot and humid. Fireflies flitted around the ankles of trees in the wood across the street. Moths, drawn by light, danced against the windows, banished outside by the incomprehensible, invisible force of plate glass. He could see the reflection of the restaurant, the bar with the chrome-padded stools, the gleaming serving counter, the cut-through to the kitchen.

He could see Kate too. She was walking toward their booth with plates of food. She was looking right at Isaac; she saw him looking at her and she didn't look away, didn't pretend like she didn't notice.

And Isaac didn't look away either.

6

One thing Isaac liked about Sunday worship was that even though sixty or so people sat in the pews around him, he felt contentedly alone. Alone with whatever he wanted to think about. A million miles away, free to drift where his imagination carried him. All he had to do was stand and sit at the proper times and go through the motions, which he was pretty good at since he had done it every Sunday since he was able to stand on his own. Unless he's got the flu, a preacher's kid can't skip church.

His dad's preaching created a spacious, imaginative space in which Isaac allowed his memory to wander. Cleaning fish after having been out all day in Mr. Watson's small wooden rowboat stirred in his head. If someone didn't sit up in the bow, a good wave head-on coupled with that impossibly heavy, old Evinrude bolted to the transom might up-end the boat. The cattails waved from shore as they poked along the marsh. Salt and wind stung his face. He smelled the wind off Tom's Cove, traces of sand and dander from the dunes and woods. His dad hated fishing but loved beating around that cove in that beat-up boat. Isaac always fished both poles.

Jenny floated into Isaac's sleepy thoughts. A soft-focused Jenny in an emerald dress beckoned him. Isaac allowed this Jenny to whisper things she had never spoken in real life. He wanted to plunge after her as she swayed behind velvet drapes, motioning with a single, manicured finger to follow. He wanted to follow.

Jenny's face faded into Kate's. Kate? Kate Bradshaw? He blinked. Sure enough, there was Kate smiling at him, bending toward him, her curves seeking liberation from her tight clothes and her minty breath filling his senses. He blinked again. There was Jenny in that emerald dress, red, inviting lips. He blinked and saw Kate. Now Jenny. Now Kate. They were alone in a vast outdoors of haloed sun. Kate was scratching the middle of her back. He reached out to help her get the itch. It's my bra strap, this dreamy Kate said. I have a mole under my bra strap and it itches.

Did the saints have this kind of vision? When the saints saw Jesus, did Jesus look this real? Did he talk about ordinary things like moles? A doctor could remove the mole, Isaac heard himself say. In real life his voice would have squeaked up an octave and would be wavering. But it was smooth and steady in this divine visitation. A doctor could help with the mole, Isaac continued, and I'd be glad to help you with the bra.

These curious visions were a little confusing, but a million times better than the sermon. And because he wasn't making this up, he understood this vision to be a gift—albeit an unusual gift—from God. The Lord does work in mysterious ways.

Something in his hormone-soaked brain warned that he couldn't let these visions—no matter how holy—go any further in the middle of worship. A wet dream on the fourth pew was an ecclesiastical embarrassment. Reluctantly but dutifully, he began to distract himself by thinking of the famine in Africa. The AIDS epidemic there. Starving children. Algebra. The Holocaust. All the world's sorrow. He wondered if Jesus got a hard-on when he was a teenager.

Then he thought of Billy Birdsong. That worked. Jenny's image evaporated instantly. The velvet drapes of his vision opened to a cinder block wall.

The sermon seemed to buck through a range of emotions. His father usually wasn't overly dramatic, but in this sermon Isaac noticed a fair amount of loud, staccato speech punctuated by whispers and long pauses. He hadn't actually listened to a word.

Isaac glanced around the sanctuary just to make sure sleepy worshippers weren't reading his lurid mind. Mrs. Greer listened to his dad's sermon with a look of earnest concentration. She had put too much powder on her face. Her mascara was smeared the color of coal. Her lipstick was an unflattering shade of hot pink. Her thinning hair had been sprayed motionless. Sun streamed into the sanctuary, and a narrow ray of blue light from the Jesus the Good Shepherd window lit her in such a way that, if it weren't for the steady rising of her chest, Isaac might have mistaken her for a corpse sitting upright. Her husband slouched next to her, head bowed and snoring lightly with his hands folded neatly in his lap.

After the sermon, Mr. Greer woke up and everyone else bowed for prayer. Isaac's dad prayed for workers at the concrete factory recently laid off. He mentioned Steve Pincus, a member in the hospital, and Albert Lange out in Ohio recently home from surgery. Ouch, Isaac thought.

Isaac glanced at his hands. The blisters had hardened with calluses. There were traces of black grease in the deep lines of his palms. He thought of Crazy Eddie, who always complained, was always crabby and often purposefully rude. Isaac was beginning to see that it was an act, a practiced put-on. On Thursday Eddie had practically sprinted across the lumberyard when Isaac had started poking around the outside eaves of the warehouse with a warped boat hook to clean out half a century of old bird nests.

"Leave it be," Eddie had said. "This part of the building belongs to the bluebirds, not Chum. They come back here to nest every year, and everybody needs a place to lay his head."

Isaac wanted to peek behind Eddie's mask. Who was this strange, old man? Why did he keep to himself? How come nobody seemed to know him really? Who was this loner from whom everyone kept his distance?

Isaac jolted back to reality when his dad stepped out of the pulpit for the beginning of a baptism ceremony. A young couple brought their daughter forward and joined with Isaac's dad at the eight-sided baptismal font. At the bottom of the font, under the water, was a scallop shell, a symbol of baptism. Most people in the church didn't know the shell was there, but Isaac did. He knew everything about this church. He had explored every crevice of it.

The couple's relatives and friends jammed into the second pew. Everybody shows up when a baby "gets done," as his father put it. Nothing brings people to a church like a baptism or a funeral. The congregation strained their necks for a good view. Isaac found himself doing the same, not knowing where the sudden emotion he felt came from. It occurred to him there were still things he didn't understand about church.

Isaac's father beamed as he took the child in his arms and touched Mary Katherine's head generously with water. "You are God's child," he said, carrying the baby gently out into the congregation. "And on behalf of the whole church, this community promises to stand by you forever." The baby clutched his ministerial ring finger. He stopped in front of Isaac. "This is your new sister, Isaac. Watch out for her. Give her something to look up to. Don't let her down."

Reverend Lawson was looking at Isaac, but talking to everyone. He waited until Isaac nodded firmly, then swept little Mary Katherine back to her parents, waiting eagerly at the front of the church.

⇂ ⇂ ⇂

He and his dad headed for lunch after church, something they did a lot of since his mom had died. His dad was a lousy cook. "I have to see Steve Pincus in the hospital, first," his dad said. "It's right down the highway and it won't take but a minute. You can wait in the car or come in."

"What's wrong with him? I played ball with his grandson on Thursday after work. Little Steve didn't say anything about his granddad being sick."

"They're testing him head to foot since he's been having dizzy spells. Last week he dropped the collection plate, remember?"

"Yes," Isaac said. "It was the most life we've had in church in a while."

"Watch your tongue," his dad said, drumming on the wheel, seeming euphoric that worship was over and he was out of his black preaching robe. "My sermons are more exciting than professional wrestling. Do you remember what I preached on last week?"

Isaac didn't like tests. "No," Isaac said.

His father squinted as if he were looking right into the sun. He drove thirty-five even though they were on the highway now and the speed limit was fifty-five. "I don't either," he said. "Have no idea. But I'm sure it was a good one." He glanced at the speedometer, then floored it. The Ford Taurus lifted off the road, surging toward Nassawadox.

His father's minutes could stretch on for hours, so Isaac opted to go with him into the hospital. Besides, Isaac liked Mr. Pincus. He used to be the town's fire chief. He'd freed cats from trees, treated shark bites, and even put out fires. Mostly, when the evenings were cool, he had grilled fish and ribs out behind the firehouse. Cooking made the waiting easier. That's what firefighting is mostly, he said. Waiting.

Every year for vacation bible school, Mr. Pincus and some of his fire-fighters would referee the giant shaving cream fight on the front lawn. Every year Isaac's dad had worked quietly to get the shaving cream fight written out of the schedule, but every year it stayed in. Barbasol wasn't good for the grass, he said. Wasting things in plain sight, even shaving cream, wasn't the best witness for the church. Each year the shaving cream fight was the most popular event. Isaac's puppet show was the second most popular attraction.

When they got to his third-floor room, the Lawsons found Mr. Pincus propped up in bed looking bored and flipping through channels on the TV. "Ho, ho, ho," he said. "Must be Christmas to get a visit from you two catbirds. What a present!"

"You, Stephen, are in very good spirits," said Isaac's dad. "But when are you not?"

"When I dropped that offering plate last Sunday, that's a time that comes immediately to mind. Ever find all the pennies?" He looked at Isaac and laughed. "How 'bout those Orioles, Isaac?"

"I haven't really followed any baseball this season," Isaac said. "I haven't had time." His father sat grinning on the chair by Mr. Pincus' bed, feet flat on the floor, arms resting on his thighs, hands hanging loosely between his widely spread legs.

"Son, you've got to make time for baseball," Mr. Pincus said, seriously. "What could be more important than catching a game or two each week? Seems to me a baseball player like yourself at least ought to find time to read the box scores each day in the paper."

"Yes, sir, seems so. I'll read them tomorrow during my lunch break. I promise."

"Lunch break?"

"Yes, sir, I'm working at Chum's this summer."

"Ha! Mr. Chum have you working in that lumberyard of his?"

"No, sir," Isaac said. "The warehouse."

"I'll bet that place is a treasure trove. Especially if you're into junk." Mr. Pincus shifted his attention to Isaac's dad. "You've been keeping up with these break-ins, David?"

Isaac's dad glanced at his son and said that he had, and that, no, they hadn't caught the culprits.

"What do you make of them, Isaac?" The question caught Isaac off guard. He thought immediately of the reward and wondered what Orioles season tickets cost.

"I'm not sure, Mr. Pincus," he said finally. "But they're offering a reward.

Five thousand dollars, last I heard." Isaac glanced over to his dad, who turned his gaze to the tiles on the floor. "I aim to collect that reward," Isaac said, hoping to get under his dad's skin. "Going to try, anyway."

"Sounds dangerous to me," Mr. Pincus said. "What do you think of your young detective, David?"

His dad answered without looking up. "He says he's going to buy me cable TV with the money. It'll be nice to have ESPN. I can't complain."

Reverend Lawson looked up to Isaac. "Of course, if he gets killed sticking his nose in where it doesn't belong, that'll be a problem since his life insurance isn't quite paid up. Funerals aren't cheap, and I'd hate to be left holding the bag."

Isaac rolled his eyes.

Reverend Lawson smiled at Mr. Pincus. "You've raised three children, Steve. Maybe some day you could tell me how you did it."

"Oh Lord, we've had our moments." Mr. Pincus laughed. He looked at Isaac. "I think it's kids running some prank, personally. You got any clues, Sherlock?"

Isaac looked at his father. "A few," Isaac lied. "I've been asking around. Somebody at the hardware store says it's kind of like arson without the actual fire. You know, the flames painted on the walls."

"Interesting observation," Mr. Pincus said. "We never had any proven arson within the town limits, not when I was in the department. And the only deaths we had in residential fires were back when I was a kid like you. When I was a kid, I'll tell you, I was filled with visions of becoming a fireman."

Isaac had no vision about what he wanted to be.

"Yes, sir," Mr. Pincus said. "It was Eddie Patrick's wife and baby. What a sad thing." He looked over to Isaac's dad. "Have you heard about that, David?"

Isaac's dad nodded. "Many times."

"Those old houses burnt easier than dried hay."

"Eddie Patrick?" Isaac asked, taken aback. "You mean the hardware Eddie? Crazy Eddie?"

"Eddie still working?"

Isaac nodded.

"I thought he retired this winter," Mr. Pincus said, "but what do I know?

He's not slowed down a bit, that old guy. He's well over seventy, I would guess. Hardware Eddie, that's the one."

"I didn't know he had been married and had a child," Isaac said.

"There's probably a whole lot you don't know about Eddie, son." Mr. Pincus crossed his legs and put his hands behind his head. He had short black hair that was slicked back and a sagging tattoo of an anchor on his forearm. "You never really know any man, son. Especially a man like Eddie Patrick."

ψ ψ ψ

They stayed in the hospital exactly one hour. By the time they got to the car it was 12:30, and the car seats were blistering hot.

The Duck Blind with its black, fake marble tabletops was cool. Isaac looked furtively for Kate Bradshaw. He didn't want to seem too eager, though he was. He reminded himself that the vision he'd had of her that morning may have been divine, but it wasn't real.

Isaac dug into the buffet and ate at least one of everything except chicken livers. By the time he got to the watermelon, Isaac could no longer wait to ask about Eddie. His know-it-all, experienced dad would probably have an answer.

"First off," his dad said, "why'd you call him crazy?"

"It's a long story," Isaac said.

"He's had a hard life," his dad said. "You shouldn't pick on him."

"I don't," Isaac said defensively. "What do you mean, a hard life?"

Reverend Lawson was picking his teeth with a toothpick, tie loosened, calendar book bulging out of his breast pocket. "Just look at his face," his father said. "He's a member of the church, but never comes. His family did, apparently. Were very active. That was before my time, of course. There's a window in the narthex in memory of his grandparents. They were Patricks from Dublin."

"I've never noticed." Isaac made a mental note to find that window next time he was at church.

His dad leaned forward on his elbows. "Did you know that he grows a garden every year?"

"So," Isaac said, dismissively. "This is the boondocks. Everybody around here has a garden. There's nothing else to do." Isaac's mom had had a small garden overrun each year by tomatoes, cucumbers, and squash. His dad had been mowing over the patch since spring, and it was slowly disappearing, beginning to look like the rest of the backyard.

"He gives it all away. We've been eating his fresh greens every summer."

"I thought Mom got those."

"Where do you suppose she got them from?"

Isaac didn't answer.

"Eddie'd drop bags full of them by the church. 'For the missus,' he'd say. Greens. Spinach. Swiss Chard. Beans. Peas."

"What about his family?" Isaac asked. "How long had he been married? How old was his child?"

"She was a baby girl. His wife was from Richmond."

"Did they meet in college?"

His dad raised an eyebrow over one eye and squinted with the other. "Why, yes, they did, from what I hear. How'd you know that?"

"He told me one day at the store that he went to college in Richmond," Isaac said. "I couldn't believe somebody like Eddie went to college at all."

The Duck Blind was getting noisy.

Presbyterians got out of worship at 10:30 in the summer. Other denominations kept their winter schedules and still got out at noon. Isaac watched the Episcopalians, Baptists, Pentecostals, and all the rest filling the tables and booths. He and his dad sometimes took bets on which group of hungry Christians would get to the town's only restaurant first. And watching them come was like a parade at the world religion zoo, Isaac thought, a beautiful, exotic sight that he always enjoyed watching: people of every shade of white and brown lining up at the buffet, some dressed up, some not, impatient little boys harnessed in clip-on neckties, women with dangerously wide hats, old men in seersucker suits the exact colors of sherbet, some people in jeans. It was a gloriously real vision. The line of people and the air conditioning streamed out the glass door into the parking lot that smelled like tar. The place filled up with the smells of cologne, perfume, and steaming batches of perfectly timed fried chicken being whisked through the kitchen serving window to the buffet.

"What else is Eddie telling you?" his dad asked as he leaned back from the table. He smiled and nodded generously to the people he knew at the buffet.

"Not much," Isaac said. "Mostly he tells me to get back to work. Every time I take a breath, he pops up. I think he likes having me around to pick on." Isaac looked out the window. It was a great afternoon for a baseball game on TV. "I can't believe his wife and baby were killed in a fire," Isaac said. "That's really awful."

"I'll say. It was very sad. They hadn't lived here long at all. Eddie's father needed help with the farm, so Eddie came home. Came home with a wife."

"Weren't there others around to help? Migrant workers, like now? And others."

His dad sipped his coffee. "Migrant workers came later, in the '50s. Others, mainly black folk, may have been available," his dad said, "but maybe Mr. Patrick couldn't pay them. I don't know. Maybe he just wanted his son around."

Out of nowhere, Kate Bradshaw appeared at their table with the bill. "This isn't my area today," she said, "but I wanted to come by and say hey."

"Well, hey," Isaac said. His voice squeaked. He couldn't wait to talk to her, but suddenly couldn't think of a single thing to say. Before he could make a lame comment about the weather, his dad chimed in.

"What?" his dad said to her, holding the bill, mock surprise in his voice. "Our bill before dessert? I've got a growing boy here."

For once Isaac was glad his dad was so quick and good with words.

"Sundays, as you know, Reverend Lawson, are buffets. What we got," she said smiling, "is all on the buffet. Help yourself. Apple cobbler, for one thing. Or," she said with a wink to Isaac, "another helping of string beans. They're all fresh, you know." She gave Isaac a big smile. "It was good to see you the other night, Isaac." She put the bill on the table. "Hope to see you later maybe."

"Thanks," he said, but she was already around the corner in the other part of the restaurant.

A man and his young son were in the buffet line. The boy insisted that he carry his own plate, while the father was trying to help. The boy was starting to squeal.

"You heard from Jenny this week?"

Thinking of her was a jolt. It kind of made him sick, then it got him mad. "Things didn't go so well at the beach last weekend," Isaac said. "I thought you knew." Without looking at it, he held up his cell phone. "And she hasn't called," he added. "So things likely aren't going to get any better."

"I'll bet she misses you," his dad said, setting down his empty coffee cup. "I would."

Why? Isaac wanted to say. But he kept his mouth shut.

↡ ↡ ↡

After lunch they went to the library. Isaac's dad volunteered in the genealogy room. "You want to come?" he had asked. "I'm surprised. Do you want to spend quality time with your old man or are you suddenly interested in genealogy?"

"Neither," Isaac had said. "I thought I'd see if they have any new DVDs in the movie collection." But Isaac had something else in mind. He had mastered the library's microfilm machine doing another project for Mr. Wilson's history class. He knew old copies of *The Shore News* were stored that way. The microfilm machine was in the reference section, which could be seen through the windows of the genealogy room, and Isaac didn't want his dad to see what he was doing, so he worked quickly, ducking his head behind the monitor. He scanned the front-page headlines from 1952. That's when he thought Eddie had said he'd started working at the hardware store; Isaac guessed that that might be the year of the fire. It wasn't; 1951 was.

The story was buried at the bottom of page three under a small headline. The half-page ad at the top of the page featured a dress shop that Isaac had never heard of. The fire trucks arrived too late, the story said. The house was outside of town at the Patrick farm. A Charles Windsor was the chief. The cause of the fire was not reported. The story didn't even list the names of Eddie's wife or child. Did they not know the names at press time? At a weekly newspaper? Isaac wondered why they were left out.

But there was a picture. Isaac's heart began to pound.

He had seen death before. His mother died at home in a hospital bed they put in the breakfast nook overlooking her flowers in the backyard. Her last days were spent sleeping, mainly, and sometimes talking. What she said didn't make a lot of sense at the end. She said I love you a lot. Even after she was too tired to make a sound, she'd mouth the words and smile that dreamy smile of hers.

But that was different. It was like she was being tucked into bed for the night, like she was just going to sleep. There was no struggle at the very last, just an occasional fidgetiness that he and his dad calmed by holding her hands, stroking her forearms. The hospice nurse came by with shots twice a day. It was very clean, very peaceful, and, by the end, very expected.

Not these deaths. Isaac hunched over the microfilm machine, intent on the screen, fingers almost trembling too much to adjust the knobs, to pull the ugliness into better focus. The middle of the house had caved in, leaving brick chimneys on either end standing above the ruins. Isaac stared at the picture, the tangle of charred beams.

Isaac remembered what Mr. Pincus had said about those old houses, how they burned so easily, like bales of hay. He stared at the chimneys, lonely, watchful, but unable to stop the fire. Unable to shout warning. Able only to stand by as Eddie Patrick's wife and baby shrieked, and burned, and turned to ash.

7

Monday night Isaac looked like a raccoon in reverse. He stood looking at himself in the hallway mirror when he came home. He had white rings around his eyes where goggles had been and a face darkened with grime. He had swept out an end of the warehouse with an electric blower. His ears were still ringing.

He had been alone all day. He couldn't get the picture of that farm-house out of his head—the ashes, the gray sky in that black-and-white photograph. He gave William and Susan Chum a polite hello and hurried through his morning sweeping in the store. Hank Grady, he heard, was at the dentist, so the conversation around the stove wasn't as toxic. In a way, Isaac was sorry he couldn't linger in the store and give everything a good cleaning, enjoying the talk, the AC. But ease seemed vulgar. So he went out back to the warehouse, pushing, shoving, and hauling the clutter.

Whenever Eddie came in, Isaac would turn on the loud electric blower again, attacking some neglected crevice. He didn't want to look at Eddie, didn't want to wonder about his family, their death, Eddie's loss.

He worked through lunch again. He wanted to see Kate, but he didn't want to see her feeling like he did.

When he got home, his dad had dinner waiting.

The lasagna tasted good. His father kept filling his plate. Salad with cherry tomatoes. Homemade cornbread muffins. Iced tea. Except for be-ing covered head to toe with dirt, Isaac was beginning to feel human again from the hot food.

He became aware that his father was watching him eat. He stuffed more salad into his mouth. The air conditioning felt good. He leaned back and stretched. He chewed with his mouth open. The stove behind him was still warm; his father didn't like using the microwave. Isaac dabbed at his mouth with a paper napkin that said Happy Birthday.

"You just drank a whole pitcher of tea," his dad said, "and ate, I figure, six servings of lasagna. That's, let's see, maybe 4,000 calories. That doesn't include four muffins made with real butter."

His dad was on a diet. Wanted to look trim for the summer, he said. Isaac figured he wanted to impress Miss Edwards.

"And you won't gain a pound," Reverend Lawson said, smiling and shaking his head. "My growing boy. Used to hold you in a single hand."

"What's for dessert?"

"The Duck Blind, later," his dad said. "Mrs. Watson outdid herself today with a key lime pie. I had some for lunch."

Isaac looked to his father's belly.

"Just a sliver. It would have been an offense not to since she came over to my table and told me about it herself." He pushed his plate back. "She asked whether we wanted to use the family house on Chincoteague for the pony penning this summer."

"What did you tell her?"

"I told her that we were still making plans," he said. "Nothing definite yet, but we'd let her know soon. She said she understood."

Isaac got up for the jug of milk in the refrigerator. "What's the latest on these break-ins? You hear anything new?" He poured a glass of milk and jabbed at the tray of lasagna on the counter, digging at its burned edges. He didn't want to turn around until his father answered.

"I don't feel good about this, about you poking around in this," he said. "I really think this could be dangerous."

"Why?" Isaac said.

"I've got this sense, this intuition. Your mother said I needed to pay more attention to that."

Isaac heard his father stirring his iced tea.

"Of course, it's pretty hard to understand what I feel without her here to help me figure it out," he said. "I'm better at the head stuff."

"I still don't understand why you don't want me looking into these break-ins."

"A gang could be doing it. That's one reason."

"And it could be just a prank too," Isaac said. "Besides, I can fend for myself." Isaac leaned over the sink, looking out the window.

"I was taught to mind my own business," his dad said, softening. "That's another reason. There's something to be said for respecting other people's privacy."

"But you're a genealogist, for heaven's sake! You look into things that aren't your business every time you go to the library."

"That's different," David Lawson said.

"How?"

"They're all dead, mostly."

Isaac didn't answer. There was no breeze outside. Water drops leaked from the faucet, but nothing came from the sky. He wasn't mad, just disappointed. All of his friends were in a different world: ball fields, late night bus rides home, early morning practices before it got hot. And Jenny was long gone. His dad was all he had left.

Isaac noticed that his mother's hummingbird feeder outside the kitchen window was empty; probably had been since she last filled it herself. The clouds looked like they would stay forever.

"I could give you some money, if you want it so bad," his dad said. "I'm not that poor. Tell me how much you want. Write a proposal for me, a business plan, so to speak. We'll go over it, make adjustments, and I'll give you the money. I'll even let you buy me cable TV."

Isaac was feeling tired and beginning to ache. A hot shower would feel good. He wanted to go to bed early. "It's not about the money," he said.

"You'll be in college soon," his dad said. "Plus you want some spending money now. I understand."

"This isn't about college, Dad."

"What do you want then?" his dad asked. "Why are you so curious all of a sudden about petty robberies?"

"Nothing was stolen," Isaac said.

"Huh?"

"They weren't robberies," Isaac said. "The houses didn't have anything taken."

Isaac didn't know why he was so interested. Like everybody else, he was curious. He liked the idea of having a pile of reward money. He also liked defying his dad, proving that he was his own person. Mainly, he was bored. What else was there to do?

"Well?" his father said.

Isaac and his father had had few serious talks since last summer. School had started and things had gotten busy for both of them. His father had been right: they had spent much of the winter in other people's homes, at other family gatherings. Being together with other people was the perfect way to avoid each other. His mom would have made it better.

"We named you Isaac because it means laughter," he heard his dad say. "You were born smiling. I said it was because you had gas. Your mother insisted it was because you were well-tempered."

Isaac had heard this before.

"And we named you David, sort of after me and your grandfather, but mainly because you were so small, just barely five pounds. David in the Bible was small too, but he stood up to giants. It seemed appropriate at the time."

Isaac tried not to roll his eyes. He had heard this before too.

"Your mom couldn't have any other children, and we never got around to adopting, though we had talked about it. Just never came up. Maybe we thought we had forever."

Isaac had never heard this before.

"Isaac David Lawson," his dad said. "Baseball star. Puppeteer. Member of the National Junior Honor Society. Detective. That's too long for a business card."

Maybe it was because he was so tired, but Isaac couldn't think of anything to say. He poured himself another glass of milk.

"You're growing up," his father said, folding his hands. "And I'm losing the little boy you used to be."

Isaac noticed in the twilight that his father's eyes were shiny.

"How's that for feeling?" his dad said, looking away to the pictures on the refrigerator.

Isaac could hear the hall table clock counting out the seconds.

"You're not losing me," Isaac said, finally, turning to look out the window again. "I'm not getting lost."

He swallowed hard. Amazing, he thought, looking at the clouds, how many shades of gray there are, and how, when you look long enough, gray clouds become black and purple and the purest white, and when you blink they are a thousand shades of gray again.

The summer before his mom died the family flew to Atlanta to see his grandparents. On their flight back home they took off at dusk between thunderstorms that had delayed flights all afternoon. Isaac remembered the plane shuddering through layers of clouds that hung like a tight-fitting metal lid over the ground. He remembered thinking as they climbed through the storm that there was no turning back. The ground was no longer safe.

When the plane lurched, his mother would pat his hand or give his arm a squeeze. His dad was perfectly serene. A book was open on his lap and his eyes were closed.

On the taxi ride to the airport that evening, Isaac had watched a wounded pigeon flail in the gutter. It had been unable to balance itself on its legs without the use of its tangled wing. On the plane, he thought of falling out of that violent air like a disabled bird. He was excited and petrified all at once. It was his father's calm that made him know everything was going to be all right.

From his aisle seat, his father leaned over him and his mom to look out the window. That's when Isaac noticed his dad's face was slick with sweat even though the air conditioning was blowing full blast and he and his mom were huddling together to stay warm.

His father battled his fear quietly and alone. Just like last summer when his mother lay dying. Just like now.

"Help me crack the case, boss, and I'll split the money with you, 60-40."

His father choked back a laugh. "What's a wealthy man like me want extra money for?"

The oven had grown cold. The kitchen was a catastrophe; the few times his father cooked, he made a mess. Isaac would clean up before his shower. The sun hadn't set, but it was past time to turn lights on in the house.

Reverend Lawson opened a magazine, but it was too dark to see anything.

8

Every day he worked hard. Every day he got dirty and tired. And every day the shadowy warehouse looked about the same. He could tell that progress was coming but he wondered if anyone else could.

His mother had taught him to clean up his room as a child. Chum's warehouse was no bedroom, but it brought him some joy to think that she had instilled in him the value of an orderly space.

Tuesday was a blur. The store was busy, there were lots of deliveries, and they got an unexpected load of lumber that day. He could have worked through lunch, but he couldn't imagine missing a chance to bump into Kate. The Duck Blind was packed. He wanted a table in Kate's section, but he didn't have the guts to tell the hostess. He ended up at the counter. He waved and smiled, but it was so crowded he wasn't even sure Kate knew he was there. And from where he sat, he couldn't watch her work. What a bust. He sulked over a Dr Pepper and BLT and was back at work in less than twenty minutes.

By late afternoon he was beat. He shuffled along the pathway he had cleared and looked at the rows and rows of half-empty and dried-up cans of paint. All of them had been opened. Drips of paint drooled down the labels. Though Mr. Chum probably wouldn't mind if he threw every can out, Isaac opened each one and saved any that weren't more than half-empty or dried-up just in case the eldest Chum showed up on one of his unannounced rambles. Halfway up the shelves, above the rows of paint cans, were boxes of light bulbs coated with years of dust and chipped clay flower pots.

Isaac paused and strained to see the clock above the bulletin board. It was 4:30. He had been lost in his cleaning. His stomach growled. He stretched his arms and back. He would be sore again tonight, he figured.

He looked at the top shelf. Besides a coating of dust, it was filled with papers, a few small boxes, and phone books. He'd have to get a ladder to clean it off. He was ready to go home, and could easily piddle away the last thirty minutes doing something easy, but leaving this small part of one corner undone to another day seemed wrong. He wanted to finish.

He wrestled a wooden ladder to a precarious spot against the shelves and staggered up. The shelves groaned under his weight. He got to the top and turned around to look at the shop. Light needled in through the holes and cracks to the outside world. Dust and light and darkness swirled together like smoke. His head filled with dirt and fumes. He had worked himself into a daze. He wanted dinner.

When he turned back around to clear off the shelf, he saw the ledger.

It was the size of a thin world atlas, the kind the library had on the lower shelves in the reference section, and it had a maroon leather spine. It stood taller than the phone books on the left and the seed catalogs and paperback almanacs on the right. "Keys" was written vertically on the spine in the script used for the numbers on the key board. Isaac resisted the impulse immediately to pull it down and examine it. It was almost five o'clock, and he was determined to finish emptying this shelf.

He dropped the phone books one by one onto the floor. Plumes of dust billowed into the light. The almanacs followed. Finally, only the ledger remained.

He opened the cloth cover. He shifted his weight to get better balance and leafed through the ruled, yellowed pages flecked with brown. The pages were lined in blue, names handwritten in spidery script, numbers preceding them. Williams. Martin. Davis. Kellam. He flipped through it. Fifty or more pages, front and back, of names and numbers, single spaced, the rest of the pages blank. Some notes and addresses had been jotted beside entries.

There were twenty-five keys listed under the Grand Hotel, which had burned down when Isaac was in grade school. There were keys that unlocked restaurants that Isaac had never heard of. He recognized some of the family names. Jones. Reeves. Miller.

He recognized a few of the business names on Front Street, too. Milynn's still did a good business selling china, sterling patterns, and other fine gifts; Isaac's mom had known the women there by name but mainly just window-shopped. She had never taken Isaac inside because she had said he was like a bull in a china shop. His dad said every bride on the shore since Teddy Roosevelt's day had been registered at Milynn's.

Isaac read each name, curious about all the people and their stories. His father loved history, but, except for his paper about P.O.T.S., Isaac thought it was boring. Until now. What treasures were these keys meant to protect? Did they unlock trunks filled with stamps or ancient coins, or sheds with human bones buried beneath the rotting floor?

There was a Thomson without a p, several Crocketts, and two people named Masters. He turned a dusty page. At the top was Nathan Parramore's name. His house was the latest hit. Isaac's dad had showed him the story in *The Shore News*. Flames had been painted on Nathan Parramore's walls. The drains had been stopped up and the water had been left running, apparently for days.

And the key to Mr. Parramore's front door was hanging on the cobwebby key board downstairs by the warehouse back door.

"What you doing, boy?"

The voice was a growl. Isaac nearly fell off the ladder.

Crazy Eddie glared like he'd just treed a coon and was looking for a way to get off a shot.

"I'm cleaning," Isaac said, annoyed that Eddie dared to think him lazy after all the work he'd done. He clapped shut the book, mildly amazed that it was dust free.

"I can see you're making progress," Eddie said. "It'll be slow going, though, especially if you're going to read all day."

Isaac felt steam rise to his head. "I've been busting my tail all day, Eddie, while you've been gone all afternoon on deliveries. You just haven't seen."

"Oh, I've seen," Eddie said. "And I know." He began singing the Santa Claus song in a tuneless way. "I know when you've been sleeping. Know when you're awake." He took the toothpick out from between his thin lips. "Know if you've been bad or good, so be good for goodness sake."

Isaac gritted his teeth. He didn't like the idea of being watched. Or threatened. He held up the book in his hands. "I found the old ledger that kept track of the keys. Mr. Chum said it was lost."

"It wasn't lost. I've known where it was all along," Eddie said. "I keep telling him that I know where everything is back here. I've been knowing since he was a little boy when he played around here. His britches weren't so big then, I declare."

"Problem is," Isaac said, "he's the boss."

Eddie fired back a hard glance. "Junior's got ideas for this place. Gonna make it a Walmart, or something. Trying to clean everything up so's we won't be able to find nothing. He has high ideas. Progress. He don't know that ain't nothing going to change on the Shore. People here got old ideas."

With a sudden flurry of wings, a pigeon darted out from under the eaves, circling up into the cavernous space at the peak of the sagging roof, then out a broken vent. Nest feathers drifted down past the rafters, streaked with white excrement.

"I'm aiming to leave this shelf clean. Those phone books," Isaac said, pointing to the floor, "are older than I am. Those catalogs and almanacs too." He looked at the ledger. "What do you want me to do with this old book?"

"Put it back where you found it, I reckon."

"And that pile of work rags?" Isaac pointed to a waist-high stack near the door.

"Same."

"They're still wrapped up, never been used, but they've dry rotted. They're not any good."

"Dumpster, then," Eddie said.

"There isn't any room in the dumpster, Eddie. Hardly any room around it. I filled that thing up last week and pick up's not 'till Wednesday."

"Well, start a burn pile out back, then. Liable to burn the whole town down, what with the fire department we have, but we'll have a clean warehouse. The boss'll be happy with that, I'm sure."

Isaac left the ledger on the shelf and ambled down the ladder. It was 5:15. "I'll start the pile first thing in the morning," he said.

Eddie watched Isaac put the ladder back against the post where he'd gotten it.

"See you then, okay?"

Eddie grunted, then headed to the big doors and began shutting them. Isaac endeavored to practice being nice, so when he got home to his father, he'd already be in the habit. He helped Eddie with the big doors, then signed his timecard, imagining dinner in the formal dining room of the Cavalier Hotel. That door was locked. He'd never have the key to that dream.

The doors in this town were another story. If you knew where the ledger was and if the key was on the board and if the locks hadn't been changed, you could walk right into somebody's house without leaving a clue. You could paint flames. You could stop up drains. You could raid the fridge if you wanted. You could do anything without leaving a trace as to how you got in.

But you'd have to know about the key board. And you'd have to know where the ledger was. And as far as Isaac could tell, the only one who knew about both of those things was Eddie Patrick.

↡ ↡ ↡

"Hey, Dad," Isaac hollered as he came in from work. He walked into the kitchen. This time no dinner was on the stove. Reverend Lawson was sitting at the table with what appeared to be sermon notes strewn about. Several magazines were open. Isaac took a swig of milk from the jug in the refrigerator. "Remember last night when you said you'd help me crack the case?"

Reverend Lawson had resumed writing on a legal pad. "What case," he said in a monotone without looking up.

"Right," Isaac said, taking a seat and putting his elbows on the table. "I want to pick your brain, okay? Have you heard anything?"

"How should I know?" He yawned. "The center of information in this town is the circle of chairs around that potbellied stove in the hardware store. You probably know more than anybody."

Isaac restlessly stood up and leaned against the counter. "You know the police chief, though, and the mayor, and people like that."

"They didn't do it," Reverend Lawson said, not looking up from his magazine. "At least that's their story."

Isaac sat back down and scooted his chair in closer to his father. He folded his hands together like he was going to pray. He'd washed them, but he could see in the half light that oily dirt was still embedded under his nails and in the lines of his knuckles.

"Doesn't sound like a gang to me," Isaac said. "They would have stolen something for sure."

His father was still pretending to work on his sermon.

"Sounds to me like a prank," Isaac said. "Whoever's doing this is going to a lot of trouble. I mean, it takes planning to find an empty house, and to know in advance that it's empty."

His father set down his pen and crossed his leg.

"And getting in, that takes some doing as well," Isaac continued. "And why a private home? This is the sort of thing you might do to a public building, like a school or the post office. But to a house? To three houses on three separate occasions?"

"Is that what they're saying at the hardware store?"

"Yep," Isaac said. "They're scared, I think, because all the victims have been elderly, just like them."

"You're right about being scared," Isaac's dad said. "The elderly folk in the congregation are locking their doors during the daytime now. Used to be, I'd knock and walk right in to save them the trouble of getting up. Not now. They're locked tight and everybody is talking." He lifted his yellow legal pad. "This sermon stinks," he said. "Anyway, what do the guys at Chum's say the motive is?"

"Vandalism," Isaac said. "It's not robbery because nothing is stolen. And they think it's local kids."

Reverend Lawson leaned forward and began lightly drawing on the table with his finger. "What do you say the motive is?"

"Well," Isaac began. He hadn't organized his thoughts yet, so he was unsure of himself. "It's not kids, not any I know, anyway. I think if it were, they would have left more clues. This is the sort of thing Pickles Jordan and his brother would do just to get the attention, but they wouldn't keep it a secret."

"Why do they call him Pickles?" his father asked, smiling.

"Nobody calls him that to his face, or they'd get it punched in. It's just ironic, I guess. Such a wimpy name for such a bully."

"Irony. Now that's an interesting way to put it," his dad said, smiling. "Who was your English teacher this term? I'll need to thank her."

Isaac drummed his fingers on the table. "No broken windows, no signs of entry. I mean, how did the crook get in?"

"Or crooks."

"Or crooks," Isaac nodded. "Unless doors or windows are left unlocked, houses aren't that easy to break into. Just for the fun of it, I tried to break into ours yesterday."

"How'd you do it?"

Isaac was silent for a moment. "I couldn't. I had to use my key."

The room was perfectly quiet except for the hall clock and the distant hum of the air conditioner.

"Did you know," Isaac asked, "that Mr. Chum makes keys?"

"Every hardware store does."

"But Mr. Chum's is the only hardware store around," Isaac said. "And did you know that the old Mr. Chum used to keep a copy of every key he made? He'd keep it on a board in the warehouse, and keep who the keys belonged to in a ledger. Said that if anybody ever lost a key, he could replace it. Just like that."

Isaac's father ceased his imaginary drawing and cocked an eye.

"So," Isaac said, "if somebody had access to Mr. Chum's keys, that could explain how the crooks get into these houses."

"Yeah, but Mr. Chum could get into these houses without a key, couldn't he?"

"Why would he want to do that?" Isaac said, wide-eyed.

"No, no," Reverend Lawson said, wiping the notion away with his hand in the air. "The owner of a hardware store, seems to me, has to be a jack of all trades. And the Chums, if I'm not mistaken, are locksmiths, right? Isn't that something Chum's full service hardware store offers?"

He was right. Under the big word Chum's, the sign said "Full Service Hardware Store." Then under that, in italics, the words "You're a friend at Chum's."

"So, don't you think somebody like Mr. Chum could pick a lock without leaving a trace?"

Isaac hadn't thought of that. He was a lousy detective. "Well, I don't know what a locksmith can and can't do, but I do know something about that key board in the warehouse. I'll bet you a hundred bucks that all three houses that have been broken into have keys on the key board. I know for sure the Parramore key is on it, because I looked. I'll bet that the other vandalized houses are listed in the ledger too."

His father rubbed his chin with a sigh. "How do you know these keys on the key board still work?"

"I don't know."

"Seems far-fetched to me. Realtors sometimes have access to keys. And that key board. Lots of people have access to that key board, right? Everybody that works at Chum's—what, twelve or more people? And all the people who've had summer jobs over the years. Teenagers like you."

"Yes, yes. I've thought of that," Isaac said, "but only one person has access to the ledger."

"Who, pray tell, would that be?"

Isaac looked right into his father's eyes and cleared his throat. "Eddie Patrick," he said. "As far as I know, only Eddie knows where that ledger is, besides me."

"You didn't do it, did you?" Reverend Lawson said deadpan to his son.

Isaac rolled his eyes and shook his head.

"I'm sure Eddie didn't do it," Reverend Lawson mused. "There's got to be another explanation."

"I'm all ears," Isaac said.

His dad smiled. "You're the big-shot detective."

Reverend Lawson jumped when the doorbell rang.

"Who's that?" he asked, then fell silent running possibilities through his head. It was nearly seven o'clock. The doorbell rang again. Then two more times.

"Oh, my goodness," Reverend Lawson said, bolting for the front door. "It's Clara! I forgot all about her and Tom."

Isaac trotted after his father down the hall.

"She was going to bring some checks by for me. I've got to reimburse Mrs. Greer for some VBS expenses, and Lottie, and, oh—it's a long story."

Reverend Lawson groped for his son in the living room. He took his shoulders. "Isaac, I told Clara that you would watch Tom while she and I went for a stroll. I forgot all about it." He squeezed Isaac's shoulders tighter. "A friend in need is a friend indeed, yes?"

Isaac thought it funny that his father looked flustered and nervous.

"Will you?"

If this wasn't dating, Isaac didn't know what was. "Sure," Isaac said. He couldn't help smiling.

Reverend Lawson opened the heavy front door and unlatched the glass storm door. He clicked on the porch light.

Miss Edwards and her six-year-old son were halfway down the walk toward their station wagon. She turned back to them and looked surprised. Her son clutched her hand, craning his head to see Reverend Lawson. The boy was small for his age, and he wore an expression that was a cross between fright and curiosity.

Reverend Lawson stepped onto the stoop. "Greetings!" he said in a big voice. The porch light made it look like he was wearing a halo. "You both are a sight for sore eyes."

They turned around and came to the door. David Lawson waved them in.

When Tom saw Isaac standing in the living room, he shouted, "Isaac!" and let go of his mother's hand and ran, hugging Isaac's legs.

Isaac was surprised, given how he'd treated Tom during their game of psycho-catch.

"I've been looking forward to seeing you all day, Isaac," Tom said. "But let's not play catch, okay?"

Before Isaac could answer, Tom opened his mouth and words poured out. "Vacation bible school is next week and I can't wait for your puppet show! Everybody is talking about it." He took Isaac's hand and gave it a squeeze.

Isaac patted Tom's head.

Before anyone else could speak, Tom said, "Don't you have lights in this scary house? Mommy tells me all the time I have to be brave, but I'm still a little afraid of the dark."

9

Isaac got to the hardware store at seven. He wasn't expected until eight. He came early to talk to Mr. Chum.

Eddie was in the warehouse sitting in a rusted metal chair that leaned to the left. His feet were propped up on an empty dappling bucket turned upside-down. He had his marlinspike out and was splicing an eye onto the end of a piece of heavy rope. He seemed surprised to see Isaac arrive an hour early.

"Nice chair," Eddie said as Isaac unpinned his timecard from the bulletin board and filled it in. The floors were clean, Isaac noticed, but the high counter was covered in dust. "I found it by the dumpster," Eddie continued. "A misguided young man I know was trying to throw it away."

Eddie sat in the chair at an angle to compensate for its slightly twisted frame. He held the end of the rope in one fist and the gleaming spike in another.

"It looked like junk to me, Eddie. But I can see now that it's a regular throne."

Eddie's ears grew red and he began digging at the thick strands of rope with his spike. "A throne," he muttered. "Clean freak."

✟ ✟ ✟

It was easier going without the old-timers around the stove. Seven o'clock in the morning was too early for them. Isaac ran the wide mop down the center aisles without having to maneuver around arthritic legs and scooting chairs. He mopped fast, working up his courage to ask Mr. Chum about door locks, how they worked, and how you would go about picking one. They bumped into each other at the front door.

"Whoa!" Mr. Chum laughed. "Who said Indy was the best place for speed?"

"Sorry, Mr. Chum. Didn't mean to take you out."

"If only we had ice hockey in these parts, I declare. You're some checker." Mr. Chum smiled and clapped Isaac on the shoulder. "You're here a mite early, aren't you?"

"Yes, sir," Isaac said. "Just trying to beat the heat."

Mr. Chum leaned a sign in the storefront window. He was running a week-long special on garden tools. "I've got an overstock," he said with a frown, nodding to the sign. "Hard rakes, fan rakes, snippers, clippers, the like. Listened to Mrs. Chum when I ordered this winter. Shouldn't have. But don't tell her I said so."

He pointed Isaac down the solvent aisle and followed him and his dry mop.

"I hope you're liking it here, Isaac. That junkyard in the back has never looked better. I want to thank you."

"No need, sir. Just my job."

"Well, if you need anything, you let me know."

When they got up front, Isaac pulled the page off the daily calendar.

Mr. Chum bumped through the waist-high swinging doors to the other side of the counter. The counter was solid, uncluttered.

"I do have a question," Isaac said.

Mr. Chum slid his palm across the linoleum countertop, like he was proud of it, Isaac thought, and pulled up a stool with his foot. He sat down and patted the counter. "Shoot," he said.

"Are you a locksmith, Mr. Chum?"

"I know a thing or two, I guess you could say. Why do you ask?"

"Do you do locksmith work? I mean, does Chum's?"

"There's a locksmith in every other strip mall along 13, Isaac. We're kind of getting out of that end of things. That's all they do. Can't beat their prices. But there was a time when we were the only ones in town. Every town had a locksmith, and we were it for this town."

Isaac nodded. "I was wondering about door locks." Isaac cleared his throat. "I was wondering how you pick a lock, you know, break in. Is it easy?" Isaac didn't know how to ease into this. He was embarrassed. He dared not ponder what Mr. Chum was thinking.

"Well," Mr. Chum said, twisting up his mouth and folding his arms across his chest, "it just depends. Sometimes it's as easy as cake. Sometimes it's impossible."

Isaac leaned his long mop handle against the counter and stepped closer. No one else except Mrs. Chum was in the store, and she was at her desk in the corner, punching numbers in on an adding machine that stuttered and clacked. Isaac didn't want to speak too loudly.

"Can you get into any door?"

"Sure I can." He pointed to the hammer aisle. "With an ax or one of my big malls and maybe a splitting wedge you can get into any door—except for the ones at the bank." He leaned forward, motioning for Isaac to do the same. Their faces met over the big counter. "You aren't thinking about knocking off a bank, are you?"

Isaac's throat went dry. "No, sir, I'm happy with my pay here—"

"—I must be paying you too much, then!" Mr. Chum practically shouted with laughter.

Isaac tried to smile as Mr. Chum's laughter died down. "I'm talking about house doors," he said. "And can you get in, can a locksmith like you get in, well, I mean by picking it. Can you pick it in such a way that you don't leave a trace?"

Mr. Chum seemed amused. He chortled and wiped his bushy mustache. "There're a lot of door locks out there, son. It just depends."

"Okay," Isaac said, "suppose it's an older door lock."

"How old?"

Isaac was trying to think of how old the houses were that had been broken into. Rooksville had sprung up around a depot where the railroad put a spur in from the main rails that went to the ferry terminals at Cape Charles. Isaac wasn't sure when that was. He wasn't thinking too clearly, anyway. He was nervous to be talking about picking locks, and he wanted this to be over. "Say, about the turn of the century. Nineteen hundred, or so."

"Well, now," Mr. Chum said, "a lot of those older locks had wooden dead bolts. And not all door locks even had dead bolts. Some were just spring latches. A credit card could get you into one of those. Of course, around here the only reason people'd lock their doors in the first place was to keep a nor'easter from blowing them open. Things have changed."

Mr. Chum, it seemed to Isaac, was growing nostalgic.

"You got a lock problem with a door at home?"

Isaac noticed Mrs. Chum watching from her desk. He smiled at her and gave her a nod.

"Hello, Isaac," she said, then picked up a sheath of papers from her desk and tapped them together neatly.

"No, sir," Isaac said, trying to be nonchalant. He didn't like acting. Or lying. "I'm just talking theoretically."

"Oh, theoretically?" William Chum narrowed his eyes and nodded. "You know," he said more quietly, "we're all interested in how those houses were broken into."

Busted, Isaac thought. He didn't say a word.

Mr. Chum nodded again. "I see," he said. "Well, theoretically I could—a locksmith could—pick most any lock with a tension wrench and a little luck. Especially an older lock. Dead latches, though, do get tricky."

"Dead latches?"

He got off his stool and slid open the pegboard door under the counter. "I think I have an old catalogue down here I could show you."

Isaac didn't think he needed this much detail. He wanted this to be over, and he tensed as the front door bell jangled. He didn't want to seem anxious, so he turned casually around to see who it was.

Hank Grady had his paper under his arm and held the door for Harvey Norris, who was swallowed in a peach-colored shirt that looked new.

Isaac leaned over the counter. Mr. Chum was halfway under it.

"That's not necessary, Mr. Chum. I'm just trying to get an idea."

Mr. Chum was about fifty, or fifty-five. Except for his white mustache and blonde hair fading to white, he looked much younger. He seemed excited to be talking shop. He stood up and wagged his finger distractedly. "Find me later today and I'll take you to my workbench at home where I do that work now—what little I actually do. I'll find you an example of a spring latch and a dead latch and everything in between. Don't know why

I keep those old things, but I have plenty of them. Anyway, those dead latches aren't on older doors; they came out later, in the sixties."

Isaac grabbed the handle of his mop. "But a locksmith could get into an older door," he asked, "by picking the lock?"

"With the right tools, a steady hand, and a little luck, yes, sir," Mr. Chum nodded.

"Without a trace?"

A sly smile crept across Mr. Chum's face. "Without a trace."

Eddie was making deliveries when Isaac's day was over. Isaac clocked out at four and found himself standing at the old key board on his way out the warehouse door.

After Miss Edwards and little Tom had come over the night before, he'd given no thought to what he and his dad had discussed. All of them had gone for a stroll. Miss Edwards and his dad went one way, and Isaac and little Tom went the other, to the Duck Blind. Kate Bradshaw was still waiting tables, but on the other side of the restaurant. She came over and talked with them anyway. It was a slow night, she said, but lunch and dinner had been crazy busy. It was nice now to have somebody her age to talk to, she said.

Isaac told her that he had come for lunch hoping to see her, which made her smile. Isaac thought she blushed, and he was glad. It was difficult to talk with Tom wanting attention; he talked about school, the alphabet, and being scared of the dark, and Kate seemed enthralled.

As they were leaving, she told Isaac that she'd be gone until after the Fourth of July. She, her parents, and little brother were going on a whirlwind tour of the colleges she was thinking about applying to: U of R, William and Mary, Longwood, UVA, Mary Baldwin, Vandy. A few weeks ago she had looked forward to the trip, but now, she said, was a little sad to be gone for nearly ten days.

Isaac tried to hide his disappointment. Ten days. It made him feel really abandoned.

"I get back soon enough," she said, biting her lip. "On a Friday."

He wanted to suggest that they call each other while she was gone, but he had never called her. Besides, he'd probably get tongue-tied.

"Well," Isaac said, "on the day you get back, I'll plan on eating at the friendly Duck Blind for breakfast, lunch, and dinner."

"And yeah," Tom broke in. "We'll all meet up for dessert, just like tonight!"

Kate beamed. "I can't wait to see you again, Tom," she said. But she was looking right at Isaac when she said it.

Isaac got home, got a late shower, and slept soundly.

Today, he tried to let locks, keys, and breaking into old homes without leaving a trace fill his imagination. It worked. He avoided Eddie for the second day in a row. Isaac had his earbuds to his iPod in his ears. When Eddie came into the warehouse, Isaac pointed to his earphones, acted like he couldn't hear, and got busy clearing a stack of junk as far away from Eddie as he could get. He needed the space to think.

Now that it was time to go home—4:07—he'd gotten no closer to seeing things more clearly. So much for concentration.

He stood in front of the board with all the keys. Any locksmith could open just about any door in the county. That didn't narrow the list of suspects at all. And even if Eddie did use the keys on the key board, and even if the keys did still work, what would an eighty-year-old man be doing vandalizing the homes of old people? Maybe his friends were right about Eddie, after all.

Still, Isaac wondered about those keys. If the Parramore house key didn't work anymore, then the whole idea of Eddie borrowing keys would prove as ridiculous as it sounded. If, on the other hand, the Parramore key did work, that would be another matter. It still wouldn't make sense that Eddie would do such a thing, but it would prove that Eddie could, at least, do it.

Theoretically.

Isaac remembered what his father often said from the pulpit. When one had a question, spiritual or otherwise, one should do as Jesus said: Ask, and it will be given you; seek, and you will find; knock, and the door will be opened for you. Knock, Isaac thought. Or, use a key.

If he got the courage to walk up to the front door of Nathan Parramore's water-soaked, ruined house, he'd be able to test his theory. First he'd have to get the key. And to get the key, he'd have to find a ladder and get up to that shelf for the ledger if it was still there—before Eddie got back from his deliveries.

The sun broiled down into the lumberyard. A big splotch of sunlight angled in from the open sliding door and filled much of the warehouse. But the shelf with the ledger, he remembered, was along the far wall, high up, hidden in the shadows. Isaac saw that the ladder leaned against the same post it had the week before. He looked at the clock above the coffeepot on the counter. It was 4:15. If he moved quickly, he could get the key number from the ledger, then pocket the key before Eddie got back. But he'd have to be quick. If he waited to find the nerve, he'd never make it.

He dropped his empty lunch bag and bolted to the ladder, which was heavier than he remembered, and awkward to move into place. He banged it against the shelf so hard, in fact, he thought that shelf and ladder might come crashing to the floor like a quail full of buckshot.

It was darker than he remembered too, when he got his head up at shelf level. But the shelf was empty except for dust, some bird feathers, and the ledger, which was right where he had left it. He opened it and began scanning the names. He had seen the name Parramore before, but on which page? The week before he had looked at pages randomly. Now he used his finger and drew a slow line down each name, page after page after page. Moore. Erickson. Carmines.

He looked back to the clock. It was 4:19.

More pages. More names. Williams. Thomson. Peterson. Hanson. His finger was shaking.

The name Thomson rang a bell. He went back to it. Thomson. 15 Conch Street. November 16th, 1933. Miss Thomson was a member of their church. She was a shut-in. Isaac's dad delivered communion to her once a month. It wasn't a physical disability that kept her from coming to church, Isaac seemed to remember from his father. It was her mind.

Isaac heard a truck pull up outside the warehouse. A door slammed. He couldn't make out the voices. On the other side of the lot, somebody started the forklift, which coughed to life.

This wasn't worth $5,000.

Miss Thomson's key number was 77. He had brought a pen up with him and he wrote the number on his hand.

Isaac turned the page and scanned more names. Where was Parramore? The names were running together. Very few began with the letter "p." There were lots of Kellams and Turners. They must be big Shore families. He wiped his eyes.

His coach had taught the team that you can't perform your best when you're out of control. You've got to find your zone and stay in it. Don't let other people or circumstances take you out of the game, he said. Get in your own little world and stay there.

Isaac closed his eyes and took a deep breath. Then he closed the heavy ledger and held it in his trembling hands. He held it loosely, his fingers laced under the spine. The covers were between his thumbs. He opened his palms and let the ledger fall open on its own. He set the book down and scanned the names.

Parsons. Adams. And there it was: Parramore. 25 Cowry Street. July 3rd, 1946. Key number 116. He didn't know if this luck was a gift from heaven or somewhere else, but there it was, either way.

The rise and fall of voices came from near the warehouse door. Three men, maybe four. Mr. Chum was one of them, and maybe his son, Will.

Isaac practically slid down the ladder, picking up a nasty splinter in his hand on the way down. He walked the upright ladder back to its post. It was hard to be careful when all he wanted to do was be quick. The ladder was maybe fifteen feet tall, so tall and old that the wood had warped. It was heavy and rough.

He sprinted to the key board and for a split second couldn't think of a single number, not his age, not his telephone number, not Jenny's, much less the right ones. He looked to his palm. The ink had run because his hands were so sweaty, but the numbers were still clear enough. He got the Thomson key from its corroded brass hook, then the Parramore key.

When he heard Eddie's shrill voice he thought his heart had exploded.

Eddie walked slowly up from behind him and picked up Isaac's lunch bag from the floor. Isaac stood still.

"You're shaking, boy." Eddie studied the profile of Isaac's face. The conversation outside was end-of-the-day chatter, talk of getting into the garden before the rain, picking up a six-pack on the way home. Somebody killed the forklift motor.

Isaac looked back at Eddie, right into his eyes. They were gray with flecks of emerald the color of the bay.

"You've worked a little overtime and now you're afraid Chum ain't going to pay you, I'll bet!" He took Isaac's clenched hand. "I see you've got yourself hurt."

Eddie laughed and squeezed Isaac's fist open. His palm was bleeding from the splinter. Blood had covered his fingers. Only now did Isaac notice the stickiness of it, and a dull throbbing running up his arm. There was blood and those two numbers scrawled right below the fingers in smeared, black ink.

"I'd call 911 if I knew the number," Eddie said mirthfully. He laughed out loud again, this time more easily. "I've got just the thing," he said over his shoulder.

Eddie led Isaac by the hand to the counter, then started banging around in a metal tool box. He pulled out a clear plastic box that held tweezers and Band Aids. He unrolled a clean, white cloth.

"Set your hand down here, son. Let me have a look." Eddie hummed a tune. "It's deep," he muttered to himself. "There's a fountain flowing deep and wide. Yes, sir." His words faded back and forth from speaking and quiet humming. And with a mother's tenderness, Eddie deftly slipped out the big splinter.

Isaac felt himself go limp. He didn't think about the sting of the wound, or the danger of getting caught, or this summer which had begun like no other, or of all he did not have and could not understand. He just stared at Eddie's steady, slender fingers with red hairs curling from freckled knuckles as he wiped Isaac's palm with alcohol, squeezed a dab of antibiotic cream into the wound, and put on a Band-Aid.

The keys were clenched in Isaac's other hand, and if they hadn't changed the locks since the break-in, and if Parramore's old key still worked, then maybe he was onto something. What, he did not know. Suddenly, though, nothing was clear. And he couldn't remember why he ever cared.

Isaac sprinted out of the door without saying goodbye. Or thanks.

10

Walking down the bumpy sidewalk to Mattie Thomson's house, he fingered the key in his pocket. His hand was so sweaty and shaky that he wasn't sure if he could get the key out of his pants without dropping it. He wondered if he could even get it into the keyhole.

This would be over soon, he told himself. His lunch break was only an hour. In less than sixty minutes he'd be back at Chum's working. Or in jail. Or worse.

Nathan Parramore's house was too dangerous, Isaac had decided. Neighbors—maybe even the police—would be keeping a close eye on things. Maybe workers had begun doing the repairs. Trying that door would be stupid, not that trying Mattie Thomson's door was any smarter, but he had to know if any of those ancient keys worked.

It was warm out, but he was shivering as he walked. He tried to talk himself into another frame of mind. Get a hold of yourself. Find your zone. Breathe.

He tried to look normal. It's just a game, he thought. At the same time, he knew it wasn't just a game.

Key number 77. 15 Conch Street.

He walked down Kingfisher and argued with himself. This was a good idea; this was madness. He couldn't understand the motivation of an eighty-year-old vandal. But he couldn't understand his own motivation, either. Was he curious about the break-ins? Did he want to know who did it? Of course. Did he want the fat reward? Why not? But something else was dawning on him now. If Eddie was behind all of this—as ludicrous as that sounded—Isaac wanted to find out before Hank Grady and his rabid disciples in P.O.T.S. They would humiliate Eddie, and gloat about the arrest in the newspaper, and say terrible things about Eddie needing a shrink or the electric chair. Isaac didn't want Eddie hurt like that. That was part of his motivation. That was why this was so important.

Walking fast calmed his shaking. Out of habit, Isaac cut down the alley. The garbage cans stunk. On Conch, he walked passed old lady Thomson's house and ran his hand along the wrought-iron arrow fence. It felt like prison bars, immovable iron bars anchored in concrete. Her yard used to be beautiful. He had vague memories of it, how his mother always wanted to drive by to see what "Miss Mattie's doing with her flowers." He could almost hear his mother saying those words.

Gladioli, full of purple and orange blooms and too heavy for their own stems, were lying in the postage stamp front yard. The tiger grass at the border had done a fair job keeping weeds out of the neglected flower beds. He recognized some colorful impatiens. There were other flowers, or flowering weeds, he couldn't tell. Summer's heat would probably kill it all.

He stood at the fence, looking at the yard, then up at the porch and the red brick house with shutters shedding black paint. That was the front porch he'd need to get up to, stand on, claim—at least for a few seconds.

Isaac had overheard people at the church murmuring about how Miss Thomson needed to be put into a nursing home so that she wouldn't hurt herself. She could have a stroke and end up on the floor for days before somebody found her.

He paced to the end of the block and played back his plan. He'd just walk right up to the front door, as plain as the mailman, stick the key right into the lock, and give it a turn. He would wave to the neighbors should any of them see him. He'd smile and look at ease and be very cool, very unsuspicious. If the door unlatches, the key works. And if the key works, it would prove his point. Sounded easy, but he was having trouble steeling himself, getting up the nerve.

It's just like stepping into the batter's box at the bottom of the ninth. Tap off your cleats, spit, and go. Don't think about the score. Tune the crowds out. Focus on the pitcher, his wind-up, on that ball in his knotted hand.

Breathe. Find that space within. That quiet place. Your own little world. Let your body lead. He could hear his coach telling him that now was the time for your training to pay off. Trust yourself.

Problem was, he knew, he'd had no training for this. But at least he had a plan. If the door unlatched, he'd pull out the key and knock real hard. She'd come to the door. He would introduce himself and ask permission to pick some flowers from her front yard for his girlfriend, which he didn't have, but she didn't know. She'd say yes or no, and he would say 'thank you' either way and be on his way. He would walk away, relaxed and casual. He might saunter. Just like a Sunday stroll. He'd remember to smile and to breathe. He'd take the porch steps one at a time. He'd open the gate, which had scraped a groove in the sidewalk. He'd close the gate, careful to latch it. He'd look up. He'd smile again. And wave a generous wave. Completely unsuspicious. Very natural.

He was practicing his smile so hard his face hurt.

When he reached for the gate, it was heavy, squeaked, and clanked. The six wooden steps up onto the porch were steep. They squeaked too. The massive wooden door had scrollwork around the edge and ornate molding. It was solid. The brass numbers blended in with the weathered wood. They needed polishing. The narrow, beveled windows on either side of the entrance way were curtained from the inside. Isaac dared not try to look into them. He focused on that keyhole. The key would likely become fused to his fingers he was holding it so tightly. He practiced his smile.

Getting through the gate, up the popping wooden steps, onto the creaky porch had taken only seconds. So far, so good. With his free hand, Isaac took the doorknob and gave it a firm twist, just like it was his own house. It felt cold and smooth. It was locked.

Stay in your zone. Play your game.

With his other hand, he tried the key. He found the hole on the first try. He gave it a twist and turned the knob. The door snapped open, but before he could knock, he felt bony fingers in the small of his back.

"Miss Thomson," he said jovially, balling up the key in his hand and pivoting around wearing his plastic smile.

Miss Thomson's crinkled face glared up into his. The door creaked as it slowly floated open. She grabbed him by the shirt, pulling him down to her level. She was short, thin, and brittle, but had a surprisingly strong grip. Her breath smelled rancid, not unlike the garbage cans in the alley out back. She had a mouth full of large, yellow teeth.

She pulled him lower. She squinted. "You," she grunted. Her loose-fitting dentures clicked when she spoke. "Who're you?" Click, click.

Isaac opened his mouth but nothing came out. The key dug into his injured hand; his knuckles were turning white he held it so tightly. His back ached from bending over at such an odd angle. She had grabbed some flesh with his shirt and her nails hurt. Rabies flashed through his mind. Muskrat claws. He shifted his weight and the porch groaned. She hadn't blinked. One eyelid was opened much wider than the other. She worked her tongue over her white gums.

"I know you, don't I?" Click.

Isaac didn't speak.

"And I know what I'm going to do." Click, click.

Isaac couldn't speak.

He glanced over her tangle of gray hair. He'd not noticed the big wicker chairs and couch stumped at one end of the porch. There was a pillow on the couch with an indentation about the shape of her head. Reading glasses on the coffee table. *A Baltimore Sun*. She must have been napping, or worse, watching him the whole time.

She huffed through her nostrils like Isaac imagined a bull might do before lowering his horns and charging. Pale, blue veins bulged in her skull.

"You're the Presbyterian preacher's boy, aren't you?"

Isaac just nodded.

"Well, aren't you?" She huffed again, which startled him.

Isaac nodded again.

They stared at each other.

Isaac managed to speak. "What are you going to do?" He practiced his smile but couldn't make it work. The door still squeaked as it drifted slowly open into the dark house on what, on any other summer day, would be a delicious stirring of breeze.

She pulled him closer, then patted his chest with her open palm. "I'm going to invite you in, of course. I got manners." Click.

↓↓↓

Mattie Thomson turned Isaac around toward the open door and gave him a shove. "There," she said. "Watch your step and don't mind the mess. Been awhile since I've gone to entertaining."

The room was cellar-cold. An upright piano stood next to the dark, spiral staircase. Antique furniture was covered in worn maroon material with wavy, golden trim. She made him sit down on a small couch. He felt the springs in his bottom and against his back. It was like doll house furniture, he thought, made for small people, for Hobbits. It seemed so fragile, he was afraid he might break it just by breathing hard.

Bags of newspapers were stacked like blocks, three bags high, along the walls and around the furniture. Yellowed curtains hung from the big windows. The high walls were papered in an off-white with a green, raised design. The room was dark and stale. Dust coated everything. Cobwebs hung from the corners of the high ceilings like mosquito netting.

"Have some," she said, pouring from a crystal pitcher that she could hardly lift. The pitcher sat on an end table surrounded by thick glasses with plum-colored rims. He took the glass from her lest she spill it on the threadbare carpet. Why she had a full pitcher in a room that obviously hadn't seen guests in a long time, Isaac did not know.

"No thanks," he said. "I—"

"Drink it," she snapped.

He held the glass awkwardly, yearning to return it to the table. He had no idea what it was or how long it had been sitting there. There was still time to bolt from this place, Isaac thought. Still time to spring over that threshold and run.

"What gives me the pleasure of your visit?" Click.

"Flowers," he said. "Your flowers are always so pretty. I wanted permission to take some for my girlfriend."

"Your mother's dead." Her gaze had drifted from Isaac to the slightly blotched, oval mirror that hung over the couch, just behind his head. She was looking at her own reflection, Isaac thought, or at nothing at all. "One of the only people who took me for me," she said. "Didn't try to change me, your mother."

"Yes. Your flowers are so beautiful," he said, trying not to let his voice quiver. He spoke quickly. "Thought maybe you'd give me a handful. I'd like to score some points with my girlfriend."

"Score some points, huh?" She huffed through her nostrils twice, then wiped her nose with the back of her emaciated hand.

He swallowed his drink in one gulp. It was lemonade, pulpy, sour, and heavy on lemon.

Miss Thomson was still staring at her reflection. She sat motionless except for the fingers of her right hand moving like the cilium he'd seen under the microscope in science class. Her vibrating fingers madly fidgeted at a pink, balding place in her scalp behind her ear. Isaac could hear the scratching.

He told himself to keep it real. She might be a little unhinged, Isaac told himself, but she was harmless. Probably.

"Yes, ma'am," he said, trying to lean into her line of vision, to snap her out of her trance. "Your flowers have been catching my eye every day on my walk to the hardware store."

She jerked back to life.

"You work at Chum's? Chum's hardware with Eddie Patrick?"

"Yes, ma'am."

She looked right at him, excitement coming to life in her eyes.

"Why do you ask?" Isaac said. This time his smile was sincere.

She was silent.

"Am I being too nosy?"

"Why, how are you going to learn anything if you don't ask?" she said. She sank back into her chair. The fingers of her right hand fidgeted along the fraying hemline of her baggy shorts. A network of blue veins twisted up her thin legs like unfortunate rivers beneath her shiny, white skin.

"When you've been friends as long as we have . . . " She seemed to be drifting away again. Her eyes popped back into focus and she continued. "We went to first grade together, in the one-room schoolhouse that they made into the funeral home, out on 126. We were inseparable."

She was smiling. She leaned her head back in her chair. Maybe she was remembering that schoolhouse. Maybe she was there.

"Yes, ma'am," Isaac said. He spoke soothingly, like he had the other night when little Tom Edwards was afraid. "Do you and Eddie visit much?" Isaac asked. "Nowadays?"

"He brings me my vegetables all through the summer, just like he did for your mama who's as dead as my azaleas. It was the bugs that got them," she said.

"You knew that Eddie gave my mother vegetables?"

"Sure did," she said. "This is a small town, boy. More water?" She pointed to the pitcher.

"No, thank you," he said. It was water! He wished he could go the rest of the day without swallowing.

"I used to do a lot more before I got so tied up in this big house. When my arthritis is acting up, I can't even get down my own front steps. Haven't been to my attic in near about twenty years. Lots of memories packed into that attic, and that's the gospel truth. My family moved into this house from the farm when I was in sixth grade. Eddie and I hardly knew what to do without being next door neighbors anymore. We had lived on practically the same plot of land. He stayed on the farm, and I became a city girl."

Isaac thought it funny that anyone would consider Rooksville a city.

"Did you used to date?" he asked.

"We were friends."

"Did he see other girls?"

She huffed again from her nose. "He didn't date much," she said with a click. "Practical men didn't have time, to speak of. And he was practical. Very polite, but very serious, direct. He's grown into the old codger role pretty well, hasn't he? Such a blustery character. I just love how he turned out."

"I'm sure he thinks the same about you, Miss Thomson."

The color was coming back to her face. She was lightly tugging on her hemline with her right hand, but the fingers has ceased their furious movement. "Do you know I used to be three inches taller? I'm shrinking away, I tell you." She laughed a squeaky laugh and shyly looked away.

Miss Thomson got up and went to the dining room. She was stooped but walked quickly. She opened the big breakfront and reached up on tiptoe.

"I can't quite reach," she said in a small voice. "Will you help?"

Isaac got up.

She pointed to a small white vase. "It's for you, if you can reach it," she said.

She must have read his blank look.

"For your flowers. For your girlfriend. Remember?"

Isaac nodded and quickly got the vase down. It was a nice one, and he felt awkward about taking it. He shut the delicate glass door and followed Miss Thomson back to the living room.

He could imagine a dinner party in this old house, the wooden window blinds opened, perhaps a fire in the tiled fireplace. Miss Thomson seeing to it that everyone was comfortable. Perhaps she would have maids. Laughter. Maybe even dancing, but not the hopping around and bump-and-grind that Isaac had seen his friends do at school dances, but real dances, Isaac thought, the kind where you have to learn the steps.

He eased back onto the couch. "But Eddie did marry, didn't he?"

"Why yes," she said. "Not many people remember about that, especially young ones like yourself." She tapped her nose with her left forefinger. "What do you know about that?"

"Nothing," Isaac said. "I don't know much about Eddie's family. I know that he and his wife met in college, in Richmond, that they had a baby, and that his wife and baby died in a house fire in 1951."

"Died? Were killed is more like it." Miss Thomson pursed her lips over those unnaturally large teeth.

"Killed? What do you mean? Killed by fire?"

"Murdered, boy," she said. "Murdered by the Klan." Her fingers had begun their mad dance again, crabbing at her hem, trying to pick off lint that wasn't there. "Would you like more water?" She glanced into the mirror.

Isaac said no. "I've read about the Klan," he said, "in the deep South. But they were here?"

"Honey, the Klan was everywhere," she said. She peered through the shadows at the brilliant light pouring through the open door.

"Okay, but why would the Klan want to kill Eddie's wife and child? I mean, a woman and a little baby. That doesn't make sense."

Isaac leaned into Miss Thomson's line of vision. She was staring at herself again.

"She had a name," she said. Miss Thomson's watery eyes seemed indistinct, like the bay overtaken by a fog. She did not move them from the mirror. "Eddie's wife had a name," she said, dreamily. "She was Celeste, short for Celestial, like the heavens. The baby's name was Josephine."

"Why would the Klan want to kill Celeste and Josephine?" Saying their names aloud made him wince. He remembered the microfilm picture in the library. He remembered the sickness he had felt.

Miss Thomson looked at Isaac. "Why? Because, sugar, back in those days—and I'm not sure much has changed—the Klan didn't take well to white men marrying black ladies and bearing into this world half-breed children." She huffed twice through her nose.

Isaac felt he was losing his hostess, like Miss Thomson would simply become invisible right before his eyes. "I don't understand," he said.

"What don't you understand?" Miss Thomson snapped. "Eddie's wife was a Negro woman, as brown as the dried tobacco leaves that they used to harvest all up and down these farms. That baby was the apple of his eye. And old Eddie's been just plain dead inside ever since."

Isaac slumped back to the hardware store and could hardly push open the warehouse door, he was so drained. He stepped into the cool darkness and let it envelop him. His father had said there were things in this world that could hurt you. He was right.

"What you got there?"

Isaac's eyes weren't adjusted yet to the shade.

"Cat got your tongue?"

It was Eddie.

Isaac held out a white glass vase filled with flowers. "For you," he said emotionlessly, putting them into Eddie's hand.

Eddie took them and cocked his head.

"Look, I think I'm coming down with something. I'd better take the afternoon off."

"I'll say, boy. You look real peaked." Eddie seemed to be trying to lean into Isaac's line of sight, but Isaac looked away, away into the concrete floor like Miss Thomson did into her living room mirror. Maybe that's what you do when the world shows you things you don't want to look at, you just look away.

"You'll look worse if you don't get back here all the earlier tomorrow," Eddie said. "You think this work'll wait, you're wrong. We're getting an order of lumber in the morning that'll take ten men to unload, except it's just you and me. Willy and the others'll be on a job all day, and I'm not taking that on alone, understand?"

Isaac nodded. "Yes, sir," he said.

Eddie looked at the flowers and scratched his leathery neck. He headed for the store. "Cut flowers'll die out here in this furnace, you should know that." He stopped at the door. "Susan Chum can use them more than me. But thanks, anyway." Eddie disappeared through the door.

Isaac was alone in the warehouse, glad to be surrounded by the familiar, but aware that nothing would ever be the same. He wrote his hours on his timecard and pinned it back onto the corkboard next to his Virginia Beach postcard. He hung up the Thomson and Parramore keys on the key board, never minding who, if anyone, was watching, and stepped from the shadows into the bright, perfect light.

11

Isaac slept all afternoon with a pillow over his head. It was a dreamless sleep. He wished he had someone to talk to.

If his mother were here, things would be different. She'd help him make sense of things. She didn't have all the answers, but she was good at asking questions. Her most frequent question was the most obvious: "Why?"

When he woke up at five o'clock, he was hungry and still tired. He rode his bike to the church. He didn't want anyone to see his mom's blue Honda parked out front because he didn't want to be bothered or have to explain why he was there, why he was poking through the clerk's record books that the church secretary kept in the top filing drawer in her unlocked office.

What he found in those books, especially in light of Mattie Thomson's revelations, made him madder than when an ump threw him out of a game for questioning one of Robbie Scare's wild pitches. He pedaled home, hopping curbs and grinding over the new gravel in the alleys, leaving a cloud of dust and a bunch of barking dogs in his wake. He couldn't wait to ask his father some questions.

He got home at seven. His dad was reading in the cluttered den.

"You missed dinner," his dad said, looking up from his book. "I had a bowl of cereal, but I drank the last of the milk. Sorry."

Isaac sat down in his mom's old recliner. "What do you know about the Klan on the Shore? Mr. Wilson never said anything about it in U.S. History, and we spent a whole nine weeks on the twentieth century."

"There's a lot you don't learn in school, you know." Reverend Lawson held out a can of peanuts.

Isaac shook his head.

"Fear is everywhere," Reverend Lawson said.

"What does fear have to do with it?"

"For the Klan? Everything," his dad said.

"So were they?" Isaac asked. "Was the Klan here? On the Shore?"

"Maybe. Certainly could have been." His father took his glasses off. "I dated a girl in college whose father still had his father's Klan hood and robe. He kept it hanging in the back of the downstairs coat closet. Old man Goodrich was some grand pooh-bah of the Klan back then. Fewer people wear the costumes, I suspect, but the hatred and fear haven't gone away."

Reverend Lawson's hands were folded, and he wasn't distracted by his book for once. He said that his girlfriend didn't know why her father kept the hood and robe. Maybe it was to remember. Maybe it was so he'd never forget. That was in Charlottesville, a long time ago, and Reverend Lawson had lost track of the girl. Isaac was glad for that.

"Why do you want to know? Does Mr. Chum have you doing research?"

"I rode my bike to the church today," Isaac said.

"What were you doing there?" Reverend Lawson asked.

"Whatever you do in churches, I guess."

Reverend Lawson nodded. "You want to go to a movie tonight up at Belle Haven? It's Friday night and I've got a hankering for some movie popcorn and Junior Mints, to hell with my diet. What do you say?"

"I looked up Eddie's family in the record book that you keep in the fireproof filing cabinet. The permanent record book, you know the one?"

Reverend Lawson nodded.

"You and Mr. Rogers showed our confirmation class how the church kept its records, how the names of members were added first to the chronological list, then each name was given a number and entered into an alphabetical list. Remember? That way you'll never lose track of a name."

"Malcolm Rogers is a good clerk. Details mean everything to him," Reverend Lawson said.

"From that roll, you can tell when somebody joined the church, when they were elected to be an elder or deacon, when they married, when their kids were baptized, when they transferred their membership, when they died—everything, right?"

"Good memory."

"Eddie's mother was Margaret," Isaac continued. "His father was Andrew. They had a child who died young, Eddie's brother, Gabriel. Eddie was born in 1925, in June. Everything is mentioned in those books. But did you know, there's no mention of Eddie's wife? No mention of their wedding. No mention of their child. No mention of her baptism. Why?"

His father lifted his eyebrows. He eased up in his recliner and took a breath to speak, but Isaac beat him to it.

"Wasn't Eddie married in our church? Didn't everybody have a church wedding back then?"

"No," Reverend Lawson said softly. "No, they didn't." Reverend Lawson explained that he presumed Eddie had been married in Richmond.

"Oh," Isaac said. In his fervor, he hadn't thought of that. "Well," he continued, "wasn't Eddie's baby baptized in the church? You don't have to get married in the church, or by a preacher, even. But if you get baptized, a preacher's there. And, usually, so is the congregation. Wasn't Eddie's baby baptized in our church? Didn't the minister take that baby in his arms and walk out into the congregation to introduce her, just like you do, just like you did last Sunday? And aren't the names of baptized children entered onto the baptized roll?"

"Yes, well." His father's mouth twisted around another word, but Isaac didn't give him a chance to say it.

"Well?"

Isaac stared at his dad. And his mother's favorite question rose up in him like the storm surge and winds of the Ash Wednesday Storm that flooded half of the Shore and left the town of Chincoteague waterlogged. "Why?" Isaac asked. "Why isn't Eddie's child written down in the baptized roll? It should be there. My name is there."

Isaac stood up and pulled a piece of crumpled paper from the front pocket of his cut-offs. He waved it at his father, then glanced at it. "My name is in that book, my parents' names are there, my date of birth, my place of birth, the date of my baptism, the place of my baptism."

Isaac was punching his finger down the list. The paper snapped with every jab like miniature rounds of applause.

"The name of 'clergyman administering sacrament.' That line's filled in," Isaac said. "The dates and places are all complete. It says I was removed from that roll on Easter of 1997 when I joined the church, was 'admitted to full communion.' You said in confirmation class that one thing that makes us Presbyterian is the way we govern ourselves. We like order. We keep records. History, you said, matters to us. 'A great cloud of witnesses.' 'We are family.' And naming one another and keeping records are things that families do, you said. You say those words all the time. And I have listened to them."

Isaac balled up the list and flung it at his father, who jerked away and struggled awkwardly with the lever to the footstool of his recliner.

"Why? Why am I on that list and Eddie's baby is not on that list?"

"It could have been an oversight," Reverend Lawson said, holding out the open palm of his left hand and shrugging his shoulders. With his right hand he continued his struggle with the lever. "An old member who has moved away returns to the church with a wife and a baby . . . maybe their names aren't entered in the book. I'd have to ask Malcolm Rogers how a clerk is required to handle that." Reverend Lawson searched Isaac's face. "What's with all this concern about church records?"

"I'm not interested in the records. I'm interested in the people who should be in the records." Isaac was boiling. "Their names should be written down!" he shouted.

David Lawson didn't move. Isaac recognized the swirl of anger and confusion registering on his father's face. The house was quiet except for the ticking of the Seth Thomas Regulator clock in the entrance hall, a ticking that Isaac never noticed except at moments like this.

Isaac was trembling because Eddie's family had been made invisible. They had been erased. Their names weren't in the newspaper story written about the fire in which they had died. Their names weren't in the record books of the church of which Eddie Patrick was a member. It was like they never had existed. Hadn't lived here. Hadn't died here. Or been killed.

"Honey, since you seem to know everything else, you know—"

"Don't honey me. Don't, don't—"

Isaac felt sick. He couldn't stop his trembling and didn't want his dad to notice. His throat felt like someone was choking him, like he had rubbed his tongue on carpet and had swallowed hot sand. He hated the church for forgetting, hated his father for being their minister, hated Eddie for letting them keep it a secret, hated the whole town. He sat down on the sturdy coffee table in front of the couch.

"Isaac—"

"—Well?"

"You know," his father said calmly, slowly, "that when the Session approves a baptism, and when the church baptizes a child, the name is entered into the roll of baptized children."

"Why isn't Eddie's baby's name recorded in that book?"

"There could be lots of reasons, Isaac. She could have been baptized in Richmond, or never baptized at all." David Lawson scratched his head. "I'm not sure I understand your obsession with the church record books."

"Don't you see?" Isaac blurted out. "Josephine Patrick's name should be written down somewhere."

Reverend Lawson had conquered the lever and the recliner popped as he eased the footstool down. He sat at the edge of the chair. He leaned into his knotted hands and slowly rubbed his forehead and the bridge of his nose with the knuckles of his thumbs. "Was that her name?" he said into his hands. He lifted his head and wore an expression that looked to Isaac to be wonderment and sadness mixed together. He sighed. "Was that Eddie's baby's name?"

Isaac's shoulder blades felt like they were sawing into the top of his back. His jaws ached. His head was beginning to throb.

"I thought I was the historian of the family," Reverend Lawson said to the ceiling. He leaned way back in his chair and crossed his legs like he had run a great distance and was too tired to move.

"This isn't about history, Dad," Isaac said with difficulty. "It's about a person. It's about a family."

They both were silent. Isaac's father looked at the ceiling, then closed his eyes and begin speaking in almost a whisper. "Eddie's wife was black. Negro or colored, they would have said back then—"

"—or nigger."

"Or nigger, yes. Back in those days they might have called her that. From what I hear, the baby was, naturally, not white." Isaac's father had a faraway look about him. There was an ache in his voice, a sadness. "From what I hear, it was a scandal," he said. He seemed reluctant to continue, but he did. "A few in the church thought that the church should not approve. I've been told that the minister tried to change their minds, to help them see things from another angle. But that vocal minority would not budge."

"What about everybody else?" Isaac whispered.

"Everybody else went along with the squeaky wheels, that's what. In effect, the church would not let her worship with him. They would not acknowledge that child. As far as I know, Josephine never was baptized. Churches in Richmond at the time, black ones and white ones, were probably no more open-minded about race than this one." David Lawson shook his head.

"And this is in the history books of the church?" Isaac asked.

"Nope," his father said. "It was never recorded, as you plainly know. There's not a word about it written down."

The black-and-white photograph at the library popped back into Isaac's mind. "If it's not in the record books that you and Malcolm Rogers prize so much, how do you know?"

"I don't prize those books," Reverend Lawson said, his eyes closed. "But I do value what's in them, the stories written between the lines. The lives and the blood." He sighed, then opened his eyes and looked at Isaac. "The written history, as you are learning, is only part of the history."

Isaac's back ached. Pain coursed through the veins in his head. "How do you know this stuff then?"

"The ladies who give me jelly," Reverend Lawson said quietly. "They know. Over the years they've told me about their sorrows, their aches and pains. Their mistakes. They tell me about swollen ankles and how they miss dead husbands. The older ones are dying out, but several of them told me about Eddie and about his daughter. They just never said her name."

Isaac noticed that his dad's hair was graying at the temples. The skin on his face seemed paler, wrinkled more at the corners of his eyes.

"One old lady in particular—she's listed in the roll book as Mrs. Robert Julius Branch—Mrs. Branch would often talk about Eddie's family and how they weren't welcomed. Doris Branch is dead now, but it hurt her to talk about it."

"Her?" Isaac spat. "What about Celeste and Josephine? It hurt them more than Mrs. Robert What's-her-name!"

He was losing his voice. He hated to keep talking. He hated to ask his father what he'd been trying not to ask all night long. "How can you be their pastor? How can you serve these murderers?"

Reverend Lawson rocked forward in his chair and gazed at the green shag carpet. "We all murder with our words. All of us do that."

"They burned down that house with fire, not words," Isaac said.

Reverend Lawson squinted, like he was trying hard to find a better focus. "Who is they?" he asked. "What are you talking about?"

"The Klan burned down Eddie's house," Isaac rasped. His voice was gone.

"Did Eddie tell you this nonsense?"

"Miss Thomson did," Isaac whispered.

Reverend Lawson laughed loudly, like a friend had told an unfunny joke in a crowd and somebody had to laugh. "You've been keeping interesting company," he said. "Mattie Thomson came unhinged a long time ago. Hardly ever makes sense, especially when she runs out of her blood pressure medicine. I should know. She's one of ours."

Reverend Lawson stood and stretched.

Isaac sat hunched on the coffee table. He put his elbows on his knees and stared into the empty fireplace. He had to whisper in order to speak.

"I searched the microfiche the other day," he said. He spoke so quietly, he could feel his father lean down to hear. Isaac could smell his father's breath, could feel the wisps of it feathering his cheek. "Found the news article about the fire. There was a picture. They had taken a picture of the house after the fire. The article doesn't even mention their names. But you've got to see the picture. Just a pile of wood and embers. A woman and baby died in that."

Isaac felt his father looking down on him. He kept staring into the bare fireplace, blackened with soot. He imagined orange flames painted on a bedroom wall, licking up to the ceiling, and the determined rise of water from wide-open spigots ruining everything.

"Eddie Patrick did this," Isaac said steadily. "He vandalized those houses."

"What?" Reverend Lawson said. "Why would Eddie do that?"

With every word, Isaac felt that shards of glass were being ground into his raw throat. "To get back at this town," Isaac whispered. "To make them pay for what they did."

Isaac felt his father's hand on his shoulder, could feel his father bending over him, coming close. He could smell his Old Spice, a hint of his breath, the faint scent of newsprint on his hands.

"Why now, son? After all these years?"

"I don't know," Isaac whispered.

Isaac turned to face his father standing over his aching shoulders. "You want to know what else?"

Reverend Lawson nodded.

"I don't think he's finished yet."

David Lawson stood behind his son, rubbing his shoulders, something he did after most baseball games, especially after the Saturday double-headers. His sturdy fingers made deep circles up Isaac's neck, behind his ears, to the hollow space at the bottom of his skull. With his fingernails, he scratched Isaac's head, which made his scalp tingle. Isaac bowed his head; his muscles were untangling, melting. His father kneaded the tops of his arms and back, then up and down either side of his spine. It felt so good.

They were quiet for a long time.

Isaac couldn't help it, but he began to cry quietly. He squeezed his eyes shut as he sobbed. He was so tired. He hadn't realized how heavy Mattie Thomson's words had been, how impossibly troubling.

He let his father's thumbs soothe his muscles. David Lawson's fingers seemed to loosen the banks of something inside that was swollen and long-dammed, and Isaac wept without a sound. He let the tears and exhaustion and sorrow go. All the scheming and counting reward money he didn't have and really didn't want. Asking Mr. Chum about locks, poking his nose in other people's business, breaking into Miss Thomson's haunted house.

"Let's give it a rest, son, what do you say?"

Isaac wiped his face on the front of his shirt.

"We aren't detectives, not really," his father said. "The guilty one, or ones, will slip up and get caught one day. Or get bored and stop."

"Or," Isaac said, clearing the gobs of snot running down his throat, "somebody will get hurt."

"You might get hurt, Isaac. Maybe you already have."

"What about others?" Isaac said. "You can't think only about me."

"Yes, I can," Reverend Lawson said quickly, his voice cracking.

It had been a long time since Isaac had played baseball regularly, since he had run laps, done crunches, hit a hundred fast balls in a row. It felt like forever. It had been a long time since his father had rubbed his shoulders.

"Son, if it's Eddie, he wouldn't hurt anyone."

"But if they find out," Isaac said, "somebody might hurt him. They've done it before. I don't want them to do it again." He looked at his father. "Do you?"

12

On Monday morning the regulars were talking about Constitution Gray, his ailing wife, and the ruined condition of their fine, 1890s house. On Saturday the elderly couple had come home to a stream of water seeping beneath the threshold of their front door. Upstairs tap water had cascaded from a stopped-up bathtub and sink. Orange flames were painted on the bedroom wall. The waterlogged downstairs ceilings had sagged and collapsed. Carpets were so sodden it took six men to haul them all out.

There was no sign of forced entry. It was just like a ghost did it, Mr. Bennett said. Just like a phantom wisp of smoke breezed in through a crack in the attic and wreaked this havoc.

Mr. Peake said that they had spent all of Sunday pumping out the root cellar. At least it was good for the lawn, he said. The grass needed the water.

Isaac was all ears as he oil-mopped the floor and rewound spools of rope and small chain. When he stopped to straighten the shelves, he peeked at the men from between the rows of carpenter's glue and boxes of trash bags. Rotund Harvey Norris looked like a ripe lemon in a bright yellow shirt. Hank Grady looked like he always did, bulging out of denim overalls. Mr. Jackson had a gravelly voice and was wearing a wide necktie that looked like it had been cut from worn drapes. Mr. Peake kept time with his nervous rocking. Even Mr. Chum stood by, leaning against the light fixture aisle. His father, Billy, had ambled in and sat like a pharaoh in a rocker.

Mr. Bennett, Isaac's science teacher, had come in for electrical tape and had joined the clot of men around the stove. And so had Reginald Williams, Rooksville's chief of police.

The talk scattered into side conversations that were hard to follow. Everyone chattered about the recent break-in. Isaac roamed the store from corner to corner, dusting everything at least once, taking extra time to put lemon treatment on his dry mop. He wanted to catch everything. Every time he saw Harvey Norris and smelled the mop, he imagined an enormous lemon sitting in the middle of the store, rotting. And it took him a moment to realize he was absently humming the Peter, Paul, and Mary song about lemon trees, a favorite in his father's stack of records that Isaac sometimes spun on their battered, direct-drive turntable.

They called John Gray "Constitution" because he was a retired judge. Played things by the book, Mr. Peake said. He said that Mrs. Gray—Page— was no bigger than a man's fist. Harvey said they were pillars of their church, Methodist as best as Isaac could tell, and they had scads of grandchildren. They had raised four boys and a girl, all of whom had done well. Only one stayed on the Shore, the girl. Lives up in Maryland, in some trendy town like Oxford or Cambridge, Hank Grady said; he said he didn't know how people could afford to live in those places, what with the property taxes. That's where the Grays had been, visiting their daughter in Maryland for the better part of the week.

None of the men could fathom what such a nice, respectable couple had done to deserve this. A breach of human decency was what Harvey called it.

But Isaac knew. If Eddie did it—and that was a big if—he did it for a reason. And that reason had something to do with his dead wife and dead child, with how they were shunned by this town, by even the respectable, upstanding citizens. Mr. and Mrs. Gray had something to do with how Celestial and Josephine were welcomed, stared-down, killed by the nice, decent people of this picture-perfect town. How, exactly, Isaac maddeningly didn't have a clue. But if Eddie was involved there was a clear, direct connection that Isaac just couldn't see, no matter how hard he tried.

Hank Grady chided the men for not being at the P.O.T.S. meeting the night before. P.O.T.S. met on the fourth Sunday of the month in their historic library.

"I was there, you dummy," Mr. Peake chimed in. "Took the minutes, which we need to get a woman to do, by the way."

"The only women who come to meetings," Harvey chuckled, "are ones who can't write!"

"You all should have been there," Hank Grady bellowed. "That's all there is to it."

Everyone stopped talking while Grady recited the meeting in detail. He'd tried to up the reward to $10,000, but their treasury only had $1,900 and nobody was willing to pledge the extra money. Mr. Peake couldn't do it, he said, because his wife did the books at home and he hadn't seen the checkbook in twenty years. He hadn't even been in the bank since he had retired a decade ago.

"The Oprahs of this world are going to take over if men don't take their place at the head of the family," Hank said, slapping the arms of his chair with his fat palms. "Only thing worse than a strong woman who doesn't know her place is a weak man."

"Go stick your fat head in the toilet, Grady," Mr. Peake said. "You could have made up the difference in our re-ward with cash, what with your recent real estate transaction."

The men laughed uneasily. Isaac had heard that Grady had sold his large farm a year before, but he didn't know what Mr. Peake's sarcasm was about.

Billy Chum's voice rose above the howl. "Calm down, gentlemen. Since when you boys gotten as rough as corn cobs?" the quavering voice of the elder Chum complained. "When I ran things here, there was none of this fractiousness."

"There was none of this irresponsibility among our youth, either, Billy. They're the ones at the bottom of these break-ins," Hank said. "Last night, P.O.T.S. issued a statement. The worst kind of terrorism is terrorism at home. Kids nowadays don't know how good we have it. They need to save up their rambunctiousness for our war with the darkies in the godforsaken Middle East."

Isaac looked down the aisle. Half the men were nodding. Some, like Mr. Bennett and the younger Chum, looked away.

Isaac oil-mopped the floor, straightened the shelves, and even straightened under the counter where Mr. Chum kept extra catalogues and boxes of file folders. Every can of thinner and water seal and cherry stain was straight and dusted with the labels facing out. Isaac emptied the plastic trash cans behind the wide counter and checked the stock of plastic liners. On his way back to the warehouse Hank Grady spoke.

"What's your theory, Isaac?" Grady asked. "Our chief of police here don't seem to have one. He certainly hasn't made any arrests. Could it be that the long arm of the law is twiddling his thumbs?"

If it was possible to stare two men down at once, that's what Hank Grady was doing to Isaac and Reginald Williams. Everyone looked over to Isaac, who was returning the broom to its hook near the mop. He hated being in the spotlight.

Some of the men smiled, like Mr. Bennett, who crossed his arms. Hank Grady stopped picking at his teeth, and Mr. Peake stopped rocking. Mike Lindvall leaned so far forward in his rocker, Isaac expected him to fall out. They were waiting for Isaac to speak.

He didn't want to let on that he'd been listening. "Theory about what?" Isaac said at last. His voice sounded like it had waves in it.

"What? Why, the biggest string of crimes ever to beset our little town, that's what," Grady said. "Don't play dumb, even if you do seem a little on the slow side."

That insulting oaf, Isaac thought. What about the fire that consumed Celeste and Josephine Patrick? Wasn't that a bigger crime than this?

Isaac wished he could launch into his father's sermon mode, firing off memorized words and finding a rhythm of sentences that flowed like a song or a boxer's sweet punches. He could feel cold sweat on his face and under his arms. The words jumbled in his head. He wanted to say that this crime spree was nothing compared to the murder of Eddie Patrick's family. And the break-ins weren't as dangerous as Hank Grady being president of P.O.T.S.

"I haven't thought about it much," was all Isaac could think to say. He felt outnumbered and insufficiently armed with only a broom.

"You got any friends getting into mischief this summer?" Grady asked.

Isaac looked to Reginald Williams. The police chief had a receding hairline and a round face that made him look like a little kid, but Isaac knew that he had a grandson in the police academy in Washington, D.C. Reginald Williams was looking up towards the top of the wall where they hung the small kiddy pools.

Hank Grady locked onto Isaac through narrowed eyes. A grim little smile snaked beneath his black and white beard.

Isaac had been so busy this summer with his job that he hadn't connected with any of his buddies much. Just one pick-up game. Just one afternoon. And Jenny at the beach. Their names floated just beyond his tongue for a quarter-second. Practically the only person he had seen lately from his school was Kate. "My friends are playing ball this summer."

"You got any friends good at picking locks?"

The room grew even quieter. Isaac despised being the center of attention, and he resented the accusations. He heard his stomach growl. He had gotten off this morning without breakfast, not even a frozen waffle. And suddenly he felt cold in the air conditioning. He felt out of place in his torn, short pants and old, pony-penning T-shirt. When he looked at Mr. Chum, Mr. Chum smiled and stared at the floor, like he wanted to help but couldn't. Isaac wondered suddenly if Mr. Chum remembered their conversation about picking locks and breaking into older homes without leaving a trace. How could he not remember?

"Anything you say can and will be used against you in a court of law," Grady said slowly, drawing a sprinkle of nervous laughter.

"The only thing my friends are good at is stealing bases, and I'm not sure they've done much of that because I hear the team's not doing so well."

Harvey clapped his hands and nodded forward, snorting back whoops of laughter. "That's a good one," he said. "Stealing bases." Harvey laughed at anything.

Hank started picking his teeth again, but he didn't take his eyes off Isaac. Mr. Peake resumed his caffeinated rocking.

"I'm sure the chief would agree that property damage of this magnitude is no laughing matter," Grady said. "You tell your friends that, Isaac. This has gone on long enough."

"Reggie," Mr. Jackson asked, "do you use the conference room at the police station as an interrogation room? And do you get confessions from guys like they do it on NYPD Blue?"

Everyone was laughing. And nobody was looking at Isaac anymore except Hank Grady.

Isaac went out to the front sidewalk, glad to get away. It was cold around that stove, and the sun felt good. He was startled when someone put a hand on his shoulder. Isaac was relieved that it was Chief Williams.

"Needed some air, huh, Chief?"

The chief shook his head and lightly kicked at a crack in the sidewalk. "I need something," he said. "That's for sure." He took a deep breath through his nostrils and rocked up to the balls of his feet. The sweet air came compliments of Pearson's Bakery. He slowly exhaled and looked slumped and tired again.

"Walk me around back, would you?" the chief said.

The chief took Isaac's elbow and turned him towards Slipper Street, which ran alongside the warehouse. Reggie Williams and his father were friends and volunteered together at the library. Isaac liked Chief Williams. Everybody did, it would seem, except for Hank Grady.

"Ever think about retiring, Chief?"

"Before Grady got this P.O.T.S. group all riled up, I was practically semi-retired. Used to be, wasn't so much to do for the police chief in a small town."

They turned from sunny Main Street to the purple shadows of Slipper. They strolled a few yards in silence, then Chief Williams stopped and leaned against the fence. He looked at Isaac with a kindly smile, then down the street past the Gas and Go.

"I'll never find who did this," he said. He glanced at Isaac again. He was still smiling. "I'll never get this guy." He dropped his gaze towards his shoes. "When I was growing up over in Cape Charles, we played hide-and-seek a lot. You ever play that?"

Isaac nodded.

"My little brother was the champion. He was so good at hiding we never found him. We'd look everywhere. We'd tear things up looking for him. He'd just disappear. I wouldn't see him until hours later, long after we gave up and started playing something else. He just wouldn't come out. Mom would ask, 'Where's John?' We'd say the last time we saw him was when I started counting in a game of hide-and-seek, and she'd just nod. There was nothing to do until he showed up, like at bedtime when he'd come into the bathroom in his pajamas to brush his teeth. I'd be sitting there taking a dump and he'd just brush his teeth and say good night, just like that. Didn't even seem happy about winning. In looking back on it, I think he might have been disappointed about never being found, but I didn't know that then. Was too stupid to think that then."

Chief Williams smiled and waved as someone drove slowly by in a new, green Volkswagen bug. "I could retire and buy me one of those snazzy cars," he said, watching the bug pull into the Gas and Go.

"Somebody like my brother is doing this vandalism," the chief said. "They're so good at hiding they won't be found. Unless they want to be."

"Could it be your brother, Chief?"

"I wish it was," the chief said, his face brightening slightly. "My little brother went to Vietnam in 1965 and never came home. His headstone is in the graveyard down by the park. But who knows where his body is. They never found it."

"I'm sorry, Chief," Isaac said. "I shouldn't joke like that, I—"

"No, no, no."

Chief Williams grasped the fence post. His hand was rough, and fat, and possibly strong. Isaac looked him in the face. "I think the detectives in there are right," the chief said, tossing his head in the direction of the store. "I think this is probably the work of bored kids. You know most kids around here, Isaac, and maybe you could ask around some." He motioned towards the store again. "They want blood. All I want is for this to stop."

"Like I said, Mr. Williams, I—"

"I heard you," the chief said. "And I believe you. I'm just grasping for straws, and I thought maybe you'd let me know if you hear anything. I just want this guy off of my back."

"You mean the vandal?"

"No," he said, patting his stomach and frowning. "I mean the guy at that stove inside who's giving me constant heartburn." The chief peeled out two Rolaids from a roll in his front pocket and popped them into his mouth. "If Hank Grady doesn't stop chewing on me, I won't be able to enjoy a thing from my summer garden, and my banana peppers are coming in real nice."

Isaac spent the rest of the morning stacking wood with Eddie. They didn't talk much. But Isaac enjoyed working with Eddie, and Eddie wasn't complaining. There are lots of ways to talk with someone without using words.

They were moving two-by-sixes and landscape timbers from the back of the lumberyard nearer to the side gate. This was the sort of lumber most people off the street wanted, and there was no need to keep it squirreled in the back, Eddie said.

Eddie would point to the big timbers, and Isaac would take his place at one end. They'd bend down together like synchronized swimmers. Isaac would stick out an elbow pointing in one direction or another. They might share a single word now and then. Eddie said "legs" when they first started, which was shorthand for Isaac to keep his back straight and lift with his legs. "Splinter." "Scrap." "Bottom." Words like those said it all. They sorted bows, warps, and knots, like a team.

Isaac thought Eddie was surprisingly strong and spry for such an old guy. He found himself wanting to do more than his share to ease the load for Eddie, but that was impossible to do from his end of a piece of lumber. The best he could do was not slow Eddie down, who moved steadily, fluidly, like a distance runner.

They worked until lunch before they began using complete sentences.

"What did you do this weekend?" Eddie asked as they headed towards the warehouse for the shade and water fountain. "I imagine a young man like you has a pretty full social life."

"Nothing much," Isaac said. "Just vandalized a house or two, went to church, watched some TV."

Eddie stopped and gave Isaac a searching look.

Isaac shuffled past him, stepped into the cool of the warehouse, and leaned into the water fountain.

"Well," he said, "the way Hank Grady was grilling me, you'd think I was a first-class criminal. He was sitting around the store with the cuss-and-discuss crowd this morning—bigger crowd than usual—and they were talking about the latest break-in. You heard?"

"I don't listen to gossip," Eddie said, taking his place at the water fountain for a drink.

"It wasn't gossip that flooded Constitution Gray's house," Isaac said. "Anyway, the geezers in the store think this is the work of teenagers just out for kicks. People of the Shore is offering a reward, dead or alive. Do I look like a criminal?"

Eddie shook his head.

"Thanks," Isaac said. "Neither do you."

"What else were they talking about?"

Isaac had to think a second. "Well, Mr. Bennett, my science teacher, brought up evolution, which got Hank Grady off my ass. Grady jumped right in and said something like if he were God, he'd have done things differently. He said he'd make man so that, when he got old, his testicles would drop off instead of his teeth falling out. That way, he said, when you got old, at least you'd be able to enjoy corn on the cob."

Eddie shook his head. "Let's be thankful, then, that Hank Grady isn't God, amen?"

"Amen."

"Pay them no mind. Just a bunch of gossips perched around that stove. In the wintertime when that stove is stoked full blast, somebody ought to push those old hens right in." Eddie's eyes twinkled. "Rotisserie chicken," he added.

He offered the water fountain to Isaac. Isaac leaned into the cool stream of water. He hadn't noticed how thirsty he was, how hot he'd become.

"Don't be fooled by Grady's community rah-rah," Eddie said. "First of all he's retired now, and the wife doesn't want him in the house. So he's got lots of time on his hands and more than a little nagging at home."

"How do you know?" Isaac asked, looking up from the fountain.

"You just learn things from time to time if you close your trap and open your ears," Eddie said. "You oughta try it sometime."

Isaac bent in for one more sip.

"Another thing is that his good-for-nothing sons didn't want the farm, and he wouldn't give it to his daughter, who's the smartest one in the whole family, so instead of selling to local interests, he sold out to a housing man from Norfolk. I think he's mad at himself, and I know everybody in the farm co-op is royally peeved. Of course he made a mint—more than he ever did farming."

Isaac tried to ask how much he got for the farm, but Eddie kept talking like he was in a trance.

"Developers are gobbling up whatever they can get on the Shore, see. We'll soon have more people and sewage than trees and soy fields. Condos. Roads. Shopping centers. The locals, real Shore people, are pretty upset about it. Our way of life is changing." Eddie blinked hard and looked at Isaac. "But the vultures can't buy what's not for sale, understand? Which is why Hank Grady is on the outs with his wife. Most of their land had belonged to her father, her people. But it's gone now. Forever."

"How do you know all this?" Isaac was incredulous.

"I listen and I have my theories," Eddie said. "So tell me for real about your weekend."

It had actually been a quiet weekend. On Saturday Isaac and his dad had paid a visit to Mattie Thomson. She hadn't remembered Isaac's visit just the day before and she wondered why his mom hadn't been by "in a coon's age." Is she under the weather, Miss Thomson wanted to know. Under the ground is more like it, is what Isaac wanted to say, but he let his dad answer.

When Isaac asked Miss Thomson if she knew Eddie, she said that she did and said he was a fox in the hen house. She said he owed her "quite a bit" of money and had been stealing her blood pressure medicine and selling it to the Chinese. Isaac admired her roses climbing up a trellis at the far end of the porch, and she said they weren't roses at all but ivy. Isaac wasn't a botanist, but he knew the difference between roses in full bloom and ivy.

Reverend Lawson said that the congregation missed her in church to which she replied that she hadn't missed a Sunday since Pearl Harbor. These are difficult times, she said, and the nation has to pray for the President.

Reverend Lawson left some store-bought hard rolls and a wedge of cheese. "We'll see you next time," he said, leading Isaac down the porch steps.

Old Lady Thomson was waving distractedly, the fingers on her right hand writhing like the legs of an upside-down bug.

At the gate, Reverend Lawson said, "By the way, Mattie, who is the President now?"

She didn't pause. "Mr. Roosevelt, of course."

Mattie Thomson looked from Isaac to his father as if they didn't have sense enough to come in out of the rain.

Eddie and Isaac took their lunch break together, something that was becoming more common. Eddie sat in the leaning metal chair he had retrieved from the dumpster. Isaac leaned against the counter. Isaac had packed a ham sandwich and about twenty Oreos. Eddie sliced a ripe tomato.

Isaac told him about the puppet show he had to do that night and how he'd probably have to wing the script. Without ever telling Mrs. Greer "yes," Isaac had agreed to do it. He had decided that it was nice being wanted even though it was also a pain. And a lot of work. The stage—three panels with curtained windows—wasn't even finished; he was toying with a spaceship motif, but couldn't get things to come together the right way. He was, after all, no carpenter. After work he was going to rush straight over to the church and bang the thing together—both the stage and a script. Eddie asked Isaac if he wanted to cut away a little early that afternoon. Isaac said he needed a week, not a few hours.

"Last year," Isaac said, "Jenny helped me. We weren't dating then, but it sure was nice to have her around."

"Yep," Eddie said. "Know what you mean."

Isaac glanced up to the postcard of the Cavalier Hotel pinned to the cork board over the work bench. He thought of Celeste. "Have you ever been in love, Eddie?"

"You're the expert," Eddie said, gesturing with a slice of tomato and a pulpy knife in one hand, and the bottom half of a dripping tomato in the other. "Young love. Stars. Moonlight on the water."

Eddie slurped up the tomato slice. "If you go back to that beach," he said between swallows, "you better wear some protection, all's I got to say."

Isaac's cookie broke in his hand.

Eddie gave him a wink. "I'm talking sunscreen, son."

Eddie put his tomato on the bench and pulled a stack of crackers out of his paper lunch bag. "It's been a long time," Eddie said. "It's been a long, long time since I've been in love, I guess."

13

Isaac told Mr. Chum that after he swept up in the store, he had some personal errands to run. He'd be off the clock for a couple of hours but would make up the time. Mr. Chum, at the counter reading the paper, glanced over his reading glasses, and smiled.

"Go, kiddo."

Isaac changed the calendar on the cash register, tearing off Monday. It was already July. Summer was half over. The store would be closed tomorrow for the Fourth of July break. On the Fourth, the town parade would begin at the fountain and end up at the wharf for live music followed by fireworks. The pony penning in Chincoteague was less than a month away. Time was flying.

Isaac's first errand took him to the Rooksville Fire Station. He might find some answers there, or questions he never thought to ask. He was nervous as he thought about what he was going to say when he got there, but if he could invent dialogue between aliens from outer space and Jesus in a children's puppet show, maybe he could do some ad-libbing with firemen. It would be a fact-finding mission. A field trip.

He had something in common with the vandalized houses, their waterlogged walls and ceilings straining under weight they weren't designed to hold. Everything just fine on the outside, a structural catastrophe on the inside. What doesn't kill us makes us stronger. Isn't that what his mother had said?

His mother had also said that taking the bull by the horns is always the best way. And that eating crow while it's warm is a lot better than waiting until it gets cold.

Isaac kicked a piece of gravel down the sidewalk, wondering what it was like to be gored by a bull, wondering where his mother had come up with her crazy expressions. Out of the open front door of the bakery, the smell of cinnamon wafted like incense. Mr. Pearson needn't take an ad out in the paper to attract customers; he just needed to keep his front door open.

The sun warmed the top of Isaac's bowed head as he walked with his hands in his pockets past the florist. An old man reclined in a chair at the barbershop, all lathered up for a shave. The man didn't move his head, but his eyes followed Isaac as he walked by the open door.

It had been one week since Hank Grady had asked Isaac what his theory of the break-ins was. Every night since, Grady had haunted Isaac's sleep.

The dream was always the same: Hank would chase Isaac into a cavernous, dark room that Isaac couldn't place. Maybe it was the warehouse. Isaac would lie down to hide but couldn't control his gasps or his shaking. He breathed louder and louder until he sounded like a storm, and Hank found him, cowering on the floor, wheezing like a broken fan. Hank would laugh and say, "You deliver my message yet, boy? Have you talked to those good-for-nothing friends of yours?" Then he'd reach out his hands, fingers curled like hooks, and bend toward Isaac on the floor, that snaky smile of his writhing inside his black and white beard. "Somebody's got to teach mischief-makers like you a lesson," Hank would say. Isaac could feel Hank's hot, vomit-smelling breath. "Your preacher father is too weak. They're all too weak. But not me. I'm not weak." He'd grab Isaac with those meat hook hands and begin pulling him apart like green husks from yellow corn. Isaac always woke when his stretched muscles began to snap off the bone.

Isaac slumped onto a park bench at the corner. The dolphin fountain at Fountain Square had been turned off. The Shore was in a drought. The summer still looked fresh, though, despite the lack of rain. The sun hadn't yet cooked the leaves to the same dull green; they were still tender, lime colored and yellow and teal and the whole spectrum of green.

His mother's little sayings jumbled around in his head like lyrics to an over-played song. The break-ins, Hank Grady, Jenny's body pressed up against his in that last hug, Tom's perplexed disappointment playing a simple game of catch in the backyard. He thought of Eddie, feeling protective of him, fearing for his safety against what Isaac worried was a building rage among some in town, Hank Grady in particular.

Isaac turned the notion of motive over and over in his thoughts. Until that weekend, he couldn't understand how Eddie—or anybody else—could get up the nerve to trash people's houses. Maybe it wasn't about nerve, or revenge, or calculation. Maybe it was about something rawer, more base, like a shark's primal attraction to the smell of blood, or a mother springing like a lion to protect her child.

Isaac knew how someone could be stirred by forces outside of or bigger than himself, forces so immediate and intense so as almost to have no control over them. But a flash of anger was one thing. Losing your cool once made sense. A flash of anger four times, taking exactly the same form each time, was something else. Maybe it was a gang of bored teens.

This detective game wasn't fun anymore. There was something dark going on, and Isaac wanted out. Going to the fire station, first, and to Miss Mattie Thomson's house, second, would be a start. They were the only steps he knew how to take.

The two fire trucks at the Rooksville Fire Station were shiny. That's what Isaac noticed first. Everything was polished. They weren't new trucks, but there was no rust, and even the little dings and dents gleamed.

Isaac wandered into the open garage and marveled at how neat the place was, how the floor of the garage looked more like the floor of a museum. There were no puddles of oil. No tire marks. No trace of use.

Lines of yellow coats hung along one wall, with big yellow overalls folded in front of the coats, centered perfectly over sturdy boots. The walls gleamed. Isaac looked to the arching ceiling. It was a mosaic of bright tiles in a hundred colors.

"They notice the trucks, first. But that ceiling really gets them."

Isaac swung around. The voice belonged to a young man, maybe in his thirties, with short, blonde hair. He wore a blue, short-sleeved shirt. The face of the watch he wore was close to the circumference of a tennis ball, adding to his rugged look, but he also had a gentle manner, like maybe he collected stamps in his spare time or was a preschool teacher at his church.

"Hi," Isaac said, extending his hand. "I'm Isaac Lawson. Don't mean to wander in where I don't belong."

"If you pay taxes in this town, this place belongs to you," the man said, taking Isaac's hand. "Jacob Emerson Finch. Emerson is a family name. You can call me Jake, though people back home sometimes call me Jeff, for my initials."

"Well, nice to meet you, Jake, or Jeff. Where are you from?"

"Come on, you're joking, right? With this accent you can't tell I'm from Jersey? Born in sight of Asbury Park. Bruce Springsteen's related to me, they say, but I've never gotten a free concert ticket yet."

Isaac smiled. So much for the jitters.

"But you're too young to know who Bruce Springsteen is, right?"

"I know Bruce," Isaac said. "Do you like Bowling for Soup or Black Eyed Peas?"

"Listen, I make it a point never to listen to bands with vegetable names. Me, I like my music straight up."

Jake looked like he was in shape and had energy to burn. He was rocking from his toes to his heels. "Pardon my rudeness," he said. "What can I do for you? I mean, where are my manners? I know you came here for something."

"I've been living in this town since I was a kid and I've never toured the fire station," Isaac said. "Do you work here?"

"I'm just the captain," he said. "But, hey, what does that mean? Means I'm in charge of everything that goes wrong, that's what! I'd be honored to show you around, though there's not a lot to see." Jake did a circle on his heels, sweeping his arm around the big garage. "This original building," he said, "was constructed in the 1930s—which is why those doors are a little on the small side for these big engines." He motioned to the ceiling. "And that tile ceiling was designed by grade schoolers in a contest before the building was built."

Jake strode towards a heavy glass door that led to another part of the building. He stopped at the big map hanging on the wall. It was the size of a garage door. It was of Rooksville and the surrounding area. Isaac didn't know anybody made such big maps of small places.

"Do you know where the Patrick farm is?" Isaac asked. "Near where 126 meets 19? They're little roads, way on the other side of the highway." Isaac was running his finger along the circuitous 126, which wound out of town into the country.

"There it is," Jake said, joining Isaac at the map. "19's right here."

He drew his finger down and met Isaac's at 126.

"That's where the farm is," Isaac said.

Jake rubbed his hand over the parts of the map not crisscrossed with roads. Jagged creeks from the bay wound like tentacles deep into the countryside.

"Yeah," he said, "it's pretty country out there. Lots of fields and beauty. I like natural things." He pointed to a road on the other side of town, not far from Isaac's school. "This is where I live." He paused. "What about that Patrick farm?"

"There was a fire there in 1951," Isaac said. "Did you work here then?"

Both of them laughed.

"Yeah, right," Jake said. "I wasn't even a gleam in my parents' eye, know what I mean?"

"The fire destroyed one of the field houses. Killed two people." Isaac rubbed the spot on the vinyl map where the two roads came together. "How long would it take for you to get out there on a run?"

"I'd say we could cover that ground in under ten minutes."

Jake looked at the map and touched Highway 13, the commercial life-blood of the Eastern Shore. Thatched lines of the railroad paralleled 13 and the business route into town.

"Most of those farm roads weren't paved in 1951," Jake said. He pointed his thumb at Engine 11. "A big rig like that might have a hard time on a dirt road. And it would sure mess up the wax job."

"What kind of person would start a fire, burn a house down to the ground?"

"I dunno," Jake said, scanning the big map. "A sicko?"

They went into the office. A window air conditioner hummed. A small desk was tidy with several neat stacks of papers.

"This is my office," Jake said. "Command central. Or, paperwork central, I should say. There's so much paperwork I got to do it's freaking unbelievable. Not only reports about the fires, which you'd expect, but building maintenance reports, training reports, budget reports, personnel reports, equipment reports. You name it. I've got to write a report to take a dump, no offense."

Isaac laughed.

"That's why I got out of the city. I was climbing the ranks, and making good time going up the company ladder, pardon the pun. But you think there's red tape here, you ought to try it up there in Jersey. Besides, my wife liked the country and we needed a slower life. My daughter, see, has Down's Syndrome, and we wanted to find a place where she wouldn't feel swallowed up. The town here is perfect for us, filled with caring, salt-of-the-earth people. A lot of people leave towns like this. We're glad to have found it."

Jake picked up a file folder from his desk and tossed it back down, onto another stack. "I took over this captain job from Mr. Pincus when he retired. They usually promote within the company, but nobody wanted the job. Must have known about the paperwork. Been here almost five years."

"What church do you go to?" Isaac asked.

"You want to save my soul?" Jake lifted his fists in a boxer's stance.

"No," Isaac said, waving Jake's fists down. "It's just my dad is the Presbyterian pastor in town, and I just ask those kinds of questions. Don't mean to be nosy."

"Reverend Lawson your dad?"

Isaac nodded.

"He tutors at the grade school," Jake said. "Wonderful man. And your mother was the art teacher. Now, she was something."

Isaac nodded again. "She was a play therapist too," he said. "But most people thought of her as the art teacher."

"Ah," Jake said. "A jack of all trades. My family went to your mother's funeral. My daughter wouldn't have had it any other way. She loved your mom. See, Angie's been in first grade twice. She's learning what she can. She loves school. And she really loved your mother, loves drawing pictures. I should have recognized you."

They had been pacing around the station and had ended up in the small dining room.

"I'm Catholic, to answer your question. And every mealtime I make sure we pray. I don't mention the Virgin or anything like that. Don't want to offend any of you Protestants, know what I mean? But we say a little prayer every time we eat. The guys expect it, look forward to it, even. I think in life, no matter what your lot is, you've got a lot to be thankful for, right? So we thank the man upstairs and ask him to keep us safe."

They had looped around the station and found themselves back in the garage. Bolted onto the wall was a bronze plaque filled with names that Isaac had not noticed before.

"What's this for?" Isaac asked.

"When they built the addition in the fifties, they commemorated all the volunteers. These guys were it."

"When was the addition made?"

"The cornerstone says 1952," Jake said.

"And were these men volunteers in 1951?"

"You got it. Why?"

"Just curious," Isaac said. "Are any of them still around?"

"Well, none of them are firefighters anymore, that's for sure," Jake said, rubbing his chin again. "But some of them still poke around. When we have the fall barbecue, all of the old-timers come out of the woodwork. Can talk the ears off a brass monkey. Probably not many from 1951, though."

Isaac looked at his watch. "Hey, got to go. Thanks for the tour." Isaac nudged Jake in the ribs. "By the way, I do pay taxes."

Smooth as silk.

"You're most certainly welcome, Isaac Lawson." He pulled Isaac aside as if for a word of advice. "Be careful this week with the fireworks. In my opinion, the world would be a lot better off without fireworks. The noise gets on my nerves, and it's just not wise shooting open flames above people's houses. I'm sorry, but I make no apologies for that."

"Sure thing, boss."

Jake took Isaac's hand, giving it a firm shake. "It's been my pleasure meeting you, it really has."

Isaac took a last look at the mosaic ceiling. "What is it supposed to be?"

"It's the sky," Jake said. "Can't you see it?"

And at that instant he could. There were clouds, all colors of white and gray, and wisps of wind, a quarter moon and a sun and shards of star light and a thousand shades of night blue. It seemed to jump right out at him.

"Well, that's cool," Isaac whispered. He looked at Jake. "My mother would have loved that."

"She did," Jake said, a look of mild shock on his face. "Didn't you know? She took her art classes here twice a year to show it off. It gave them inspiration, she said."

There was so much I didn't know, Isaac thought. And no matter how well you know someone, there's still much to learn.

↓ ↓ ↓

There were twenty names on that bronze plaque. All of the names were familiar. In the middle of the second row one name stood out.

Nathan Parramore.

Isaac left the fire station and passed the post office on Angel Wing and then cut across Fountain Square toward Conch Street. After three blocks he stopped in front of Miss Thomson's house, opened her squeaky metal gate, and climbed the three high stone steps on the sidewalk leading up to the squeaky wooden steps of the porch. He took them two at a time because this was just the first part of his second errand, the easy part.

He stood before Miss Thomson's thick, weathered door and knocked as hard as he could. It was almost ten o'clock, and it was getting hot. The softness of the morning had all but burned away.

When she opened the door, she looked like a child in hiding. She wasn't wearing her teeth.

"Good morning, Miss Thomson," Isaac said, reaching out both of his hands.

She handed him her hands as if she wasn't quite sure they belonged to her. They were cold and fragile with too many bones. He gave them a gentle squeeze.

"Miss Thomson, I'm Isaac Lawson—David and the late Marie Lawson's son."

She had a quizzical look on her face. She glanced down at her hands in his like she wanted hers back but didn't know what would be required to complete the operation. He could feel her restless fingers wiggling.

"You know your pastor, Reverend Lawson, Miss Thomson?"

She nodded vacantly.

"He's my dad," Isaac said. "Miss Thomson, I hate to bother you, but I'd like your permission to pick a handful of your pretty flowers. May I?"

When he mentioned flowers, she smiled. Her shrunken face beamed.

"Yes," she said. "Take what you need. They're meant to be enjoyed."

She disappeared into her living room. The wide door creaked open, and the coolness of the darkened rooms tickled the hair on his legs in the draft. She had put her teeth in, and they were as big and yellow as before. She stood there tentatively smiling. She was holding her cut-glass water pitcher in both hands.

"Here," she said. Her teeth still clicked when she spoke, like she was also communicating via Morse code. "Put them in this." Click. "And pick as many as you want." Click, click. "They're meant to be shared." Click.

He'd return the pitcher. He knew that to refuse it would confuse her. Besides, she'd never miss it. He thanked her, took the pitcher, and filled it with flowers. He had hoped to be finished with his errands by now, and he hurried straight back to the shop trying to make up time.

When Isaac stepped into the warehouse with the flowers, Eddie was there, pouring the leftover coffee down the water fountain drain.

"You shouldn't have," he said, looking at the flowers.

Isaac blew the dust off the counter and spread out the flowers. He cut the stems at a careful angle with a pair of wire cutters from the pegboard above the work bench, pulled off the damaged leaves, and arranged the flowers neatly in the pitcher. He went to the water fountain and filled the pitcher up. Eddie leaned against the door frame leading into the store, watching.

"Do you suppose I could borrow the keys to the pickup truck?" Isaac asked as he rearranged the flowers in the pitcher. "My car's at home, and I need to run a quick errand before any more of this morning slips away."

"You're not allowed, boy. Name's not on the insurance list."

"Give me the keys, Eddie. Don't be a prick."

"A what?"

"A prick is somebody who won't loan you their car. Look it up. Please. A friend in need . . . "

Eddie didn't move.

"I won't be gone long," Isaac said, softening. "Fifteen minutes, tops."

Eddie put the coffeepot upside down on the coffee machine and fumbled in his pocket for his keys. "I'll take you."

"This is private," Isaac said. He followed Eddie out to the truck.

"Get in the truck, son. Ain't nobody more private than me." Eddie hopped in and started the motor. Country music was on the radio.

"Well?" Eddie called.

Isaac climbed onto the passenger seat. The hot vinyl burned the back of his legs. Eddie looked over to Isaac and popped the truck into reverse.

"Kids today," he said under his breath, looking out the rearview mirror. "So big for their dang britches, if you ask me."

He turned around in the lumberyard, then nosed out onto Main Street. They lurched out onto the empty road. Eddie continued his mumbled complaining. "We ought to have mandatory military service for all teenagers. Might do the country good, I declare, and save the rest of us from such trials and tribulations, yes, sir."

They drove across the Kingfisher bridge and along Norman Creek. Isaac told Eddie to stop in front of the small house with the pink shutters that matched the blooming crepe myrtles in the front yard.

"Wish me luck," he said as he got out of the truck and headed up the walk.

When Clara Edwards opened the door, little Tom stood peering around her with each arm wrapped around her waist. Isaac knelt down and looked at Tom, who quickly hid his face behind his mother's stomach. "I just wanted to tell you that I think you're going to be a fine baseball player."

Then he stood up and thrust out the flowers to Miss Edwards. There was a long moment that Isaac wasn't sure she was going to take them. Sometimes in baseball games there are moments when time seems to stop, like when a guy slides home and it takes forever for the dust to clear and the ump to make the call.

This was one of those moments.

When she took the pitcher with both hands, Isaac backed down the four stairs of the porch. "See you guys," he said, nodding, then turned and jogged back to the truck idling on the street. Eddie didn't say a word as he dropped into gear and chugged around the corner.

14

They were out of eggs, waffles, and oatmeal. They didn't have juice, butter, or bread. The cookie jar was empty. There were no leftovers in the fridge. There was no bacon, lunch meat, grits, or cheese. They had jelly. They also had milk, but no cereal except for bran. They were even out of peanut butter and tea bags. That's why Isaac went to the Duck Blind for breakfast on the Fourth of July.

When he looked up from the menu, he was shocked that Kate Bradshaw was his waitress.

"I got back a whole day early," she said, "and wanted to come to work. I'm working the morning shift. How's that for dedication?"

"I'm really glad to see you," Isaac said. He didn't try to cover up his enthusiasm. He awkwardly stood up. "Sit down," he said, motioning with an open palm to the other side of the booth.

"It's busy now," she said, "and—"

Before she could finish, Isaac quickly and lightly hugged her. That was awkward, he thought.

"I can't sit now, silly. I'm working."

He sat. "How was college?"

"They're all too expensive," she said. "I'll have to stay in Rooksville waitressing until I make enough money. If I save every single dime, I'll be here until I'm fifty."

They laughed.

"I'm really glad to see you," he said.

When she brought his two fried eggs, bacon, toast, sausage links, hash browns, and large orange juice, she sat down in the booth across from him.

"Who cares that we're busy," she said. "It's almost a sin that somebody should eat breakfast on the Fourth of July all by themselves. This is my mission of mercy, Isaac Lawson."

She leaned across the table, grabbing his hand, which was wrapped around his orange juice glass. "And just so you know," she said in a lower voice, "I don't do this with all the guys." She cocked her head to the counter. Four old men were eating alone.

Isaac explained that he had come alone because his father had rushed over to the hospital in Nassawadox to see Ina Greer's husband, who was in the emergency room with chest pains.

Kate looked at Isaac's plate and shook her head. "You'll have chest pains if you keep eating like that."

She asked if he had plans for lunch. A picnic sounded good to her, and if he couldn't go, there were four other guys at the counter to choose from. She said that she would take care of the food if he'd pick the spot, which he agreed to do. He said he would bring a plan and a Frisbee.

Isaac pulled into her driveway at noon. It took two trips from her kitchen to load a red-and-white blanket, a heavy basket of food, and two backpacks into his car.

All the regular picnic places would be crowded on a day like this, Isaac had thought. He didn't want to picnic at Fountain Square right in town where he'd have to fight off ants and crowds of people. Same thing for Norman Park; people from all over the county would descend there. The wharf would be busy and was set up for the concert and fireworks that evening. The field at the new high school didn't have a single shade tree since it used to be the site of one of the biggest potato farms on the Shore.

That's why he had settled on the hill on the other side of the highway at the hedgerow between farms where 126 and 19 met. From the top, you could see Wampum Sound in the one direction and the Patrick farm in the other.

∀ ∀ ∀

"Are you running away?" he said as he lugged the baggage from his Honda to a slight rise under some cottonwoods. "You've packed everything."

"Are you trying to kidnap me," she said back, "taking me all the way out here in the middle of nowhere?"

"They'll find us eventually," Isaac said, spreading the red-and-white blanket. He set the basket and bags on three corners.

Kate stood at the top of the rise. Isaac joined her there.

"Beyond that field there is Wampum Sound," he said, pointing. "Beyond that are the barrier islands and the ocean. Can you hear the waves?"

They were silent. A nearby locust started making a racket. She followed his finger. "And along that row of trees is a creek, which you can't see from here. These hedgerows and creeks used to mark the boundaries of these farms. Still do, I guess."

"And those houses," she said, pointing to clusters of homes in the midst of the wide fields, "are they farm houses?"

"Used to be," Isaac said. "A lot of them are abandoned now."

"What about that one?" she said, pointing to the nearest one.

"Nope," he said. "It just looks abandoned. That's the Patrick farm. Eddie Patrick still lives there, though I don't think he's farmed the land in years. Probably leases it out."

"And those are his barns?"

"Guess so," he said.

"So we're not in the middle of nowhere," she said. "And even if we were, I'm trying to fit in as much traveling as I can, so I could mark Nowhere off my list."

They sat down on the blanket, and she started pulling out food. She had cut melons in a plastic container, a bag of strawberries, chips, dip, and a big tossed salad with grapes and bean sprouts and three kinds of lettuce.

She was a vegetarian, she told Isaac, and he, judging from what he'd had for breakfast, could use some healthy food for a change. No, she said, the little white cubes on the salad were not some kind of fancy feta cheese, it was fried tofu, and not to complain, he'd love it. She sliced tomatoes and cut pears so ripe she was soaked to her elbows. She spread chunky peanut butter on celery stalks.

All that food reminded Isaac of Thanksgiving, minus the turkey. In his mom's *Southern Living* he'd seen picnics like this.

"We're ready," she said.

When he began to fill his real china plate, she cleared her throat.

"I would think that you of all people would pause to give thanks." She jabbed her finger up to the clouds and cleared her throat again.

He bowed his head and said what came most naturally. "God is great, God is good, let us thank Him for our food—"

"—and everything else," she interrupted.

He joined her on the "amen."

"That's better than my little brother's prayer," she said, putting salad on Isaac's plate. "'Watch out teeth. Watch out gums. Watch out stomach, here it comes.'"

Isaac laughed.

At school, Kate was always friendly to him and others, but he respected the invisible line that separated younger boys from older girls. There was no line out here. Summer allowed that kind of freedom from the rules.

"My brother's a terrible brat," she said, "but to tell you the truth, I helped to spoil him rotten. When he was born, I was ten. I was into playing with baby dolls and having tea parties. When he was born, I thought I'd gotten a real live baby to play with. And I did. Dressed him up. Curled his hair. Mama wouldn't let me do his nails—until he got older. Now he avoids me like a disease. I'm so uncool."

"You're a girl," Isaac said. "You've got cooties." He touched her freckly arm with his pointer finger. "Yuck," he said.

"You've got the disease now," she said. "And there's absolutely no cure."

She stuffed a heaping fork full of salad into her mouth.

"You know what?" she said between chews. "He, my brother, just finished the second grade. And sometimes when all of his friends are around, I'll kiss him on both cheeks. It's so fun to watch his little face turn red."

She had brought a backgammon game with her. It was an ornate board, in its own maple wood case with golden hinges. The board was set with inlaid wood. The pieces were heavy and hand carved. Her grandfather had made it. He had died at Easter. Isaac knew about the heaviness she tried to explain, how sometimes she felt like an actual weight was pressing on her. He didn't say anything, but nodded a lot and said "yeah."

They played the best out of five games twice. She won.

They laid down and looked at clouds. She saw the strangest things. He saw clouds shaped like horses and fish. She saw armies of trolls and bearded women at the fires blowing handmade glass. He saw balls and wheels. She saw bowls of sherbet and clapping hands. He'd not see it, until she'd point it out. "There," she'd insist. "Right there." And then it would come together and he wondered, like with the ceiling in the fire station, why he hadn't seen it all along.

He had no idea, he said, what he wanted to do when he grew up. College is the place when that sort of thing comes together was what his dad has always said, so he hadn't thought of it. She made him want to.

She wanted to write plays or be a veterinarian or work for the ACLU. Isaac didn't know what the ACLU was. She wanted to work with people, though she thought she could probably work all alone and do just fine. She mentioned a movie she had seen about a guy who lived in Alaska doing research about wolves. "Marvelous," she said. Isaac liked her use of that word and vowed to use it some time himself. Lunch was marvelous.

She talked about the Dakota on the reservations, and the poor people and migrant workers right on the Shore. We've got it so good compared to them, she said. Money. Property. Being part of the mainstream. That's why she wanted to give something back to the world, since she'd gotten so much from it.

She was like a *National Geographic* article. No, he'd never been to Santa Fe. Yes, of course, he'd flown, but, no, he'd never ridden on a train. Even though Rooksville was once a railroad town, a passenger train hadn't run those tracks for years. He hadn't ridden a motorcycle either. Or a horse. He'd never been to the Louvre, though he'd seen pictures of its collection, which interested her. He'd never thought about going to the Great Wall of China.

He talked about wanting to get out of town, though, moving off the Shore. She was surprised, however, that he had no idea where he wanted to go. When you're called away from a place, aren't you simultaneously called to another place? she asked. He'd have to think about that, he said. And he was intrigued by her use of the word call. In confirmation class at church, he'd learned about "call" being the thing that God wanted you to do and to be. The word call was from the Latin *vocare*, and another translation besides "call" was "vocation." Kate would be impressed that he knew this, but he didn't bother to tell her because she was leading this conversation and she was leading it at a gallop. He didn't want to interrupt.

She said she'd be happy to live on the Shore or Katmandu. She was limited only by her imagination—and frequent flyer miles. Katmandu, she had to explain, was the capital of Nepal. Isaac had heard of neither.

↓↓↓

Isaac helped Kate pack everything back up. They couldn't make everything they took out of the picnic basket go back in. They stuffed, and repacked, and finally gave up. They loaded up the Honda.

"Is there a part two to this picnic?" Kate asked.

"Do you mean, are we leaving?"

She nodded.

"By no means," Isaac said. "It's time for our hike. You game?"

"I'm as game as a duck," she said.

"Follow me, then."

At the top of the rise they looked around at the farms and trees that divided fields of different colors. It looked like a patchwork quilt.

"Let's go that way," Kate pointed.

"No," Isaac said, nodding due east. "I'd like to go that way." He pointed beyond the Patrick farm, towards the hedgerow that concealed the boundary creek leading to Wampum Sound.

"There are a lot of old houses in these trees that have been abandoned, overgrown with kudzu. Neglected. Burned down. I'd like to stomp off in that direction and see if we might find something at the end of one of Eddie Patrick's old dirt roads. What do you say?"

"Are there dragons in those woods?"

"Many," Isaac said.

"Then let's go."

They skirted well around Eddie's house and the barns out back. They walked along a ditch, through the edge of the new, tall corn, and then found what may have once been a road. They followed it for a mile to the cover of trees. Isaac grew quiet as they stepped out of the sun into the cool shade of the woods. The road disappeared into the underbrush. Kate took his hand as Isaac stepped over a fallen tree.

"Oh," she said. "I could sit under these trees forever."

It was like the warehouse it was so dark. Only the narrowest beams of sunlight made it through the foliage. It was cool and hushed. There was no grass in the woods, just pine straw, which padded their steps. It was like being in an empty sanctuary.

Isaac began looking for those chimneys that had etched themselves into his brain from the library microfiche machine, but he couldn't see any. Just trees, and vines, and green. They walked for a while then hit a patch of sun. The grasses were tall again, and golden. They held hands so as not to be separated. Isaac had been leading the way, and he looked back, afraid that he was walking too fast, wearing her out. Kate glowed like a sun and smiled so fully when he turned around that he lost his footing and fell. She laughed and offered her hands to pull him up. He just lay there looking up at her reaching down for him, covering him with the splash of her smile, freckles running across the tops of her cheeks and over the bridge of her nose. It was a split second that felt like forever. He tried to look away, but couldn't. He couldn't smile and for a moment couldn't move. She blushed, then reached down and slapped him lightly on the top of his head. She grabbed his shirt and he struggled up, grinning now. She was strong.

They took their shoes off and waded through the shallow creek. They skipped stones. They explored the other side without talking. When they put on their shoes and walked down the creek, then out again to the main woods, they crossed the lower part of that same sun-drenched field. There, they stumbled over what Isaac thought were stones. He paused. They were not stones. They were bricks.

Kate picked one up. "I'll bet these are handmade," she said, tossing it down and reaching for another. "Look how squatty and solid they are. And irregular."

Isaac held out the two he had picked up. She put hers next to his.

"None of them is exactly the same," he said.

Isaac looked up and what he thought was a rotted tree covered with kudzu at the edge of the woods was something else. Too big around for the windblown cedar that grew up here. Not tall enough for the loblolly pine. They walked unsteadily though the field of bricks, and Isaac whacked the tower of vines with a stick. It was solid. Solid brick.

It was a chimney.

And they were standing in Eddie Patrick's old house.

Kate and Isaac paced out what they thought was the foundation, which was difficult because part of the field was under the waist-high grass, and the other part was choked with kudzu. There was no wood they could find, no beams, no fireplace mantle. For fear of snakes, Isaac didn't dig through the grass too thoroughly looking for other signs of habitation. At the end of what they imagined the shape of the house to be there was no other chimney. But there were plenty of bricks, perhaps enough for a chimney. And perhaps, Isaac thought, some of the bricks had been hauled off. It would have been fitting to use them for something else—a wall, or drive, or another home. Perhaps it would have been more fitting to let them alone. Maybe that's what Eddie had done.

They sat in the shade with their legs in the sun and leaned together against the same cedar. Isaac opened one of Kate's backpacks that he had brought along and pulled out the container of melon.

"Good," she said. "I'm hungry."

He took a swig of water.

"Smell that cantaloupe," she said, closing her eyes for a moment, enjoying the fragrance. "I've got granola in that front pocket."

"Kate, when I'm around you I always smell flowers. Am I imagining that, or do I actually smell flowers?"

"It's orchids," she said. "My perfume. Just a touch, here," she pointed to the spot at the crook of each arm. "And here," she said, pointing to her neck, under her ears. "Just a little bit. Is it too much?"

"No," Isaac blurted. "Not at all. I just like the smell and I only smell it, faintly, when I'm around you. I thought I might be going crazy."

"You're not around me very much," she said. "That could change, though. And," she added, "you might be a little crazy."

He smiled. "Yes, but a little crazy is a good thing."

"What do you suppose these stones would say if they could talk?" she asked.

"They'd tell the story of the family that used to live here," Isaac said.

"What was that family like?"

"I don't rightly know," Isaac said.

"Make it up, then," she said. "Use your imagination."

She took two bricks and made them like jaws. "Well," she said in a deep voice, snapping the bricks together. "Let me tell you two what it was like in this old house." She gave Isaac the bricks. "It's your turn, now," she whispered.

"There was a family who lived here," he began slowly. He set the bricks gently into his lap.

"Were they happy?"

"Of course," he said. "Aren't all families happy?"

"No, but go on. Tell me about them."

"A husband and wife," he said.

"Did she cook him breakfast every day?"

"Of course not. He cooked her breakfast every day. They had oatmeal and toast."

"What did he do?" Kate asked, drawing up her knees in her arms.

"Do?"

"For a living."

"He was a farmer," Isaac said. "Which is why they lived on a farm."

She nudged him. "Not a preacher?" she said.

"Who'd want to be a preacher?"

"Anybody who loved people," she said. "Somebody like you, for example. You love people, don't you?"

"Not really," Isaac said.

"That's not what I've heard," she said. "But go on. What did he farm?"

"A little of this and a little of that."

"Corn?"

"Sure."

"Soybeans?"

"No. He grew only things you could eat."

"You can eat soybeans," Kate said, nudging Isaac again, this time harder. "Tofu fried up with a little soy sauce. Umm."

"He grew all kinds of berries," Isaac said. "Raspberries and blueberries and strawberries and blackberries."

"What else?"

"Tomatoes and cucumbers and banana peppers."

"They must have had great salads," she said, licking her lips.

"They did," Isaac agreed. "He had a barn full of equipment. And every summer the whole town would come and help him pick his crops."

"And," Kate said, "at their summer feast they'd make homemade berry ice cream."

"Of course. And have corn on the cob and clam fritters."

"He grew clams?"

"Everybody brought something," Isaac said. "The watermen brought clams. Do vegetarians eat clams?" he asked.

"Some do," she said. "I do. By the bucket. Go on."

"The summer feast was kind of like a luau."

"Did the women wear grass skirts?" The sun had turned her cheeks red, and her face was glowing.

"No, they did not."

"And no one brought tofu?"

"Certainly not. Real food."

"Like salads and berry ice cream," she said.

"Yes," Isaac said. "The fruit of all the neighbors' fields."

"And they loved one another very much?"

"Yes, the townsfolk loved and respected each other, despite their differences."

"No," Kate said. "I mean the farmer and his wife."

"Yes. Their love was like what you read about in storybooks. She was his queen and he—"

"—This sounds entirely too mushy," Kate interrupted. "There have never been kings or queens on the Eastern Shore of Virginia. No knights in shining armor, either."

"What about dragons?" Isaac asked.

She shook her head.

"Who's telling this story?" Isaac asked. "Me or you?"

She pointed to the bricks resting in his lap. "The walls are, remember?"

He touched the rough bricks. He grew quiet. Somebody fashioned mud and straw to make these bricks maybe 150 years ago, he thought. A long time. He thought about Mr. Chum's calendar on the cash register in the store. Every day he tears a page off. Every day another day is gone.

"Yes," Isaac said. "The walls. Well, the walls would tell us that the farmer and his wife loved each other very much. Is it too hokey to say that?"

"That'll pass."

"It's kind of a lonely life out in the country, and except for harvest time, people didn't come out to the farm much. So they had each other."

"They had each other," Kate said, reflectively. "And they were passionate lovers."

"I thought you didn't want mushy."

"Go on."

Isaac thought of Kate's grandfather. He patted her hand. "They played backgammon together on the front porch and dreamed dreams."

"That's marvelous," Kate said. "Did they have children?"

"Yes, one. A girl."

"What was her name?"

"Josephine," Isaac said, something welling up in him.

"That's a silly name."

"Not to them it wasn't," he said, his voice wavering just slightly. He put his fingers to his lips. "It was a beautiful name. And she was a beautiful little girl. Their daughter." Isaac's voice trailed off.

She stroked the back of his neck lightly with the long piece of grass she'd been toying with.

"He'd hold little Josephine on that porch in the late evenings after her bath and point out the fields of berries and trees and stars. She'd smell of baby powder and bath soap."

"That's nice," Kate said. "That's very nice." She sighed. "What happened to this family, O great stones?"

The afternoon was warm but the breeze that ran along the brackish creek and through the woods was cool. Isaac imagined that he could smell the ocean, which wasn't far off, that he could pick up the distant fragrance of the gulf stream, oil from Houston, spices from Africa, the music of Brazil.

When Kate kissed him lightly on his sunburned neck just below his ear, he stirred sleepily.

"Do you do that to all the guys?"

"No, indeed, Mr. Lawson. No, indeed."

She perched her chin comfortably on his shoulder. "What happened to this wonderful family?"

Her breath smelled of mint.

"That should be obvious," he said. "They lived happily ever after."

Isaac got home close to seven. His father met him at the front door. Isaac said that he had lost track of time. He had had such a blissful afternoon that he wanted to say that he'd almost lost track of reality, but he didn't dare say it.

"We're going to be late," his father said.

"I didn't mean to hold you up," Isaac said. "I didn't know you—we—had plans."

"Well, I—we—do," his father said. He seemed befuddled. "Or, I'd like to. I do. Us, tentatively." He took a deep breath. "By the way," David Lawson said, regaining his composure. "A Martha Bradshaw called a little while ago and wanted to know if her daughter was here."

"What did you tell her?" Isaac said, trying to cover his grin.

"I told her she wasn't. Then I searched the house to make sure. Who is Martha Bradshaw's daughter?"

"Kate," Isaac said. "Remember our waitress at the Duck Blind? We went on a hike today, sort of a picnic. A drive in the country. We had a marvelous time. I dropped her off before coming home. Said hello to Mrs. Bradshaw myself."

"Oh, a date—"

"A picnic-hike sort of thing," Isaac said. "It was very nice, but who said anything about dating?"

"Dating," his father said absently. Reverend Lawson straightened and pointed to the ceiling. "Speaking of a date, I've got one tonight, a real date, and want you to come along. Clara, Tom, and I would like you to come with us to the fireworks show."

"I'm doing something else tonight," Isaac said.

"What?"

"Something," Isaac said, looking away.

His dad gently took his son's shoulders and looked him in the eyes.

"You go ahead, Dad," Isaac assured him. "I'll be home by ten o'clock, safe and sound."

"I wanted to tell you, son, that the flowers the other day were nice. Clara was appreciative. Me too."

Isaac nodded. He felt cramped standing in the living room with his dad holding his shoulders. "I'm still so sorry about the other night, scaring Tom like that. I was so pissed that night, so tired, so—"

"—No need," his dad said. "Come along with us tonight. It'll be fun."

"I've really got something else up my sleeve for tonight, Dad. Actually, I'm just tired, you know?"

"I can stay if you like," his dad said. "I'm not used to this. Having a teenage son. You going on dates. Me going on dates. It is okay, isn't it?"

"It feels weird," Isaac admitted. "But it's life."

"I guess I could call and cancel. We said we'd kind of play this evening by ear."

"No," Isaac said. "I—"

"—We could play some chess. We don't have cable, yet, but we could watch the fireworks on TV. They always do that program from Washington—"

"—You go, Dad. I'm sure Miss Edwards and Tom are looking forward to this."

"Okay, okay, okay. I'll go. Okay?"

Isaac nodded.

His father studied Isaac's eyes. "As blue as ever," he said, pulling Isaac close and sternly kissing him on the cheek.

Isaac squirmed away, mocking disgust, but smiling awkwardly.

"Okay," his dad said. "Be safe. Have fun. We'll miss you."

His dad slapped Isaac's shoulder and then sat down on the couch and started putting his shoes on.

"Hey, speaking of Tom," Isaac said, jogging to his bedroom. He came back into the living room. "Give him this," Isaac said, holding out his baseball glove.

His dad looked up from leaning over his shoes. "That won't fit Tom's hand," David Lawson said. "He can hardly pick it up."

"He'll grow into it, don't worry."

"But it'll take a lot of years."

"A good glove takes a lot of years to break in, every baseball player knows that. Here," Isaac said, tossing the glove to his father.

"What are you going to do for a glove?"

"I'm buying a top-of-the-line, brand new Rawlings," Isaac said. "You know, what with all the reward money I'll be collecting soon enough, I can afford it. And, besides," he said, pointing to the glove, "everybody needs to know they have a fan. Tell Tom I'm one of his fans."

His father followed him into the kitchen. Isaac stood before the open refrigerator door and took a swig of milk from the jug.

"Your mother gave you this glove. I was against it," Reverend Lawson said, laughing. "I said it was too big. But she said she wanted you to have a good glove and that, like everything else, you'd grow into it. She didn't know a thing about baseball, or gloves, or sports. She just wanted you to want to be outside. I think she was secretly afraid you might turn out to be too bookish. She wanted you to want to know what it was like to play outside with other children, on a team, maybe, to win and to lose, and to get hurt and to get better. I said that you were only . . . How old were you?"

"It was the summer after fourth grade."

"I told her you were too little for that glove and that you'd learn those things soon enough. But she insisted." He smiled and hummed a few lines from a song that Isaac thought he recognized. "I guess you could say that she was your biggest fan."

Reverend Lawson pulled the glove to his chest.

"See what I mean?" Isaac said. He shut the refrigerator and headed down the hall towards the shower. "Time's a-wastin, Dad. Tonight is the glorious Fourth, and you better get going."

Isaac cleaned his room. Cleaning up messes was getting into his blood. He straightened the rows of books on his shelves. Just about every book he'd ever read was there. He had never known his mother had worried that he'd be too bookish. He scanned the rows and rows of his books. There was the hardback of Tom Sawyer covered in fabric that his father had read aloud to him one summer when he was little. All the Misty of Chincoteague books were lined up; they had been read aloud too, but then he went back and read them himself later. There were the Harry Potters and Hardy Boys from his grandparents. Charlie Bone books, Terry Pratchett novels, nearly a dozen Pendragon books, and Eragon were stacked there, as were some of his favorite school books: short stories by O. Henry, *To Kill a Mockingbird*, *Animal Farm*, poems by Edgar Allen Poe, the complete stories of Sir Arthur Conan Doyle. Maybe he was, in fact, a little on the bookish side. There was the thin paperback *Preacher's Boy* by Katherine Paterson, which his father had wanted him to read for months before he finally did. Now he was beginning to understand why. *Bridge to Terabithia*, another Paterson book, was a sad one that was making better sense now too. Stacks of comic books, Naruto graphic novels, the Goosebumps books, which he'd outgrown, and *Hank the Cowdog*. And *Goodnight Moon* and the Shel Silverstein books that he'd probably never outgrow, even though they were just children's books. And half a row of oversized art books, which they had stacks of in practically every room.

Isaac sat down at his desk. The sensation of Jenny's final hug that Saturday had faded. Kate's kiss on his neck seemed momentarily to deepen the beating of his heart. The strength of her hands. The smoothness of her skin. Kate, Kate, Kate.

He turned out the light and sat at his desk in the dark, then tumbled into bed at 10 o'clock and lay awake listening to the faraway sounds of fireworks exploding from the wharf downtown. A slightly out-of-tune band was playing patriotic songs. A spattering of firecrackers popped madly. He could smell the burnt powder, could hear kids' yelps of laughter.

Jacob Emerson Finch was on duty tonight, no doubt, not very far away from one of those fire trucks, playing through his mind a list of where all the town's fire hydrants were.

Isaac's ceiling fan cast shadows like silent, black panthers bounding around his room in a protective ring. The scent of honeysuckle and distant smoke stirred in the faint breeze breathing through his screened window. Isaac felt the wisp of that silent panther's great tail. Miss Thomson's teeth clicking out a Morse code greeting to the stars. The smell of his old glove, the faint scent of oil and leather and sweat. A soft piece of grass tickling his neck; the humming sound of a young father cradling his baby daughter on the front porch, rocking her to sleep under a living Van Gogh sky.

When he closed his eyes, slipping off into the billows of sleep, Isaac imagined himself standing under the tiled ceiling of the fire station, looking out of those large, open doors into the night, the shiny fire trucks safe in that garage, as safe as rubies secure in a vault, or identical twin girls tucked in for the night.

On the not so distant skyline, Isaac saw the throbbing, orange glow of Eddie Patrick's house burning down.

15

When Isaac stopped by the fire station on his lunch break, both engines were gone and no one answered the door when he knocked. He'd come to get another look at that bronze plaque.

It had occurred to him that Nathan Parramore wasn't the only name he'd recognized. John Gray was on it too, he thought. He stood on tiptoes and looked in the garage window, but because of the angle and the sheet of light glaring off the polished stone, he couldn't make out the names.

Isaac knocked on the side door again. A printed sign warned against trespassing and solicitation. Out of habit, he jiggled the door handle. It was a bad habit. The door was unlocked and, since he was in a hurry, he went in.

He remembered what Jake had said about paying taxes and this being his building. He called out. He whistled as he grabbed the pencil and notepad by the kitchen phone and headed for the garage. He made a lot of noise so as not to appear sneaky. Then he scrawled the names down, returned the notepad, and left. It wasn't breaking and entering if you didn't break anything and if you owned the building in the first place.

Hank Grady, no doubt, thought differently. Isaac caught a glimpse of him leaning against the flagpole at the post office across the street, wiping the sweat from his forehead. Mr. Peake was with him and so was Mike Lindvall. The P.O.T.S. executive committee must have had lunch together to plot its next civic improvement—leash laws for cats maybe. They had probably seen Isaac go into the station, and they certainly saw him come out. They glared at him now and swaggered across the street towards him. Isaac pretended not to notice them, but his pulse quickened, anyway. He did what was natural. He waved.

"What were you doing in the station house, boy?"

"Hello, Mr. Grady," Isaac said. He nodded to the others. "Just making a delivery to Captain Finch."

"I thought Eddie made all the deliveries for Chum." Grady looked hard at Isaac's eyes as if he were giving a visual lie detector test. Isaac tried not to flinch. He was aware of the frequency of his blinking. He felt his left eye beginning to water.

"Eddie is the delivery man," Isaac said, "but I had a question to ask Jake. So I made this one."

"You're on a first-name basis with the fire captain?"

"I am," Isaac said without flinching. "My mother taught his daughter. We both like Bruce Springsteen."

"Were you going to ask him about our break-ins? There were flames painted on all the walls," Grady said. "Firemen know a thing or two about flames."

"Nothing's wrong with asking questions."

"I've been asking a few questions my own self," Grady said, hooking his thumbs in his overall straps. "You know, my theory is that who ever is doing these break-ins has got brains. What do you think?"

"I don't have an opinion," Isaac said without thinking.

"That's not what I heard. I talked to Steve Pincus just the other day. I'm curious about these odd clues too. I figured our retired fire captain might be able to make some sense out of things. He said you were bucking to collect the reward. Said you already picked his brain on the subject."

"Mr. Pincus is right," Isaac said. "I'd like to get the reward. But to get the reward, you have to get information that will lead to an arrest. And I don't have any information. Just like you, I'm stumped."

Hank Grady stiffened and took a step closer. His belly cast a Volkswagen-sized shadow across the sidewalk and into the street. The flags snapped and tugged at the halyards, slapping at the pole. Gulls screamed as they drifted just above the rooftops.

"Who said I'm stumped?"

"You seem stumped," Isaac said, "that's all. We all are, Mr. Grady."

"I used to think it was teenagers," Grady said. "But these jobs are too clean to have been done by teenagers—"

"—or, teenager," Mr. Peake said. He had a pointed face that reminded Isaac of a lab rat.

"—unless, of course, that teen happened to be real smart." Grady stroked his heavy beard with one hand and jingled change in his pocket with the other. "Are you a smart teenager, Isaac?"

Nervousness wasn't Isaac's problem anymore. Anger was.

The men had surrounded Isaac on the sidewalk. They circled him slowly. Mr. Peake kept pushing his glasses up the bridge of his greasy nose with his pinky. His maimed hand with three missing fingers looked like a frog gigging stick. Isaac could smell Grady's breath; he was picking his teeth with a toothpick. Isaac could see Mike Lindvall behind his right shoulder; he was facing Grady but looking at Isaac sideways.

"I'm smart enough," Isaac said. "And I'm also running out of my lunch break." He sought a way through the tightening circle without bumping into any of them. Between Lindvall and Peake would be his best bet, he thought. Grady wouldn't budge, he knew.

The men fell back like bowling pins, though, when Chief Williams and another man walked up.

"What do we have here," Chief Williams said, "a quilting party?"

Grady had bitten his toothpick in two. He rolled one half between his fat lips drawn tight and held the other like a dart.

The black man with the chief wore a blue suit. He looked like an undertaker who went to college on a weight-lifting scholarship.

"Just talking to our smart friend, Isaac, here, Chief," Grady said, waving his toothpick now like a baton. "Just asking him some questions."

"They wouldn't be about our break-ins, now would they? People have been telling me," Chief Williams said, "that you've been asking lots of people lots of questions about these break-ins." The chief looked up the street. The fire trucks were lumbering slowly back toward the station, exhausted dogs after the hunt. "The people over at the utilities department, an ex-fire captain."

Chief Williams pushed his hat back on his head. He usually didn't wear a hat and sometimes didn't even wear a uniform. The badge was what mattered, he'd told Isaac once. It was the gun that mattered most, Isaac had suggested, but the chief had said no, it was the badge. The badge and brains and treating everybody with respect.

The chief looked at the other men, then leveled his gaze at Hank Grady. "You wouldn't be after the P.O.T.S. reward yourself, now would you, Grady?"

Mr. Peake laughed through his nose. Mike Lindvall just looked away. Hank Grady clenched his jaws and stuck his hands in his pockets.

"I'll tell you what, Grady. You can ride my backside all you want. And you can raise all the stink you want in the paper about my police work—"

"—or lack thereof," Grady said coolly.

"—but you've no right to bug Isaac here, or to go out to John Gray's house interviewing his wife when he's not home."

"What are you going to do about it, Chief?" Grady shouted over the rumble of the fire trucks idling by the curb. He leaned toward the chief as if to prove who was taller. "Unlike somebody in this town," he glanced at Isaac, "I'm not doing anything illegal."

The chief hadn't moved. It seemed he was beginning to turn purple with rage, Isaac thought, but it was hard to tell in the bright sun.

Grady was smiling more broadly and latched his thumbs in his straps again. "You haven't been able to make an arrest, and you can't take it out on me by squelching my freedoms."

"I can throw you in jail," Chief Williams said.

Grady made a sound like the rush of air from overfilled tires. "For what?"

"For being fat," Chief Williams said calmly.

Mr. Peake doubled over, wheezing laughter. Grady was the one turning purple now.

"And for being ugly," the chief continued. "And for hindering a federal investigation. And for a few other things, I'm sure."

"A federal investigation?" Mr. Lindvall asked, eyebrows angled up like teepees.

"Breaking into a retired federal judge's house is a no-no," Chief Williams said. He motioned to the black man in the suit. "Agent Tennyson is here from Norfolk to lend a hand."

"God knows we need it," Hank Grady said.

"God knows everything," Mr. Williams said. "And since we don't, we ought not act like we do. It's rude."

A fireman climbed out of the back of Engine 11 and stood in the intersection in front of the station's narrow doors. The engine issued a high-pitched beeping as it began backing up into the garage. The firemen looked tired.

"Agent Tennyson will be here a few days, and I'm sure you'll all cooperate by staying out of his way."

"I will," Isaac blurted out. He looked to his watch. "Gotta go," Isaac said over the sound of the loud beeping. "I'll be seeing you, Chief."

He reached out his hand to Agent Tennyson. "Enjoy your visit on the Shore, Mr. Tennyson."

Chief Williams hadn't taken his eyes off Grady, but he tipped his hat in Isaac's direction, and Agent Tennyson took Isaac's hand and gave it a crushing squeeze.

"You be careful, young Isaac," Grady said. "I'd hate to see you get into any trouble or mix with the wrong crowd."

Isaac felt like they were watching him walk away. He tried not to walk like he was guilty, or nervous. After a block, he turned around. Chief Williams and Agent Tennyson were still on the sidewalk, having an animated conversation with a few firemen. Grady and his sidekicks were gone.

Isaac had hoped to stop by the Duck Blind for a to-go order, an iced tea, anything to say hello to Kate. He had woken up that morning wondering if the picnic the day before had been a dream, some improvisational riff of his imagination.

He couldn't get her eyes out of his mind. It was the way she looked at him. It was the way she wanted to be with him. He wanted to play backgammon with her soon, or go to a movie, or take another hike. But Kate Bradshaw would have to wait because his lunch break was almost over, and the Duck Blind wasn't on the way to the clerk's office. Isaac slipped quickly in a side door of the courthouse and said hello to the woman at the window of the clerk's office. She was wearing a tropical print shirt and a hat with a banana-colored bird's beak on the front of it. Isaac looked into the large office. Lime and yellow streamers hung twisted from the corners of the ceiling. Paper umbrellas were strewn across the counter. A woman beyond the counter was digging through a filing cabinet; she wore a grass skirt and a lei.

"It's Freaky Friday," the woman said with the slightest sneer in her voice. She pushed up her beak. "What can I do for you?"

"I've got a strange question, ma'am," he said. "Are there any court records in which I might find out about what the KKK was doing here on the Shore in the 1940s and 1950s?" His face was getting hot.

"That's an interesting question, young man," the woman said. "Why do you want to know?"

"I'm working on a project for school," Isaac said.

"I suspect that even year-round schools aren't in session on the fifth of July."

"I wouldn't know, ma'am. I'm just getting ahead for the fall."

"Your dad must be too."

"My dad?"

"Aren't you David Lawson's son?"

"Yes, ma'am," Isaac said, trying too hard, perhaps, to be casual. "But don't hold that against me."

She gave him a long look and pushed up her beak again. "Reverend Lawson was in here this morning. He asked the very same question," she said. "It must be an interesting class."

16

Reverend Lawson stood at the fellowship hall sink over a load of dishes. He wore a ruffled apron and yellow rubber gloves. He swayed back and forth to the tune he was humming.

"You've been busy," Isaac said to his father.

Reverend Lawson turned around, leaving his soapy hands hanging loosely over the sink. "Ah! The lost son has returned. Go, fetch my robe and ring," he said, waving his dripping hands. "Let us kill the fatted calf. For this my son was lost and now he is found."

"I'm glad to see you too," Isaac said, not sure of what to make of his father's euphoria.

Reverend Lawson pointed to the fridge. "You look in the plastic tub of wedding mints in there and you'll find a bit of food I snatched for you before these hungry people ate everything up. They cleaned the plates so good, there's hardly any need to wash. I'm just going through the motions."

Rufus Greer was backing into the kitchen, guiding the wheeled steam table in. He was a slight, hunched man with an enormous nose. His natural expression was a scowl, but he was really a kidder.

"Watch your knuckles, honey," said a matronly voice in the hall. "If you knick yourself you're liable to bleed all over this linoleum, which the P.W. cleaned just yesterday. It was a wreck after vacation bible school."

The P.W. was the Presbyterian Women, and nobody in the church crossed the Presbyterian Women. Bleeding on that floor would be a big mistake.

Mrs. Greer, ruddy faced, followed the steam table through the door. "It's the blood thinner, Isaac. He's near about one hundred percent water, thanks to the medicine."

"You're looking good, Mr. Greer," Isaac said. "I thought you were in the hospital."

"Was," he said. "They got my medications out of whack. Had to do some fine-tuning. Problem is, see, I've got these practicing physicians. And I'm their guinea pig." He gave the steam table a sharp tug. He slapped his hands together with a little clap and gave a regal bow to Isaac. "I came home this morning and I feel great," he said. "Now, if this woman would quit hovering around me I'd be able to breathe better. Other than that I'm just dandy."

Mrs. Greer gave Isaac's arm a squeeze. Her forearms were so big, her gold-plated watch looked like a child's charm bracelet.

"He's just a big baby on the inside, but he puts on a tough front," she said. "Your puppet show was wonderful. Thanks, sweetie."

"Yes, ma'am," Isaac said.

Miss Edwards came in with the donation basket. She pushed herself up on the counter next to the sink and wrapped her arms around the basket. She was in stocking feet. "Ninety dollars and eighteen cents," she said with satisfaction. "Twenty-two adults and nine children. Not bad for the summer."

"On the week of the Fourth of July, at that," Reverend Lawson said as he sprayed off a big pot.

Miss Edwards looked at Isaac. "I saved you some food in the fridge, Isaac. There's a little of everything, except the Jell-O. I didn't want your fried chicken to be orange."

"Thank you," Isaac said, grinning. "My dad said that he's the one who saved the food."

"There he goes," she said, "taking all the credit."

"We're out of here," Rufus Greer said, poking his head back into the kitchen. He was carrying his wife's oversized purse and a plate of green olives covered in plastic. "Except for the AA in the annex, we're the last to leave."

"Thanks, Rufus," Reverend Lawson said. "You get some rest."

"Stop sounding like my wife," he complained. "But thank you."

Reverend Lawson gave him a sudsy thumbs up.

Rufus lifted his arm, and Ina said, "Good night."

Clara Edwards scooted off the counter, opened a drawer, and pulled out a plastic baggy. She stuffed in the cash and poured in the change.

Isaac and his father were watching her. She lit up when she noticed them.

"You count it five times and come up with four totals." She looked at Isaac. "But who's keeping score, huh?" She shrugged her shoulders and smiled. "I'd better go. Tom's with the neighbors tonight at a birthday party. He's probably wired on ice cream and cake."

Isaac watched her brush Reverend Lawson's shoulders lightly and step away. She put her hands on her slim hips and looked at him approvingly. "I like the ruffles," she said. "And the gloves bring out your eyes."

Isaac watched his father drink her in. It had been a long time since he'd seen his dad look so relaxed and content.

Miss Edwards turned to Isaac. "Let me know if he starts wearing ruffles at home," she said. "We can get him help."

David Lawson snorted.

"Or," she said, "maybe a bunch of hand-picked flowers would settle him down." She reached behind the salad bowls and pulled out Miss Thomson's glass pitcher. "Thank you, Isaac," she said. "They were very nice."

Isaac nodded and took the pitcher. "I'll fill it up for you again," he said.

"You needn't," she said. "The past is over."

"For the future then," he said.

She smiled at Isaac and David Lawson, each in turn, and ran her hand along Isaac's shoulders as she had his father's and then padded quietly out into the fellowship hall. Isaac listened to her rattle a folding chair, then heard the clicking of her heels fade to the far side of the room. The fellowship hall lights went out, the swinging door groaned open and sashayed closed, and Isaac and his father were alone. It was so quiet Isaac could hear the bubbles in the sink popping.

"You've been busy," Isaac said again, opening the refrigerator.

"They did all the work," Reverend Lawson said, turning back to his dishes. "I just do the big pots and leftovers that won't fit in the dishwasher. It's a great way to unwind. I should try this at home."

"I'm not talking about dishes," Isaac said, pulling a stool up to the counter by the stove. He opened the plastic container of food and dug in. "What did you discover today?"

"I don't know what you're talking about," his dad said.

"At the clerk's office," Isaac said. "Miss Hawaii told me everything."

↯ ↯ ↯

Isaac ate his dinner, and Reverend Lawson washed the pots, lids, and serving tongs. He took off his gloves, shook them, and dried them with a dish towel. He hung up his ruffled apron, then draped the gloves over the hook. He dried off the counter around the sink, then hung the towel carefully on the oven rack. He eyed the towel and adjusted it slightly so that it hung with all edges perfectly even.

Reverend Lawson pulled another stool up to the counter. "Miss Hawaii was more colorful than helpful," he said finally. "But she sent me to *The Shore News* and said if I found a case or some legal matter having to do with the Klan, she'd be glad to look it up. I can't imagine her being glad to do anything, but that's beside the point. I didn't tell her that you had already scoured the newspaper at the library. I didn't want to let on that I had an accomplice."

"Then I spilled the beans," Isaac said.

"I saw the picture of Eddie's house," his dad said. "You're right. It's awful."

Isaac shoveled in another bite of Mrs. Love's fried rice.

"You didn't scour the paper well enough, either, because I found this." His dad pulled a paper out of his back pocket and unfolded it. He slid it to Isaac. It was a photocopy of a news article from the dedication of an integrated private school near Accomac. It was dated September 1951. "The dedication speech is included with the article," Reverend Lawson said. "Do you see here the allusion to recent racial violence?"

Isaac read the lines that Reverend Lawson had circled.

> Social customs must be let go of when found to be counterproductive to the common good, wrong, evil, or all three," the speaker had said. "The common good includes everybody, of all colors and backgrounds, no matter what the status quo would lead us otherwise to believe, and no matter how forcefully the status quo would attempt to hold its sway.

"This doesn't say anything about racial violence," Isaac said.

"A preacher from Washington gave that speech," Reverend Lawson said. "It's hard for a preacher sometimes to be as clear from the pulpit on political issues as he'd like to be. When I read between the lines, I get the definite sense that something was up."

"Like what?" Isaac asked.

"Well, I talked to Mary Sue—"

"—the elderly lady down the street from us?"

"Mary Sue Wells. Episcopalian," Reverend Lawson said. "She's the one. She was a principal at the old high school. Way before your time. She knew the school district pretty well, but she doesn't remember any particular troubles between the races or between anybody. Schools were devoutly segregated then, of course. Nobody had even thought of having it any other way here on the Shore, except for the people who started that integrated private school. A pretty brave move, if you ask me. Mary Sue also said that whatever the Klan did, they must have done it very quietly because she never noticed."

"So," Isaac said, "you didn't learn much."

"I'm getting there," Reverend Lawson said. "I went to the police station and asked to see the arrest reports for those two years, 1950 and 1951."

"Did you tell the chief what you were doing?"

"Didn't have to," Reverend Lawson said. "He didn't ask. In my other life I'm a respected genealogist, remember? And every record is a matter of interest for an historian. Chief Williams knows that because I taught it to him at one of my genealogy seminars at the library. He's a quick study. Been learning the ropes with the card catalog."

"Chief Williams is into genealogy?"

"In a big way," David Lawson said. "He traces his wife's roots back to a member of John Smith's crew, from England, Devonshire, to be exact—"

"—What else did you find?"

"Nothing that rang any bells," Reverend Lawson said. "I did learn that Rufus Greer's grandfather—by that time an old man—spent a night in jail while the goats in his backyard were forcibly removed by the order of the county judge. Goats, see, weren't allowed within the city limits then, but Mr. Greer refused to remove his despite three separate court orders."

"Sounds like something P.O.T.S. would do," Isaac said, rolling his eyes.

"P.O.T.S. people are in every town," his dad said. "Anyway, I went back to the microfiche. These old records aren't on the Internet. I don't know why I didn't think of it before, but I started giving the editorials a closer read, the letters to the editor in particular. On the week after this speech was printed, two letters to the editor were published. Both said that 'the Negro' played an important role on the Shore, mainly in getting in the crops. And both said that 'the Negro and the white man' needed to live with space in between. Here," Reverend Lawson said, reaching into one back pocket, then the other. He patted his shirt pocket and pulled out a paper along with his reading glasses. "Here," he said again, unfolding two photocopies. He put on his glasses and read aloud. "'There's nothing wrong with keeping the Shore the way it's always been: the Negro in his community, and the whites in theirs.' One letter was unsigned. The other was written by Ralph Jackson."

He slid the letters over to Isaac. Isaac took a moment to read them both, then he asked his dad, "What does this mean?"

His father looked pensive. "Mean?" Reverend Lawson said. He looked at his son. "It means that maybe old Mattie Thomson isn't as nuts as I thought. Maybe you got her talking on a clear day. Maybe the Klan was more active here than anybody seems to know or is willing to talk about. It seems that there was tension between the races, which is no surprise, but that something was going on, specifically, around the time of the fire, in 1951."

Isaac went to the sink and washed his fork and plastic tub, which he'd emptied.

"I've done some work myself," Isaac said. "Four houses have been hit. All four have keys on the key board. I've looked each one up to be sure. The keys are there, though I have no proof, exactly, that any of the keys work. Miss Thomson's key is on that board and it works, I know, but how I know is a long story." He dried his hands on a dishtowel and started pacing around the chopping block in the center of the room.

Isaac continued, "Each house had flames painted on the wall. So, I went to the fire station just to look around. Seemed logical to me, and, I might add, it seemed logical to Hank Grady." Isaac explained what had happened outside the fire station. "Grady and his cronies gave me a hard time. I thought they were going to beat me up right out on the sidewalk until Chief Williams and the federal agent from Norfolk rescued me."

"Federal agent?"

"You heard me," Isaac said.

"What were you looking for at the fire station?" Reverend Lawson asked.

"I had no idea," Isaac said. "But here's what I found." He pulled out his crumpled note from the front pocket of his cut-offs. "There's a plaque on the inside garage wall. It lists all the volunteers from 1952, when the addition was built. There are twenty firemen listed on the plaque. Nathan Parramore was one of them," Isaac said. He tossed it on the counter in front of his dad and pointed to Nathan Parramore's name. "I copied down the list, wondering if these guys have anything in common with Nathan Parramore. Guess what?"

His father looked up from the list.

"All four houses hit were those of firemen. Look at the names," Isaac said, pointing them out. He'd written the dates of the break-ins next each of the four names: Horace Abbey, May 28; John Gray, June 29; Donald Martin, May 22; Nathan Parramore, June 8.

Isaac looked at his father. "Every one of these guys used to volunteer at the fire department around the time of the fire that killed Eddie's family." Isaac paced to the other side of the kitchen. "I know this is a small town," he said, "but that seems to me to be more than a little coincidence."

"These men—these families—could have had a lot in common besides being volunteer firemen. I mean, they could all be related, married into the same family, for example." Reverend Lawson tapped his finger on the counter and looked to the ceiling. "That would take some time to research, but I could do it."

"Dad, there may be other coincidences, sure," Isaac said. "But doesn't the fact that they were all volunteer firefighters mean anything?"

"Perhaps it does," said Reverend Lawson. "But like I say, there may be other so-called coincidences. They might have all been members of the same church at one time. Or Masons, or had interest in the same local business. We'd really have to check each of these things out before we jump to any conclusions."

Isaac groaned. "I'm not jumping anywhere," he said. "I'm just pointing out something that's clearly significant."

But Reverend Lawson didn't seem to be listening. He absently studied the list. He cleaned his reading glasses on a napkin and put them on again as if dust-free magnification would help. "Most of these men are dead," he said. "Some of the names I don't recognize, so they must be dead, or moved away." He started humming. "Mr. Walton lives in the nursing home; he's a Methodist. Mr. Miller moved away; he's Mrs. Roberts' brother, I'm pretty sure, and she's Episcopalian. I serve with her on a community board. Sad to say, I don't think I've ever seen her sober." He was holding the list up to the light as if another angle might yield more information. It was like he was thinking out loud, because his words didn't seem directed particularly to Isaac. "There are the four you mention as having been vandalized," he said. He touched each name with his fingertip. Then he perked up. "Looky here: Mr. Ralph Jackson is on this list."

"I know," Isaac said. "I wondered how long it would take you to notice."

"He was a volunteer firefighter and—" Reverend Lawson held up the letter to the editor from 1951 "—he thought blacks and whites could get along fine just so long as they didn't have to get along together. Of course, just about everybody on the Shore probably thought the same thing back then."

"The fire captain, Jake Finch, thinks most of those old-timers are gone too. That makes Ralph Jackson the only volunteer fireman still living around here whose house hasn't been sprinkled."

Reverend Lawson stared perplexedly at Isaac over his half glasses.

"That's what the old guys at the hardware store are calling the vandalisms," Isaac said. "Sprinklings." Isaac yawned. "I think Mr. Jackson's house must be next."

"Next? That's wonderful," David Lawson said gloomily. "Mr. Jackson is a hard-shell Baptist," he mused. He was absently looking up at the ceiling again. "I don't see Mr. Jackson often. Wonder what he's up to?"

"He's fine," Isaac said. "He was in the store just this morning. Says he and his wife are taking the grandkids down to Lake Gaston for the week."

Isaac paced around the chopping block and took the list from his father.

"All of these houses were sprinkled," Reverend Lawson said, "when their owners were out of town. When do the Jacksons leave? Did he say?"

"They leave Saturday at noon."

"Maybe we should tell Reginald about this, so he can keep an eye on the place."

"I've done something better," Isaac said.

"What?"

"I told Mr. Jackson that if he needed a house sitter, I'd be glad to do it."

"What did he say?"

"He said he'd leave the fridge stocked and pay me a hundred bucks. I start Sunday."

17

Isaac called his father from the warehouse as soon as he got in on Monday morning. He told him that everything went fine at the Jackson house the night before. It was a peaceful night, he said. The guest bed was comfortable and the satin sheets were tucked in so tight he nearly slid off the bed when he rolled over. Isaac did not tell his father that he didn't get much sleep lying on the living room couch next to the front door behind which he'd stacked ten cans of tomato soup. He'd booby-trapped every door with metal cookie sheets and pans, bottles of salad dressing, a jar filled with pennies, and anything else that would make noise if knocked over by an intruder. He jumped awake every time the central air conditioner purred on and off.

His father was miffed that he had gone through with spending the night, but Isaac had insisted. He had reminded his father how far-fetched their speculation had been, how myriad other coincidences were possible, how flimsy their links to Eddie were, and how unlikely Ralph Jackson's house was next. This is real life, Isaac had told his dad, not a television show. His father had seemed placated, if not convinced.

But the more Isaac thought about it, jolting awake all night long, the more his theory made sense. Of course, the more he thought about it, the later it got and the more punch drunk he became with exhaustion. Eddie was doing this to get back at the town that killed his family. The flames and water were part of his message, which Isaac hadn't deciphered yet. Old keys were being used, which is why no trace of entry could be found and why the key ledger was never dusty when everything else in the Chum warehouse was. The Klan was somehow involved; Isaac couldn't figure out how or who, and Miss Thomson was little help. The volunteer firefighters listed on that bronze plaque figured in somehow too. The jelly makers knew more than they were telling. Police Chief Reginald Williams was on the verge of retiring or running over Hank Grady with one of the town's two police cruisers, and the P.O.T.S. executive committee was ready to lock and load.

Those were the facts as Isaac saw them, and by sunrise, with less than a thimbleful of sleep, Isaac was convinced he was on the right road, which is why, all day long, he had the feeling he was about to have something in common with road kill.

Isaac shuffled through his work that morning. It was hot and still. He barely had the strength to move a pile of broken and rotted pallets, so he gave up and just sat down on a bucket in the middle of the warehouse, looking around for the easiest job to tackle. He decided about all he was good for was straightening shelves, so he went back into the air-conditioned store and repeated all the chores he'd done first thing that morning. Mr. Chum may have thought Isaac had had a heat stroke, but Isaac was too tired to care, and Mr. Chum didn't ask.

At lunch Isaac drove home for a quick nap. He thought he could get some sleep in his own bed. He set the alarm for fifteen minutes. Anything would be better than nothing.

When he closed his eyes, he tossed and turned and dreamed. Hank Grady towered above him. Isaac couldn't move. Grady stepped on his hip, then reached down like he was going to start a push mower. When Grady yanked, Isaac jerked awake.

He lay on his bed shaking. He had seven minutes left on the alarm. He wasn't rested, but he was decidedly awake.

When he sat up, it occurred to him that the vandal could break in anytime. Until then, Isaac had presumed the houses were flooded at night. But why not in the middle of the day when so many neighbors would be at work or running errands?

Isaac remembered that Eddie often wouldn't come back after lunch until near closing time. There was no telling where Eddie was on some afternoons, no telling which deliveries he was making first, or whether he was on deliveries at all. Eddie could be at Ralph Jackson's house that very moment, turning on faucets and slopping orange paint on his master bedroom wall.

Isaac grabbed a banana from the kitchen and slumped into his car. He coasted through the three stop signs and stopped by the Jacksons' on the way back to work. The doors were still locked and, except for a slow drip from the elegant kitchen faucet, the water spigots were turned tightly off.

After work Isaac napped until dusk. He took a shower and stood in the Jacksons' renovated kitchen. Two new bay windows opened to the backyard. The appliances were shiny and black. The stove had a grill built in. He explored the refrigerator and freezer for dinner options and decided on garlic sticks and a frozen dinner. He ate a small package of cherry tomatoes while he waited for the microwave to ding. He was still hungry after the chicken balsamico, so he had another, this time beef tips portobello. When he finished, he opened a new pint of Ben and Jerry's Cherry Garcia and spooned a bite right out of the carton. It was kind of funny, he thought, that old-timers like the Jacksons would buy hippie ice cream, but it suited him fine. The big chocolate chips lodged uncomfortably in his teeth, so he put the ice cream back and opened a new half-gallon of store-brand French vanilla. He distractedly savored a few big spoonfuls as he looked at the snapshots of children on the refrigerator. Smiling faces. Children in pools wearing water wings and exuberance. A couple leaning together at a crowded dinner table. A bare-chested Ralph Jackson holding a saw while posing formally in front of what looked like a newly constructed shed.

The house was spotless. Unlike the kitchen with its new counters and modern appliances, the rest of the house was filled with old things. Little stained-glass nightlights the shape of sailboats and balloons were plugged into the wall sockets of each room, so Isaac didn't have to turn on any lights as he rambled through. A dimly lit glass cabinet was filled with figurines and strands of twisted, blown glass. The old house had settled unevenly. The dining room sloped towards the ocean. If Isaac had dropped a marble in the doorway, it would have rolled like a dribbling grounder toward the windows. The claw-footed table had done nothing to scar those wide, gleaming, blonde floor boards. A bowl of waxed fruit sat in a silver dish on the hunt chest. Isaac looked at himself in the solid mirror that hung above it. He wondered if anybody had ever before shuffled barefoot through this room, eating ice cream out of the box with a serving spoon.

In the front living room Isaac could see the patterned marks in the plush carpet where the vacuum cleaner had been. A gun cabinet with a full-length pane of thick, bowed glass stood in the corner. There were two .22s, a couple of larger rifles with scopes, and a double-barrel shotgun with a scarred butt. The drawer beneath the cabinet wasn't locked. It was filled with neatly stacked boxes of Remington shells. It was a lot of firepower for a man who had said at the store that he had long ago given up hunting. And the boxes of shells looked new.

A brass canister stuffed with canes sat by the front door. One cane was black with a white marble knob on top. Isaac picked it up. It was solid, heavy. Another cane was fatter, made of blonde wood with snakes carved into its shaft. Isaac pulled this one out and clumsily twirled it like a baton. It got away from him and clattered onto the floor, seeming to writhe for a second like it was alive. Isaac jumped, then scooped it up like a fast grounder to first. His heart was pounding. He expected dogs to start barking or an alarm to go off.

As he slid the cane back into the canister, he noticed the shaft was loose. He gave it a twist and yanked the top. Out from the shaft came a gleaming blade. It was seven inches long with dull edges but had a perfect, sharp point. Isaac put it back into the canister and tested another cane, twisting and pulling at its shaft and head. He noticed in the crook of one what looked like a crude trigger; he popped off the rubber end cap at the bottom of the cane and the shaft was hollow. It was the long, hollow barrel of what seemed a very small-caliber pistol. He tugged at the top of another and it produced another dagger, this one the color of a dull nickel and corroded.

James Bond leapt into Isaac's mind: a thin, suave secret agent. But potbellied Ralph Jackson was no James Bond. Isaac never would have guessed that Mr. Jackson was so enthused by weapons and violence, or that he felt such a need for lethal protection. You never really know anybody, Isaac thought.

Upstairs, the small bedrooms were tidy. Slippers sat neatly on the floor by each side of the bed. There was a wide stool by one side of the bed with ornate caning. In the guest room Isaac noticed a trap door to the attic.

The first things he saw as he climbed the rickety ladder and pulled the hanging light cord were what appeared to be the pointed hoods of Klan robes. As he stood halfway inside the sweltering attic, he got chills. But as he looked closer, the hoods turned out to be two old bird cages on heavy floor stands covered by sheets. But he imagined one of those sheets pulled over Mr. Jackson, his hairy, thick belly protruding like that of a pregnant woman. Isaac remembered what his father had said about his college girl-friend, how her father had kept his father's Klan garb hanging in the coat closet.

His eyes adjusted to the light. Two bare bulbs lit the long, narrow attic. Oddly matched old planks had been nailed down for flooring in the center of the room. Pink insulation was stuffed between the exposed floor joists and roof timbers.

Besides the ghostly sheets, what most grabbed Isaac's attention was how sturdy and rough-hewn the lumber was. He had heard people come into the lumberyard and ask Will Chum for some real, untrimmed two-by-fours, and Will would say that such a thing wasn't made anymore. Lumber was on the small side now, he'd say. Now Isaac knew what they were asking for as he admired the workmanship of the underside of this old roof.

His ice cream was melting, and just as he turned up the box to take a swallow, the phone rang. He hustled down and closed up the attic, bolting downstairs before the fourth ring. The machine picked up and Isaac listened to Mrs. Jackson, in her formal Virginia drawl, explain that they were out of the how-se. There was the beep, but no one left a message.

Surely, Isaac thought, whoever was doing these break-ins would call before they came over to do the deed just to make sure nobody was home. He imagined Eddie on the other end of the line, listening to the sound of an empty house. The Jacksons were at Lake Gaston, and the dogs had been kenneled. But Isaac wanted to say that the house wasn't uninhabited. I'm here, he wanted to say. I'm here and this house isn't empty.

Isaac put the box of melting ice cream in the sink. He had eaten more than half. He washed his hands and looked at pictures of more happy peo-ple on the bulletin board by the phone. A doctor's prescription was posted there. A grocery list. A thank-you note. He picked up the phone and lis-tened for a dial tone, then hung it back up. He did that twice.

He'd have to set the pace, he told himself. Find his groove. No use getting worked up about a simple wrong number or sales call. He looked at the black clock hanging above the bulletin board. It was nine o'clock. Isaac pulled his cell out of his pocket and hit the speed dial. Calling Jenny was a hard habit to break.

Jenny's Aunt Frances answered and told Isaac that it was another perfect day in paradise at the Wild Flower. The toilet stopped up yesterday, and the clothes dryer gave up the ghost this morning, she said, but other than that, things were fine and they were running at full occupancy. They chatted. Yes, she said, she was still squeezing her own juice for those big breakfasts.

His heart sped up while he waited for Jenny to come to the phone. Isaac's mother had always said you have to be careful not to read too much into someone's look or tone. The best way to know how to tell what someone is thinking is to ask them. But Isaac's mother also had always said you need to learn to trust your instincts. When Jenny picked up, he knew immediately that things between them were still out of tune and always would be.

She was fine, Jenny said, but getting ready to go out. You know what they say about all work and no play, she said. They were going to a 9:30 movie. She didn't say who "they" were.

How's Tube, he asked. Fine, she said. He didn't care to ask about Billy Birdsong, that tattoo of orange flames streaking up his lower spine from his ass. Was she enjoying herself? he asked. Yes, she'd said. What about him? He was doing fine, he said. Everybody was fine, he said. Everything was okay. He'd met a few new friends. She was glad. She didn't ask who they were either. He imagined Kate telling him, "You better believe you've met a new friend, bucko," then punching him in his arm. He hoped Kate would say that, or something like it, but he wasn't sure. Not absolutely.

A few new friends, he had told Jenny.

He thought of making deliveries with Crazy Eddie, critiquing country song lyrics with him in a Chum's Hardware pickup driving ten miles an hour under the speed limit all the way up to near Arbuckle Neck. He thought of the gentle games of catch he was planning to play with Tom Edwards. He thought of Miss Edwards' quiet word of thanks for the flowers, and how those words were like a cool lotion that soothed the scorch of the fastballs he had aimed at Tom's plastic glove. A great cloud of witnesses, his father might say. Natives is the word his mom might use.

Isaac half-listened to Jenny talking excitedly about the art show on the boardwalk. Artists had come from everywhere, she was saying. It was sunny. Different kinds of art. Photography. Jugglers.

Isaac thought of John Singer Sargent and his drowsing lady on the couch, of Degas' ballerinas, Van Gogh's sunflowers. He thought of his mother, who had introduced him to these friends. She was as dead as a doornail, Mattie Thomson might say, but as alive as ever in her only son's heart. The past is never dead, his dad sometimes said, quoting William Faulkner; it's not even past.

"You would have loved it," Isaac heard Jenny say.

He wanted to tell her that she didn't need to pretend things had not changed. "You're right," is what he said. "That sounds real nice."

He told her he was working hard and that, not to worry, everything on the Eastern Shore of Virginia was on an even keel. She shouldn't worry about a thing. And that she'd better go, or she'd miss her movie.

As soon as he hung up his cell phone, the wall phone rang. He instinctively picked it up this time. There was a slight pause, then a click.

Nobody was there, again.

Isaac was afflicted by voices. He stood at the phone thinking about what his father might say about his situation. Seek and ye shall find. He imagined what Kate might say, if he explained everything and told her about the telephone calls and how he was house-sitting an empty, old house, and that a stranger with a gallon of orange paint might be standing outside one of those kitchen bay windows, looking in at him that very moment. He heard Kate say one word, only half smiling: Run. He pictured his mother. She stood with her arms loosely crossed in front of her and with her head cocked to one side as she often did when she admired something; Eddie walked into his mind's picture. He was holding a bag of fresh greens. His mother's face lit up just as Miss Edwards' had in the church kitchen. Isaac's mother and Crazy Eddie were standing there together looking at him like he was a Mary Cassatt painting. They both spoke at the same time. And they both said the same thing.

Listen to your father.

∀ ∀ ∀

Cookbooks lined the counter. Asian cookbooks and Southern cookbooks and Betty Crocker. Isaac was looking for a phone book in that wide collection of cooking and sundry other books. A gourmet cookbook, a collection of slow-cooker recipes, a fat copy of a repair manual for a 1988 Ford pickup.

Cooking seemed easy. Everything is prescribed. Everything is laid out. Just follow the instructions exactly as written. What could go wrong?

There was a church directory. The Jacksons were still Baptists. There was a church cookbook, a bartender's guide, a travel guide of Italy, a bunch of folded maps of Florida, and a thick book with no words on the spine, just a picture of a shimmering glass of wine.

Cooking by the numbers required no original thought. Do what the recipe says. Don't vary. See what patience and even heat can bring.

Isaac found the phone book next to the huge *Webster's Third New International Dictionary* and, with trembling fingers, found the residential numbers. He scanned the names. This time he used his cell. One finger held the name and number in place. The other finger dialed.

It took three rings before somebody picked up, plenty of time to run through the other titles. Homemade Bread! The Wonders of the Wok. Virginia Hospitality.

Precise measurements. Fresh ingredients. Follow the recipe. Hundreds of meals perfectly rendered hundreds of times. Nothing can go wrong.

Isaac had to say his own name two times before it came out clearly.

"Can you meet me at the church in twenty minutes?"

French Cuisine. The Butter Breaker's Diet.

"No, it's not about vacation Bible school."

A Kenmore owner's manual. A tattered *Field Guide to the Birds. The Eastern Shore of Virginia Guidebook.* A King James version of the Bible.

"There is nobody else to talk to about this. I need to talk to you. Face to face. Come when you can. Tonight, please."

Isaac tried to make sense of the silence in his left ear. He couldn't break its code.

"Please," he said again. "I'll meet you at the church, Eddie. I'll be waiting."

18

Isaac let the lobby door slam heavily behind him. He stood unmoving in the silence, attentive to it like a heron at the marshy edge of a tidal pool. The church smelled faintly of the flowers from Sunday. Mrs. Ober, the arthritic flower lady, had arranged a big spray of what she had said were the very last of the mimosa blooms. They were wispy, Isaac remembered, and fragile. He was nearly sick last Sunday, in a dark mood, feeling very much like he had slipped beyond the point of what honest penitence could fix and what grace could cover, so the flowers helped. They lifted his spirit, if only slightly, and what a relief that was. That's why, he remembered, he was so eager to walk Mrs. Ober to her car after the service. She yammered on about how the summer heat would cut down on her fresh flower options. She said she might have to start using artificial flowers. She whispered the word artificial like she had lapsed into a conversation about feminine hygiene or the dreaded Atlanta Braves.

"I'll have to bring that old plastic fig tree in from the parlor," she said. "Or go to the florist. But I hate spending money on what God gives us for free. Blame heat."

"Yes, ma'am," Isaac said.

Now the church was dark and chilly, not unlike the warehouse in the mornings before it got too hot. The church lobby was a welcome relief from the humid night, heavy with salt and pine and honeysuckle. The cool air made the hairs stand up on Isaac's bare arms and legs.

He remembered standing at this door as the children streamed out of the sanctuary after his puppet show on their way to their classes. He remembered how their high fives stung his palm, how some of the sixth grade girls looked demurely away as they passed him, then broke out in a chain reaction of giggles. The adults nodded firmly, smiling satisfied, tight smiles. Isaac remembered Tom Edwards' enthusiastic hug.

Isaac began to make out shapes in the shadow and dark. A half circle of chairs in the lobby. The table on which the church secretary lined up the mail. Moonlight from the upstairs classroom windows filtered in as if from some dome light indicating a cosmic door was ajar, as if something in the universe was out of balance. He hadn't moved yet. His church smelled like a cedar hope chest.

He could make out the transom windows above the office doors to his right. To his left, a strip of light under the swinging door into the sanctuary looked like a long, flat bar of gold. He stepped to the door, and the whole building adjusted to his weight. He pushed the scarred door open, and walked into another world.

The sanctuary was dominated, day and night, by the big Jesus the Good Shepherd stained glass window, which climbed the wall up towards the high ceiling. In the daytime sunlight streamed in, coloring the pews and the people. Jesus, with a sheep in his arms and several at his feet, looked into the church, down into the faces of his other flock. At night a small light from the inside lit the window so that the image could be seen from the outside. So, in the daytime, Jesus stood in the window looking into the church. At night, Jesus stood in the window looking out onto the town and into the woods. The light was on a timer and went off when the 11 o'clock news came on. That's when church neighbors said they usually went to bed.

Isaac went to the back pew and sat quietly in the dark corner. He looked at the choir loft where his mother had sung alto. She'd watch him during the service and smile when their eyes met. His father would glance at him from the pulpit when he preached. Jesus never took his eyes off of him. Isaac always sat in the back, a true Presbyterian, his dad would often say, but he could never escape being looked at. Except at night. He liked being in the church at night when it was empty because nobody was looking at him. Not even Jesus, who was busy watching passersby on Angel Wing Road.

Isaac stretched out onto the pew and put two hymnals under his head. He could see the patterns of the high, tin-paneled ceiling and the dark chandelier hanging by its big chain. His thoughts raced.

"Tonight is the night," he whispered.

He was going to—well, what was he going to do? He was going to confront Eddie, straight out. Eddie would be mad coming down to the church at this hour. He was an early riser. He probably would be in bed by now on most nights, on nights when he wasn't breaking into people's houses. He wouldn't appreciate being bothered. And on top of that, being accused of ruining four homes would send him over the top. Isaac knew he was in for it, so he'd have to talk fast.

But how to begin? Isaac turned it over again and again. His story had many gaps; mainly, why now? Eddie had access to keys that might actually work. Revenge may have been his motive. But after so many years of doing nothing, why now?

And why were the likes of Nathan Parramore and Constitution Gray targeted? Why not Mattie Thomson? She was an old-timer who represented the status quo, wasn't she? Or, why not Reggie Williams? As police chief he represented authority. Maybe they were on the list.

Eddie would launch right in. Where's the proof? You got pictures? Fingerprints? Witnesses? You're a bored little boy with nothing to do with your time except to dream dreams. You and your farcical hunches.

Isaac had a notion to leave. But leave and go where? Back to the Jacksons' house? The last thing he wanted to do was to be in that house alone, especially after opening this can of worms with Eddie. And he didn't dare go home. He felt like he had flying through that storm over Atlanta. Fear, exhilaration, uncertainty. One thing was certain: there was nowhere to go but forward. There was no backing out now. He'd better hold tight, he resolved. Hold tight and get ready to take his lumps.

He took a deep breath. Though he could see nothing but the ceiling, it felt good to be lying down on the crushed velvet pews.

At that moment keys made a violent rattling in the office door. It banged open. The building seemed to inhale. Isaac heard footsteps in the lobby, voices. He heard a light snap on. The sanctuary door punched open, and the fluorescent light from the lobby rudely swept in. More than one person came in. A scuffling of feet. The door swung shut. A moment of silence while the room adjusted to this outside presence. The smell from outdoors reached Isaac—the pine, the salt, a trace of honeysuckle, but also perfume. A set of feet thudded down front to the pulpit.

Lighter, more frequent steps followed. They were the sounds of high heels on the hardwood floor. And they had a female voice to go with them.

"I can't believe you do this."

It was Miss Edwards.

Isaac wanted to sit up and say hello, but he didn't want to explain why he was there. He didn't want to disturb them, either. He decided not to move.

The other voice was a male voice, his father's. "There are things you got to do to stay sane around here," Isaac's father said. "And, for me, this is one of those things."

If Isaac got caught spying, he'd say that he had come to church to think and had fallen asleep. But if Eddie showed up before Reverend Lawson and Clara Edwards left, Isaac didn't have a clue how he would lie himself out of that.

He was aware that his breathing had sped up to keep pace with the rising anxiety he was beginning to feel. If he were more rested, he thought, things would make a lot more sense, his mind would be working more smoothly, and things wouldn't feel so desperate. He recalled that in his recurring dream of late—the panting, the shadows, the dark room—things never turned out well. Every tiny sound he made seemed like a booby trap was going off, like empty pans were hitting a slate floor.

Isaac leaned up a bit to get a peek at what was going on. He moved as a glacier might move, imperceptibly across the eons. He wanted to see what it was that his dad did in the sanctuary in the half light in order to stay sane.

Their walking had stopped. Isaac heard a distinct humming from his father and a smaller vaguely musical sound from Miss Edwards. Were they practicing a humming duet for Sunday? It took a moment for Isaac to make anything of what he was hearing. When it came to him, he could feel his face go hot. It was a long, slurpy kiss, the kind Isaac deeply missed enjoying. Another kiss, impossibly loud. They were humming while they kissed, while they tasted each other's lips, mouths.

It was gross. And hilarious. And Isaac was pierced with a deep ache.

He knew that he ached for the things he missed, the past season of his own kisses, when he was a baseball hero, when Jenny's lips were willing and curious, when she was glad to have him around. He thought of Kate and he knew that he also ached for what might be. The ache deepened when he thought about his mother.

He felt a blistering anger at his father for daring to kiss another pretty woman. And relief. He felt relieved for his lonely father, glad for his old man. But he missed his mom so much.

More sounds. Isaac didn't want to listen, couldn't help but hear. He could hear his pulse beating in his ears. He could hear the sound of his own breathing. He heard words. Isaac imagined his father speaking close to her face, holding her in his arms. He imagined how their bodies must fit together, how they kept their balance standing so closely.

"There are times when my heart breaks for him," his dad said quietly.

Breaks for whom? Isaac wanted to know. This must be the conversation they were having before they came in, Isaac thought.

"Sometimes I'm not sure how to love him, you know? I don't want to crowd him."

Love whom? Crowd whom?

"This is the part," his dad said, "when you're supposed to say something wise that puts everything in perspective."

"If I said anything," Miss Edwards said, "you'd accuse me of preaching."

When they spoke, Isaac lifted himself in painstaking increments in order to get a look over the pew. When they stopped talking, he'd stop. Every muscle was steeled to control his slow rising.

Who was the he they were talking about and why was he so difficult to love?

"When Tom was in kindergarten, I wanted to protect him from every possible hurt," Miss Edwards said. "I found out that I just couldn't do that. Nor should I."

His father was talking about little Tom. Isaac couldn't figure out what made Tom so difficult to love. Whenever Tom walked into a room, Isaac always wanted to pat his head, or give him five, or lightly slap his back. He was adorable, though a little hyper. Maybe that's what made it hard for Isaac's dad.

"I was nervous about him making friends," Miss Edwards was saying, "fitting in, riding the bus, minding his manners. I was worried about bullies—"

Isaac's heart sank.

"—and a hundred what ifs."

"And?" his dad asked.

"And I still worry," she said. "It's hard."

A car swooshed past just outside on Angel Wing Road.

"Whatever emotional stuff I couldn't handle," Reverend Lawson said, "his mother could. We were a team, Marie and me."

It was him. His father was talking about him. Isaac slumped down again on the soft pew and laced his fingers together over his beating chest and strained to hear what his father was saying. Was saying about him.

"Now I've got to handle it all by myself, and I'm not sure sometimes what to do, what to say. I deal with other people's emotional stuff every day, but when it comes to my own son . . . I feel like I'm all thumbs."

There was a long, silent pause.

"I don't want him to feel smothered," Reverend Lawson said. "But I sure want him to feel loved, and safe. I know he's not a little kid anymore, but . . . "

Another long moment of silence.

"He knows you love him, doesn't he?" Miss Edwards asked. "Doesn't he? He knows it intuitively, of course, but you have told him, haven't you?"

There was a long silence.

"David?"

His father cleared his throat. "With words?"

"Oh, David, of course with words."

"But actions speak louder than words," his dad said.

"Both are necessary," Miss Edwards said, raising her voice. "I should write your next sermon, Reverend."

"Sanctimony isn't allowed in the pulpit," his dad chuckled.

An empty cattle trailer clanked noisily down the road.

Isaac did, indeed, feel loved. He knew his father loved him. There was no doubt. But it had been a long time since his dad had said so. And Isaac hadn't said it, either. Surely his dad knew he loved him.

And then it came back in a fraction of a second, and it all came at once, the heat, the smells of the fresh-mown grass, the feeling of sun on his face, the strange blur of people made to stand so closely together, hunched, weeping, looking determinedly off into the distance, the distortion of their words, their dark eyes, and the beads of sweat herded above their tight upper lips.

It all came forcefully back.

Isaac squeezed back the tears and he held on. He held onto the pew and gritted his teeth and put one foot slowly to the floor because he needed the extra grounding. It was so real and so fast and so uninvited. Was the world turning upside down? He was digging his fingers into the pew cushion, holding on, trying not to let go. He couldn't believe his tears, wasn't sure if he could handle this molten time warp, this spinning. He could hardly breathe. And he didn't care if the pew creaked, didn't care if they found him hiding here, didn't care if gravity lost its hold and he tumbled in a heap up to the ceiling.

It was August, at the graveyard, that impossible graveyard on a vividly bright day where the flowers were wilting on a silver metal casket and the minister friend of his father's had just pronounced the benediction. The pallbearers, limp like the flowers, had shaken their hands, and the air smelled of fresh clods of dirt. The service was over, and his father tried twice to stand, and arms came from everywhere to help him, and they pushed him and his father up into the sky that had no right to be so blue. His father stood for a moment, seemingly not knowing what to do with his hands, what to latch his gaze upon. Isaac remembered his father closing his eyes, his father's head rolling slightly back, and more arms and well-meaning fingers reaching, offering, steadying. Isaac remembered how he and his father stepped into one another, then someone pulled away the plastic chairs in a flurry. Someone else said, O God. Isaac remembered the feel of his father's arms around him, heavy like sandbags. Isaac remembered his father's sweat and tears and Old Spice rising up and mingling with the smells of dirt and grass and dying flowers, and how all the hands from all directions seemed to lift them up off the ground.

Slowly he relaxed again on his narrow pew. Miss Edwards and his father were still up front. Still talking, still laughing.

"Wait here," Reverend Lawson said quietly.

Isaac heard his father step up onto the small, hollow-sounding chancel area on which the pulpit sat. Did he hear his father drop to his knees? Is that what he did to stay sane, pray? Is that it?

Isaac slowly began sitting up again.

Then, the rattling of something metal, his dad making a slight straining sound. He heard Miss Edwards shift on her feet on the hardwood floor. Isaac was almost there. He let his legs swing down off the pew. His feet found the floor soundlessly and—the hardest part—he eased his torso up. He rested the bridge of his nose on the pew in front of him. He didn't want to watch, but couldn't help himself. Didn't want to listen, but couldn't not hear. This was wrong, he knew. This liaison was not meant for him.

He blinked to find his focus. His face was smeared with tears and sweat.

His father was, indeed, on his knees. He was tugging on the air vent in the wall behind the pulpit. The metal grate popped off easily, and he put it aside. Miss Edwards bent over to look in. Reverend Lawson reached into the rectangle of darkness and, with his right hand, pulled out a clear glass jar filled with something orange that made a dull rattling sound. With his left he pulled out a putter.

"Ta-da!" he said, smiling back at Miss Edwards. "I keep them here, because this is the only place I use them."

"In the sanctuary?"

"In the sanctuary."

David Lawson got up and stepped off the chancel. He dumped three orange golf balls onto the carpeted runner in front of the communion table and gave Miss Edwards the empty jar. "Put it over there," he said. "On its side, facing me."

He walked to the rail of the choir loft, and squared up over a ball. "This is how I sort things out when things get crazy," he said. "I come in here and practice my putting. Very relaxing."

He hit a ball. Isaac couldn't see the ball, but could hear it as it drum-rolled lightly over the carpet and clinked into the jar.

"I'd practice my driving in here if I thought I could get away with it."

"But you don't even play golf," Miss Edwards said, rolling the ball back to him.

Isaac took a good look at his dad in the dim light. He had been thinking lately that his father looked a little pudgy, graying hair, a little off his game. As recently as the day before, in the church kitchen, Isaac had said to himself that he wouldn't let that happen to him. He'd stay fit, keep working on his timing at the plate, always be able to reach big and keep his foot on the bag.

But his father didn't look so bad tonight. He was confident. He was loose. He was in the zone. Maybe he was getting pudgy, but he seemed taller, or lighter, or something.

"That's right," Reverend Lawson said. "There are some in this congregation—any congregation, I suppose—who look at golf as a bit frivolous. And expensive. They might think they're paying their minister too much."

"I, for one, know that's not true."

"I don't need eighteen holes," he said, taking another shot. "Just a pickle jar. This gets me through."

The ball pinged off the jar and dribbled onto the hardwood floor under the pews. As Miss Edwards bent down to get it, Isaac hastily lifted his legs so that she wouldn't see an orange golf ball and his tennis shoes.

He had hit the hymnal rack in his effort to lie down. It made a bump. The pew creaked as he flattened on it. He felt his whole body grimace.

"What's that?" she asked.

"What's what," Reverend Lawson said.

"That creaking."

Isaac froze. He breathed through his open mouth, his heart pounding. He heard the ping of the putter on a ball.

"That," Reverend Lawson said slowly as the ball made the two-second roll across the carpet, "is the sound of an old church settling."

The ball rattled in the jar.

"Kind of creepy here at night, all alone," she said. "And I'm not easily spooked."

The office door thumped open.

"What's that?" Miss Edwards asked.

Isaac heard heavy footsteps inside the lobby, then the sanctuary door fling open.

"That," Reverend Lawson said with a question in his voice, "is our very own Eddie Patrick."

19

Isaac lay frozen in the pew. He had rolled slowly over from his left side onto his back. He noticed small cracks in the ceiling paint and gazed at the big central chandelier, hanging from burnished bronze links of chain. Things could get worse if the chain snapped and the chandelier plunged and killed him. Otherwise, this was as bad at it could get.

Eddie spoke first. "Reverend, ma'am."

"Eddie," Reverend Lawson said, voice rising. "Come in. You're out late."

"Out walking, Reverend. I drove into town for a late dinner. Don't have sidewalks out at my place, and the way some teenagers drive, it's not safe walking on those country roads at night. Thought I'd get a walk in before I went home. Saw the light on in the lobby, figured somebody left it on by accident. Door was unlocked. Didn't know it was you. Playing golf."

"Yes, Eddie," Reverend Lawson said. "It seems that church is a sanctuary for many things, many things. You know Miss Edwards, Eddie?"

"Yes, ma'am. Knew your grandpa, I believe. Paid his accounts at the store every month with silver dollars. A bit odd, as I remember. Howdy do?"

"Fine, Mr. Patrick, thanks."

"Besides being interested in golf, Miss Edwards is our church treasurer," Reverend Lawson said.

Isaac could hear his father walking, probably towards Miss Edwards.

"We were just trying to find a way to extort enough money from the church treasury to send our youth group to the Bahamas."

"Whatever you say, Reverend," Eddie said. "Judging from what I heard about last week, what with all the young people helping out at vacation bible school, they deserve a little trip."

There was a moment of perfect silence.

"How's that son of yours?"

"He's fine, Eddie. Thanks for asking. Thanks too, for being patient with him at the store. This is his first real job, you know."

"Yep. No problem," Eddie snorted. "He doesn't give me too much grief, most of the time. Is he around here too?"

"No," Reverend Lawson said. "He's out. Can't keep him in. It's summer, you know."

"Yep. Okay, we'll see you later."

"We were just leaving. Can we give you a ride to your car?"

"Nope. Walking'll do me good."

"We'll walk you out, then," Reverend Lawson said.

Isaac heard the sounds of all three walking through the sanctuary door. He heard the lobby light snap off and the lobby door slam shut. Someone tried the door knob and gave the door a shake to make sure it was locked. Isaac heard their voices fading away outside. The inside of the church fell into the sighs and ticks of abandoned auditoriums.

The only thing worse than facing Eddie and his dad and Miss Edwards all at once was facing Eddie alone later. And he knew that moment would come. He could call in sick tomorrow. But sooner or later he'd be back to work with Eddie, and he could expect fireworks.

He sat up in his pew and looked over to the choir loft. "You couldn't help me out of this jam, Mom, even if you were here." He put his forehead on the pew in front of him and looked down at his tennis shoes. "If you were here."

He got up and found the putter and jar of balls on the first pew. He took them to the air vent behind the pulpit and put them inside, replacing the grate. He stood and stepped to the pulpit, which he held with both hands, and looked out over the empty pews. He imagined looking into the faces of all those people filled with secret, dark pasts. All those crooked hearts.

He wondered if his mother would be proud of him, or ashamed, or a little of both. As he looked for her seat in the choir loft, the light on the timer clicked off, and he was plunged into darkness.

↓ ↓ ↓

When he opened the door into the night, someone was sitting on the steps.

"You've got a lot of explaining to do, young'un."

Isaac jumped back. "Who's that?"

"Who d'you think, Mickey Mantle?"

The man stood up on the sidewalk and slowly turned around. It was Eddie. Isaac could tell by his profile in the street light that he wasn't smiling.

"You scared me to death," Isaac said. "How'd you know I was in the church?"

"I didn't know you were in it. I just know you told me to meet you at it. I came earlier and found your daddy with his girlfriend. Where were you?"

"It's a very long story," Isaac said, "one that would take me two weeks to explain. I'm just glad you're here."

Isaac sat down, leaving room for Eddie to sit next to him.

"We better walk, kid. My back was feeling fine when this late night game began, but now it's stoving up. We'd better walk." He set out down the sidewalk. "This'd better be worth it," he said, walking away.

"It is," Isaac said. "Sort of."

The road bent into the woods that fringed Norman Creek. They walked for a while in silence along the sidewalk of the homes that looked out over the creek.

"When it floods," Isaac said, "these yards really take a beating. Good thing these houses don't have cellars."

"We're not talking about the weather," Eddie scoffed.

The roots of the oaks had buckled the sidewalk. Somebody had repaired some cracks but now the concrete patches were thrust up.

"Well?" Eddie said.

"Miss Thomson says the Klan burned your house down. Killed your wife and child."

"Mattie Thomson is crazy as a loon," Eddie said, picking up the pace. "She's crazier than a loon."

"She says they were murdered because your wife was a black woman," Isaac said, trying to keep up. "And, yes, Miss Thomson is crazy, but sometimes she's as clear as a bell. When she told me was one of those times."

Isaac's shoulders tingled as if a weight had been removed. At least the ball was rolling. They walked without speaking. At first Isaac thought it was quiet out, that the sound of their feet on the sidewalk was the only sound within blocks. Then he started hearing night noises: crickets and frogs down by the creek and other sounds that he didn't recognize.

The sidewalk ended at the corner of Whelk and Waxwing, and they continued on the street. Through the trees, he caught glimpses of moonlight on the creek. For a while he tried not to look at Eddie, except at his shoes, letting the old man set the pace. Finally he risked a glance. Their eyes met, and Isaac guessed that Eddie didn't want to look at him any more than he wanted to look at Eddie. It was the same old, lined face, Isaac noticed, but his eyes were round.

"Why you bringing this up, boy? It's ancient history. Older than ancient. More dream than history, anyway."

"Did the Klan kill Celeste and Josephine?"

Eddie stopped. He leaned his head back, patted his thighs. Then he looked Isaac full in the face.

"It's not a secret, but how'd you know their names?"

"Like I said," Isaac said, "sometimes Miss Thomson's not crazy. Did they? Did the Klan kill your family?"

Eddie turned and walked slowly away. Isaac found his place by his side, closer this time. The streetlights had ended. So had the road. They were at the corner of Norman Creek Park, which bordered the south side of town. They stepped over the low boundary chain onto the damp grass.

Isaac wanted to break the silence but did not know how. Everything he could think to say, he'd said. His doubts stirred like a great wind. If Eddie wanted to play dumb, was that okay? Did he have a duty or right to put Eddie through anything he didn't want to talk about? Isaac seemed stuck now as Eddie led the way through the empty playground. Isaac resolved to forget about it. The reward never meant anything to him anyway. In the meantime, if Mr. Jackson's was the next house, so be it. Who was he, Isaac mused, to try and stop these forces. Let things run their course. It'll all come out in the wash, his mother used to say. Eddie wouldn't hurt anybody, and if anyone hurt Eddie, so be it. We all make our own beds and, sooner or later, have to lie down in them; his mother also used to say that.

Isaac resolved to find a way out of this bog of talk. He'd go home to his own bed and check in at the Jacksons' in the morning. He was wrong to be putting Eddie through all of this. Eddie was old, after all. Isaac didn't want to kill him by putting him through a past he didn't want to revisit—or couldn't let go of. Isaac knew how painful the past could be.

"They didn't do it on purpose," Eddie said quietly.

Isaac just nodded as they walked. The air smelled clean. Isaac identified more night sounds: cicada calls sawed through the cool air, at least one owl hooted insistently, and the frogs made a droning racket.

"How did Miss Thomson know?" Isaac finally asked. "Nobody else seems to know that the Klan did it, didn't even know the Klan existed here on the Shore. If they didn't know, how did she?"

"The old-timers know," Eddie said roughly. "They just won't say. And the younger ones, like you, don't want to know, don't even know to ask."

"How did Miss Thomson know? I mean, know for sure?"

"Her father was in the Klan," Eddie said. "Funny thing is, so was mine."

Eddie looked at his feet as they walked. "The house was old, falling down. It wasn't the main house. My old man had given it to us because he didn't have a choice. If I was going to give him the help he needed on the farm, he needed to give me and my family a place to stay. I had gone up to Crisfield with Mama to make some bids on machinery. Mama liked the ride. Celeste was tired and just wanted to stay home. The old man thought that Celeste and Josie had gone with us. He couldn't get a thing straight without Mama doing it for him.

"The Klan met in the back of Mr. Johnson's grocery. Whenever there was something that needed setting straight, they'd meet and decide how to do it. Like when the Jewish servicemen down at old Fort John Custis started having meetings in town. The Klan let them know in no uncertain terms that they were welcome to serve in the Army and shop for what they needed in town, but meeting to worship a Jew god could be done on base."

Isaac had never met a Jew that he knew of, though he felt a kinship with them, having heard about the Jews and Gentiles in Sunday school all his life.

"They got a hankering to put me in my place too. I knew about it, of course. I thought it was just talk. After all, I grew up here. These were my people. I didn't think they'd do anything to hurt us. I thought we'd be able to make a life here on the Shore. Unbeknownst to me, they had other ideas. Bastards."

Eddie stopped and looked at one of the two empty baseball fields. The bleachers stood black on black, skeletal contraptions without people sitting on them. The infield had been dragged for Saturday's games. The renovated cinder block concession stand was so new it still smelled of paint.

Eddie set out again. Isaac followed a half step behind.

"I'll say this now, but I could never admit it then. My old man was under a lot of pressure to go along. A lot of people, not just him, felt like they had to go along, do the right thing."

"It wasn't the right thing," Isaac sputtered.

Eddie looked shocked that Isaac was even there, much less able to speak.

"Anyway, the old man insisted that no one get hurt. So, he arranged the whole thing himself. They'd burn the house. Celeste would go back to Richmond with the baby. I'd see the error of my ways and let them go. And Papa would get some insurance for the burned house, to boot. That horse's ass."

Eddie growled up some phlegm and spat. He dabbed his lips on the sleeve of his white, buttoned-down shirt. "Like I said, Papa didn't want anybody to get hurt. But it failed."

"It sure did," Isaac whispered. "It sure did."

Isaac was exhausted and longed to sit down, on the damp ground if need be. They were making a wide sweep around the park, around the ball field and all the way to the picnic benches on the bay. Eddie churned steadily along, watching where he walked and showing no signs of letting up.

"What about your father?" Isaac asked. "What did he say about it all?"

"He didn't say and I wouldn't have listened."

"I can't believe this," Isaac said. "Your own father."

"They were very different times," Eddie said. "And not all fathers are like yours. Not all sons are like you, for that matter." Eddie put his hand on Isaac's shoulder. He nodded to the woods. "Let's cut through here."

"He killed your family," Isaac said.

"He and they," Eddie said. "Yes, sir."

"Who is they?"

Eddie didn't answer at first, like he wasn't sure if he wanted Isaac to know. "The leader—" he hesitated and shot Isaac a quick glance "—was Nathan Parramore's old man. Nathan was young and gung ho and was looking for mischief. Thought he was a big man, the punk. He was a hateful kid and grew up to be a hateful man. Go talk to him sometime and see if I'm not right. His father's hate suited him well. The rest of them," he huffed, "came from families in town."

"Hank Grady?"

"Naw," Eddie said. "Hank Grady hardly has the courage to get his own mail. He's probably sorry he missed it, but Grady wasn't there. Nor any of his kin. What's that group he's got all riled up? PISS, PITS, PONG?

"People of the Shore," Isaac said.

"P.O.T.S.!" Eddie blurted out. "That's right. Fanatics. Too much time on their hands."

"So who were the rest of the men who burned down your house?"

Eddie didn't say anything.

Isaac thought of the names of the firemen on the bronze plaque on the firehouse wall, of the owners of the flooded houses, and of the key board. "Nathan Parramore, Constitution Gray, Horace Abbey, and Donald Martin?"

Eddie was silent. Isaac nudged him.

"Yep," Eddie said, finally, kicking the grass as he walked. He took a deep breath through his nostrils. "You're really too big for your britches," he said, glancing over at Isaac. "That's all that's left."

"Except for Mr. Jackson."

Eddie didn't say anything.

"They wore hoods at night," Isaac said, "and fire uniforms during the day?"

"They never wore hoods, is what I heard. Said they were Southern gentlemen and had nothing to hide. And yes, it's hard," Eddie said, "to put out a fire when you're the one setting it."

"I wondered how the firemen fit in," Isaac said. "Volunteer firefighters and Klansmen. What a combination. Burning crosses—"

"They didn't burn any crosses," Eddie interrupted.

But Isaac wasn't listening. "—and burning down houses." Isaac was putting his thoughts together with words, saying what came to mind, not trying to make sentences but sense. "Fire and water," Isaac mumbled. "Orange painted flames and stopped-up faucets."

Isaac looked at Eddie, who had stopped ten yards ahead. "You're getting them back." It was a statement.

"I don't know what you're talking about," Eddie said. "You're starting to sound like old Mattie Thomson—on a bad day."

They resumed walking, Eddie shuffling more slowly and favoring his right leg, but still keeping a taxing pace. They had covered lots of ground, cutting through the woods and heading for the cemetery road.

"Boy, you think you're so smart."

Eddie walked now like he'd never slow down. Isaac fought to keep up. He wanted to curl up and sleep. He was so tired, so weary. But he was afraid for Eddie, afraid that this elderly man might drop from exhaustion, or run off and do something really foolish, so he didn't dare lag behind.

"Is Jackson your last house?" Isaac practically shouted, panting.

There was silence except for the cacophony of nature and their shoes scuffing through the thick, wet grass beside the gravel cemetery road.

"After you're done with Jackson, what next?"

Eddie was almost jogging now and his limp was pronounced. It was difficult for Isaac to keep up and talk at the same time. They had crossed the whole park and passed the picnic shelters along the bay. Eddie stumbled onto the narrow road.

"I'm house-sitting for the Jacksons, did you know that, Eddie? They'll be gone a week. Lake Gaston with the grandkids. I'll be at work all day tomorrow. May even try me some fishing before I come home; haven't gone all summer. Ten or so hours of running water ought to do the trick. I'll call Chief Williams and he and that federal agent will come over and take a report. They'll call the utility company to come over and cut the services. Another unsolved mystery."

They had reached the entrance of the graveyard. Two stone blocks squatted on either side of the road. Black iron rods anchored in each block arched over the road. Eddie stopped and surveyed the headstones that were the color of eggshells in the moonlight.

"Eddie, I don't blame you. I won't tell."

"It's wrong," Eddie said, wheeling around, glaring at Isaac.

"Nobody needs to know," Isaac said.

"It's wrong! Didn't your mother ever teach you two wrongs don't make a right?"

Isaac shut his mouth when he became aware of how angry Eddie's face was getting, and how his jaw muscles rippled when he grit his teeth.

"I'm sure she did," Eddie hissed, jabbing a finger into Isaac's chest.

"Ouch, Eddie. Stop."

"She taught you that and lots of other things, like not to meddle." Eddie was shouting, his voice quavering, rising in pitch. Froth had lined his thin, blue lips. "But you didn't learn those lessons very well, did you?" Eddie poked him again. "Did you?"

Isaac kept stepping back. Eddie easily closed the distance. He moved like an agile cat, balanced and strong.

"I'll tell you what," he said, grabbing Isaac's shirt and yanking him closer. He was breathing heavily through flared nostrils. Eddie hadn't shaved. Isaac could smell the decay of his breath. He was jerking Isaac around, had lifted him to his toes. Isaac held on to his thin forearm with both hands, could feel the cords of steel and hard bone.

"I'll tell you what," Eddie said again, jaw clinched, eyes narrowed. "They can't get away with this. I know who did it, and I won't let them forget. Nathan Parramore, the punk. The worthless son of a bitch. I won't let him forget, won't let him sleep, none of them. There's no sleeping in hell, damn dogs, lousy excuse for a—"

"—I'm not Nathan—"

"—human being. Hard, yellow, stupid—"

"—I'm not them—"

"—Nathan and the yellow others, sons of bitches. Such small men trying to be so big—"

"—Eddie!"

Isaac felt Eddie freeze, then go slack, his eyes growing round, jaws yawning slowly open.

"Nathan Parramore isn't here," Isaac said quietly. "Or Mr. Jackson, or Donald Martin . . ."

Eddie eased his grip and started absently patting Isaac's chest. He looked ghostly in the light of the moon, an expression of shock washing over his face. He looked hunched and tired and suddenly very old. He was still patting Isaac, rubbing his chest with trembling fingers.

"I didn't, I didn't . . . "

"It's okay, Eddie."

"I didn't mean to hurt you, son. You've got to believe . . . "

"I know, Eddie," Isaac said. "You're all bark." He took both of Eddie's hands. "It's okay, Eddie."

Eddie gave Isaac's hands a squeeze, then fumbled with the straps of his overalls. His arms were shaking. He rattled as he breathed.

"They still did a terrible thing," Eddie whispered, spitting, then pulling out a handkerchief and wiping his face. "They still did an awful thing, and it's still hard for me even though it all happened a long time ago." He wiped his eyes with the handkerchief. He stuffed the hanky into his overalls and looked at Isaac. "It never really goes away, does it?"

"I don't know," Isaac said. "I don't know."

Eddie lurched into the cemetery, shuffling under the black, iron arch, down the gravel road that twisted into the plots marked by a sea of gravestones. They all looked so heavy. Isaac followed.

"Sorry about your mother," Eddie said over his shoulder. "Didn't mean what I said. She taught you well, and, except for a few things, you're turning out just fine. She'd tell you to mind your own business, though."

Eddie stopped and put his hands on his hips. He surveyed the stones on the left side of the road. He rubbed the gravel with his steel-toed shoe.

"Eddie, I didn't set out to meddle in your life. I got curious. And one thing led to another. It just sort of snowballed."

"You wanted the reward," Eddie said flatly.

Isaac looked away. Part of the cemetery had been recently mown. The smell of grass was strong.

"I can't blame you. Five thousand dollars sure beats working at Chum's, eh?"

"I got curious," Isaac said, ashamed. "And once I started, I just couldn't stop."

"Or wouldn't," Eddie said, turning to look into Isaac's face.

Isaac looked down at Eddie's veined, freckled hands planted like claws on his hips.

"I got more and more curious," Isaac said. "Then I wanted—I wanted to save you, I think. Protect you."

Eddie snorted and spat. "Never needed protection before, boy. Made out fine all these years all by my lonesome." Eddie scanned the cemetery. "That's not the only way to do it," he said. "But it's the way I went and lived my life, by my lonesome. Probably not the best way, no sir."

Eddie resumed his walk, this time less hunched and at an easier pace. Isaac walked near his side.

"Does it feel better?" Isaac asked.

Eddie did not answer.

Isaac thought that the crunching of gravel under foot might be answer enough. An owl hooted.

"No," Eddie said finally, "it doesn't feel better. And yes, it does. But mostly no. They didn't have the courage to stand up to me man to man fifty years ago, and I don't have the courage to stand up to them now. Funny, back in 1951 there wasn't a jury on the Shore that would have convicted those guys for burning down my house and killing my family. Nowadays, there's not a jury around that wouldn't send me up the river for what I've done. Two wrongs . . . " Eddie's voice trailed off. He was getting hoarse.

"A jury back then wouldn't have convicted them even though they deserved it?"

"Even though they deserved it," Eddie said. "There wouldn't have been any arrests in the first place."

They had stopped in front of an old tombstone. Isaac would have sat down on it had he not noticed how intently Eddie was looking at it. Isaac strained to read the inscription.

1950–1951
Josephine Mary Patrick
infant
most tender rose

The tombstone next to Josephine's was that of Eddie's wife:

1923–1951
Celestial Walker Patrick
daughter, wife, mother,
martyr

"This is a white graveyard," Eddie said. "Was back then anyway." He was in no rush to get the words out. An owl hooted again, its call chased by an eerie echo.

"But no one dared not allow me to bury them here. No one dared."

"Why did you stay here, Eddie? With these—" Isaac couldn't think of what to call his neighbors. "With these people?"

"I stayed because I had obligations." Eddie stared at his wife's gravestone. He was perfectly still. "At first I couldn't leave." His voice was a quivering whimper. He bent over and caressed the rough top of his wife's marker. "Then I didn't know what else to do. Where else to go. They were all I had and all I ever wanted." He looked at Isaac, his face twisted and sad. "They were all I ever wanted."

Eddie bowed his head, then patted the stone twice and stood up straight. He snorted and spat towards the road. He sidestepped along to the next stones and pointed. "He died the next year."

Isaac strained to read Eddie's father's name.

"I handled the funeral. Made the arrangements, every detail. Saw to it that he had a church funeral. I didn't want to, but I wanted to do the right thing, even if he didn't. Especially because he didn't. Next to him, Mama."

"And," Isaac said, "next to her, your baby brother? His name was Gabriel?"

"You have been doing your homework," Eddie said, a look of surprise registering on his now-haggard face. "Gabriel, like the angel, announcing Good News."

Isaac walked over to the tombstone and read the name out loud. He had trouble doing it partly because he couldn't see the words well and partly because saying them made him choke up.

1924–1932
Gabriel Philip Patrick
eight years old
forever young

Isaac thought he could make out the voice of two owls calling to one another from across a great distance.

"Why now, Eddie?" Isaac asked quietly. "It's been so long and you're only now getting around to doing something about it?"

Eddie wiped off the top of Gabriel's gravestone and sat down. He motioned to Isaac to join him. There wasn't much space, so Isaac had to sit closely to Eddie to keep from falling off.

"Bernie Dunn was just a snotty-nosed kid and didn't know anything in 1951. His father had left. His mother was doing her best, helping old people in their homes, taking in sewing. They was as poor as August is long. Bernie needed somebody to look up to, and he found it in the back of Mr. Johnson's store. Or he thought he had."

Eddie snorted and spat. He dabbed his mouth with the handkerchief.

"He helped them burn my house down. See, he wanted to fit in, needed to be a part of something big and important. It put a bad taste in his mouth, the whole thing did. He was still in high school. He came whining to me once, all frantic, and asked me if I knew what had happened, who the players were. Begged me not to turn him in. Said he couldn't sleep. Was sick with worry. He didn't know anybody had been in the house, especially a woman and a baby. Didn't know, he said. Was a bad idea all along, but the other men, my own father, said it was okay and he went along. He pulled his weight too, he said. And now he couldn't live with himself. He begged me to forgive him."

Eddie had closed his eyes, seeming to savor the night air. It had become chilly, and Isaac rubbed his own arms to keep from shivering.

"Did you?" Isaac asked quietly. "Did you forgive him?"

Eddie opened his eyes and looked off over the graves. A duck started quacking from the direction of the marsh. The sound of beating wings. Then silence.

"He dropped out of school and left town. Sent his mother checks, from what I heard, though in those days I didn't listen much. His mother died, and he did not return for the funeral, though he paid for it, was the rumor. In the 1960s I started getting Christmas cards from Bernie. Would you believe it?" Eddie looked at Isaac. "He'd send a postcard once in a while. I saved them in a kitchen drawer and looked at them every now and then, like you do with your postcard from Virginia Beach."

Eddie looked to the stars and rubbed his whiskers with his left hand, which trembled still.

"What did he say?" Isaac asked.

Eddie looked at him blankly.

"In the postcards. What did he say?"

"Oh," Eddie said, putting his hands on his knees and straightening his back. The stone was hard. "Not much," he said. "Just small stuff like maybe he wanted to sell me a new car or something. Called me Mr. Patrick, even when we were both old men."

Eddie bent his head back. Isaac could see his knotty Adam's apple work.

"I got a card from his wife this Christmas. She wrote to tell me that Bernie had died that previous January. Yep, she wanted me to know that her husband really was sorry for what he'd done when he was a boy. Wanted me to know he'd passed."

Isaac's nose had started to run. He wiped it on his sleeve. "Wow," Isaac mumbled. It was a stupid thing to say, but he couldn't think of anything else, and he had to say something.

"I was surprised, to be honest. That he'd carried it around that long. That his wife knew. I wasn't the only one who lost, it seems." Eddie eased off the stone and stretched his back. He grimaced. "I had done my best to put the past in the past, and Bernie Dunn all the way from California had remembered. I have to say I was touched that somebody still remembered when I'd done my very best to forget."

He looked at Isaac. "But Mary Dunn's letter made me remember that fire. And it started burning in me all over again. Had any of the other men tried to apologize? No. They lived their lives like it never happened. Just like I did. But it did happen. It did." Eddie licked his teeth and shook his head. "That's about the time I came up with this harebrained idea to make them pay, to help them remember. It just came to me from nowhere, or from a part of me I didn't even know. I'd ruin their houses with water and paint."

"And?" Isaac asked.

"And they don't have a clue what it all means. They think teenagers are doing it. I could sign my name and they still wouldn't get it. Guess I don't get it, either, son. It's gotten way too big. I'm what they call in over my head. Way over." Eddie's hands were in his pockets. He was kicking at the grass. "There are times I feel so guilty that I've wanted to go apologize. Two thoughts stop me. The first is that they probably care more about their ruined carpets than an apology. These men were cads when they were younger, and that's hard to grow out of."

Eddie was silent.

"What's the second reason?" Isaac asked.

"The second is I remember . . ."

Isaac had been looking through tired eyes at his shoes and it took a moment for him to realize Eddie was crying.

"I remember what they did," Eddie whispered through silent sobs. "I remember what they did."

He looked to Isaac. "I've ruined your house this summer because you ruined my life fifty years ago? Doesn't it sound stupid?"

Isaac stood up. He didn't know what to do. What to say. How to reach out, though he wanted to. He put his hands in his pockets, like Eddie. He took a step closer.

"They deserve it," Isaac finally said.

Eddie took out his handkerchief and wiped his face and blew his nose. He groaned a loud, cleansing groan. "I'll grant you that they deserve punishment." He blew his nose into his handkerchief again. It sounded like a horn. He started folding the handkerchief, neatly. He looked at Isaac, then around the cemetery. "Should have buried my hate in this cemetery too. But I just couldn't. Or wouldn't." His body jerked, and he blinked as a man snapping out of a trance. He stuffed his handkerchief back into his pocket. "Couldn't or wouldn't," he said again slowly.

Isaac felt weak.

"I'll be seeing you, young Isaac. I've got some business to take care of before the SWAT team comes to get me."

He had only taken a few steps but his long legs had carried him a good ten yards away. Isaac was suddenly petrified to be left alone deep in that cemetery, but he knew Eddie needed to leave alone.

"They won't come to get you," Isaac called out, "if they don't know who to get."

Eddie stopped and turned around. "And they won't know if they aren't told?"

"That's right," Isaac said.

Eddie waved Isaac off and said something under his breath. He took a few more steps and stopped at the second row of gravestones. He didn't turn around this time, but said, "If you're late for work tomorrow, I'll tell Mr. Chum to dock your pay." Then he walked off in the direction of town. "You think I'm kidding?"

Isaac tried to find his way out through the woods the way they had come in but ended up in the newer side of the graveyard instead. With some difficulty he found his mother's gravestone. He hadn't been there but once since the funeral. He stood before it and wondered if his father would occupy the spot next to hers. He wondered if there'd ever be a new Mrs. David Lawson. He pictured Eddie's tired face and wondered how deep a hole it would take to bury a man's hate, and, if hate were a seed, if buried long enough, could it grow into something beautiful? A tender rose, perhaps, delicate with thorns. Or a willow, its wispy branches forever weeping.

20

The warehouse was locked when Isaac got to work at 8:05, so he hustled around through the store. Mr. and Mrs. Chum glanced up from their crossword and said hello. "Hey, Isaac," Mr. Chum said. "What's a four-letter word for friend?"

Isaac shrugged. "Chum?"

Harvey was dozing by the stove with *The Shore News* on his lap. "That's what I said, Isaac. Friend or bait, one or the other," Harvey chuckled. Harvey opened his eyes, shook the paper, and turned the page. He was wearing a shirt the color of Mrs. Watson's key lime pie. Mike Lindvall was clipping his nails. Mr. Peake was scribbling in a notebook. Hank Grady watched Isaac come in, giving Isaac his customary glare.

"But it has to begin with a b." Mr. Chum announced. "A four-letter word for friend that starts with a b.'"

Isaac tore Monday off the calendar and leaned over the cash register watching the Chums. He had gotten to the Jacksons' house just after midnight and had never slept so well. That's why he was late this morning. He didn't want to get out of bed.

Isaac felt rested enough for two days of work. He looked forward to the weekend. He didn't have weekend plans yet, but he had been thinking about it all morning. A cookout at his house with the Edwardses and some catch in the backyard with Tom sounded good. Maybe Kate would want to come, or maybe she'd enjoy another hike. Something. Anything. He hadn't seen her since the Fourth, and he was dying to see her. He wanted to spend some time with his father too. Listening to him and Miss Edwards the night before had made Isaac realize how long it had been since they had really connected. Maybe they'd throw a line in the water at the wharf, see what was biting. And he might try to catch up with some of his buddies to see if there was another baseball game he could get in on. He'd have to borrow a glove, he remembered. There was more than he could fit into just two days, but he was eager to get started.

It felt like the first day of summer.

Mr. Chum stood leaning over counter. The newspaper was spread before him like a map.

"The back's locked tight," Isaac said. "Where's Eddie?"

Mr. Chum didn't look up.

"That's a good question," Hank Grady scoffed.

Isaac was sorry Hank was listening.

"He was here earlier," Mr. Chum said. Isaac noticed the way he lightly ran his fingers over the top of his wife's shoulders. "He must have stepped out."

The front door jingled open. Isaac still leaned contentedly on the counter. From the reflection in the clock on the back wall, he could see Lester Mellande's circus-reflection waddling up the narrow aisle to the circle of chairs around the stove. He had a box of Krispy Kremes in each hand. Harvey was talking to whomever was listening about how he hated not having his driver's license anymore.

"Why would Eddie have locked up out back?" Isaac asked.

"Maybe he didn't know when he was coming back," somebody said.

"That man ought to retire," Hank said. "He's older than dirt and not doing much around here."

"He's pulling his weight," Mr. Chum said, looking up over his glasses.

"Eddie don't have as much weight as you to pull," Mr. Peake said to Hank, his rat-like snout twisting into a smile.

"Get back to your notes," Hank said. "If you wrote them so's somebody else could read them, I'd pay to have them typed. At your pace, the Historical Society may never get these minutes and the old train depot may never get on the register. We've got to enclose minutes from P.O.T.S.'s last meeting or our application won't be complete."

Mr. Peake ripped out a page and balled it up. "Got my spacing off," he said. "If you'd just shut up for once, Grady."

"You write like a fourth grader hitting the hooch," Hank Grady said. "P.O.T.S.'ll never get anywhere with you as the secretary."

"Recorder," Mr. Peake whined without looking up. "I'm the blasted recorder, not secretary."

"He doesn't have the legs for a secretary," Harvey said, tickled with himself.

Mr. Chum looked at Isaac. "Is bud spelled with one d or two?"

"When my wife dropped me off," Harvey said, "old Eddie was getting into a police car."

The words police and Eddie in the same sentence tripped an alarm in Isaac's brain. "Police car?" Isaac asked. He straightened and turned to face the guys. His voice was high and it cracked embarrassingly when he spoke.

"Yeah," Harvey said. "A police car." Harvey yawned and stretched.

Isaac leaned awkwardly by the counter, frozen. He turned nonchalantly to face the Chums feverishly poring over their puzzle. He tapped his fingers on the counter but absently yanked them away when he noticed they were shaking, dancing erratically like a crab's legs in an empty pot on the stove. An ache was rising through his body like a flood of oil-slicked water.

At the end of his burly yawn, Harvey bellowed, "The wife's gone shopping and doesn't want me along. Says I buy too much junk."

Isaac studied Harvey's reflection in the clock on the back wall. The men looked like grotesque cartoon characters, misshapen, floating above the perfect numbers on the clock.

Harvey, ceremoniously patting his rotund belly, said, "Good thing I have you guys to babysit me."

"Or," Mrs. Chum said, "what's a six-letter word for a hostile encounter between opposing military forces? We wrote battle."

"What about combat?" Harvey asked. "Lord, we have enough of that in this world."

Mr. Chum counted the squares.

"Isn't a man in this town weirder than Eddie Patrick," Hank said. He sounded more agitated than usual.

"He's an odd one," Mike Lindvall said. Isaac watched Lindvall's distorted reflection; he was picking at his nails with talon-like fingers.

"It fits!" Mr. Chum said, clapping his hands together.

Mrs. Chum pulled out her eraser. "A little finagling," she said, "and it all works out."

"Rents out his land," Hank resumed. "Works here during the day. He's at home the rest of the time. Stays to himself. Loner. What does he do all alone on that farm except give his dog VD?"

Isaac wheeled around and glared at Hank Grady.

Grady noticed. He feigned shock. "What you gonna do, boy?"

Everyone looked to Grady, then Isaac. Isaac felt his face go hot, and his temper. He swallowed hard. "Why do you have it out for Eddie?" Isaac said, anger choking up from his stomach. "What'd he ever do to you?" He could feel his mouth going dry. Isaac glanced around the room; the Chums looked up from their crossword. The men stopped rocking and looked back and forth from Grady to Isaac. "Eddie's been through enough," he eeked, voice cracking.

"Hah!" Grady grunted.

Isaac could feel everybody watch him take a deep breath. "He grows a garden and gives every widow in this town more string beans than she can use. That's what my dad says." Isaac's voice cracked and wavered, but he was beginning not to care. "He doesn't gossip. He doesn't expect anything from anybody." He swallowed hard waiting for someone to speak up.

"Hah!" Grady said again, shaking his head dramatically.

"What's Eddie done to break the law?"

"Hah!" Grady groaned again.

Isaac wanted to smack Hank Grady. Self-righteous bastard. Didn't Hank go off and sell his wife's farm to developers right from under her feet? It had been in her family for generations and in one afternoon Grady sold it to a company that would divide it and subdivide it so that the only thing that land would ever grow again would be houses and tool sheds and rusted carports and green lawns. Wasn't that a betrayal of all that P.O.T.S. stood for? Wasn't that a crime—even if it was legal? What did Hank Grady know about morality?

To Isaac's left, within easy reach, stood seven polished hickory ax handles. He could snatch one and in one fluid movement sling it over his shoulder, take a single, even swing, and pop Hank Grady's head like a ripe cantaloupe.

"Eddie puts up with people like you," he said, nodding towards Grady, "without saying an ill word—except maybe that you've always been a coward."

Somebody hiccuped a fragile, nervous laugh.

Hank Grady was hunched awkwardly in his rocker. His face was scarlet. "Eddie came home from college early to help his father out on the farm. You know that, don't you? The Klan burned his house down. Right to the ground. You know that too."

Grady turned white. His narrow eyes widened into perfect circles. "What are you talking about, boy?" he said weakly.

But they knew. Isaac could tell that Grady and the others—even Chum—knew exactly was he was talking about.

"The Klan killed his wife and daughter," Isaac resumed evenly, each word spoken clearly, deeply, with the slightest hint of growl. He scanned each face as he paused. "The Klan murdered his family and you, Mister Grady, are talking trash." Isaac nodded at the other men. "And you guys are letting him."

Mr. Lindvall nervously picked at his trousers with immaculate fingernails. Harvey wore a screwed-on smile and glistened with oily sweat. Lester Mellande sat primly with his knees together, feet flat on the floor, and two unopened boxes of doughnuts neatly stacked on his lap. They all leaned farther from Isaac as they met his gaze, which they did not hold for long.

"All you seem to care about is how tall the grass gets around here."

Nobody was looking at Isaac now, not even Grady. Everyone sat perfectly silent.

"All you care about is putting the old train depot on the historic register," Isaac said. "Seems to me, there's a lot of history nobody around here ever wants to talk about." Isaac had been leaning on the counter. He stood up and turned towards the warehouse.

"Mr. Chum," he said, still staring down the men around the stove, "I'll be back later to clean the store and to take the trash out." He spat out the words and strode out on wobbly legs without waiting for an answer.

✟ ✟ ✟

Isaac wanted to forget everything, Hank Grady, everybody. He paced to the back of the dark warehouse four times until he calmed down. So much for his earlier enthusiasm for the weekend. He hung over the water fountain and let the cool water splash his face. As the water revived him, he remembered Eddie, and the dread he had felt earlier seized him again.

He opened the big sliding door and went outside to Eddie's truck. It was unlocked and empty except for the clipboard that Eddie used to keep track of the delivery orders. The free delivery service surely didn't make Mr. Chum any money. It was a throwback to another time. When Eddie was gone, Isaac doubted Mr. Chum would replace him.

Eddie was getting old, well past retirement age, and Isaac figured that pretty soon they'd take his driver's license away too, just like they did to Harvey Norris. Isaac thought of Eddie spending his last years isolated on that farm.

Or in jail.

A police car? Locking the warehouse up because he didn't know when he'd be coming back? Eddie never did anything out of order. He made a pot of coffee just after eight o'clock every morning. He ate his lunch exactly at noon. He shaved every other day. His white, buttoned-down shirts were always pressed. It would have to be something big, really big, to get Eddie to step out of his regular schedule.

Isaac walked to the back gate and looked up and down Heron and Slipper streets. Mr. Pearson was sweeping his sidewalk at the bakery. In the other direction, Mr. Morris was up on a ladder changing the price of gas on the sign at the Gas and Go. He could see just a glimpse of Mattie Thomson's front yard. There were no signs of police cars coming or going. The sun had climbed above the slate roofs, and the houses that faced east looked like they were shingled with uniform squares of yellow light.

Calling the police chief couldn't possibly do Eddie any favors. Waiting was all Isaac could do.

Routine. The coffee wasn't made. Isaac reached above the workbench and pulled down a filter and the can of coffee. He opened it, and the smell reminded him of so many things. Frances' friendly kitchen at the Wild Flower. Mornings at the Duck Blind eating those big breakfasts with his dad. Kate Bradshaw. The social after church every Sunday in the fellowship hall. Eddie.

Isaac had seen Eddie make coffee every day, but he never paid attention to how many scoops to add. The scoop was small. He put one into the filter, but that seemed too little, so he added half another one.

When he reached for his timecard, there was an old black-and-white picture pinned up next to the Cavalier Hotel. The picture wasn't there when he had clocked out the day before. It was brittle and yellowed at the edges. A man and woman were holding a baby. Isaac unpinned it and held it gently by its corners.

On the back, written in Eddie's spidery script, was a date: spring, 1951. Isaac turned the picture over and held it in his palms like a sand dollar. "Ooh," he said softly, exhaling slowly.

It was Edward and Celestial Patrick, and they were so young. They seemed so eager and ready and poised. But it wasn't Eddie that Isaac first recognized. Isaac immediately knew the beautiful woman and the baby clad in a long white gown with bows of ribbon tied at the hem were Celeste and Josephine. A younger version of Eddie simply confirmed this. He was smiling a shy smile, and the wavy, thick hair combed back slick must have been strawberry red.

Celeste sat close to Eddie and leaned slightly into him, something like John Singer Sargent's lady reclining contentedly into the puckers of that soft couch. They were close like dancers are close, holding one another, feeling each other's presence. Eddie's big right hand held Celeste's arm, which cradled the child. Josephine wore a lace bonnet, and Isaac could see only part of her sleeping face and one tiny hand, delicate, curled fingers reaching out above her gown. Celeste had a calm face. She was smiling a contented, thankful smile. Her face reminded Isaac of the ocean on a placid day when the water looked like glass: there was power beneath Celeste's smooth skin. Power, competence, and passion. Isaac knew this because he knew Eddie.

There they are, Isaac said to himself. There they are. He got so lost looking into their faces, he didn't notice that he was no longer alone.

"This boy has an aversion to work."

Isaac startled, closed his eyes, and tried to gather himself. It was Hank, he figured, back to have the last word. Isaac turned around slowly. Two people darkened the warehouse door. It took a moment for Isaac's eyes to adjust to the light. And it wasn't Hank Grady who mocked him. It was Eddie wearing his best snarl. He stood at the open warehouse doorway with Agent Tennyson.

"He probably hangs out with his good-for-nothing friends till all hours of the night, and then comes dragging in here with nothing better to do than stand around looking at pictures all day long. I'll tell you, kids today."

"Hello, Isaac," Agent Tennyson said.

It was Eddie's turn to be startled. He looked from Agent Tennyson to Isaac.

Eddie said, "You know my coworker, eh?"

"We met briefly at the fire station the other day. He was making a delivery, I believe, for the store." Agent Tennyson smiled and nodded. "Nice to see you again," he said.

Eddie didn't look like he was in trouble. He wasn't wearing handcuffs, anyway. In fact, he was holding a Frisbee.

"Making deliveries for Chum, now are we? Bucking for my job?"

Eddie would have looked sinister if Isaac hadn't learned to see the slightest grin beneath his snarl.

"I'm not in the grave yet, and, until then, there's no way you could out-work me, no sir." He took three strides toward Isaac and tossed the Frisbee on the counter. It was Isaac's—had his name written on the underside. He had taken it along on the picnic with Kate when they went looking for the burned down house. He must have left it where they had leaned against that tree, imagining what life in that ruined house was like.

Eddie leaned over Isaac's shoulder. "Nice picture," Eddie said in a kindly, soft way. "They look real happy."

Eddie looked over to the coffeepot and let out a groan. "You see, Mike, when the kid's not lazing around, he's messing things up." He took the coffee filter out of the trap and poured the dry coffee back into the can. He measured out six rounded scoops and put them and the filter back in. Eddie took the upside-down pot and walked to Agent Tennyson. He shook his hand warmly. "You come back later for that key, and I'll have a real cup of coffee for you."

"See you before lunch, then," Agent Tennyson said. He had a radio announcer's smooth voice. "Isaac, Eddie's been talking about you. I look forward to spending more time with you later." He waved and was gone.

Eddie was filling up the coffeepot at the water fountain. He had a look on his face like he was pleased with himself.

"Why does a federal agent look forward to spending more time with me?" Isaac asked. "And why has he spent all morning with you?"

"Seems he's going to be our new neighbor," Eddie said. "When he came by the store earlier, maybe while you were making your 'delivery' to the fire station, I heard him say he might be interested in some property. I told him I might have a lot I want to sell cheap out on my farm, a lot at the edge of the woods. We met this morning."

"So you talked to Tennyson about property?" Isaac quizzed. "You didn't talk to him about anything else?"

Eddie explained that it was none of Isaac's business, but, no, he hadn't talked to Agent Tennyson about anything other than a lot on his farm. "But," Eddie said sheepishly, "I did turn myself in, if that's what you're getting at."

Isaac was confused. "So, you did tell the FBI?"

"No, I didn't want to bother the entire federal government," Eddie said. "The feds need to use their collective brain cells to fry bigger fish. This is a local matter." He paused.

Isaac wanted to shake him.

"I told Chief Williams. Went by his house this morning early on the way to my meeting with Tennyson. Told him over a cup of coffee."

Isaac's heart pounded heavily.

"Eddie, you're going to go to jail."

"Maybe," Eddie grunted, "but it don't matter."

"There's no maybe about it," Isaac groaned. "You can't ruin people's houses and get away with it."

"I'm not trying to get away from anything, or with anything," Eddie said, annoyed, "which is more than they can say. I'm not like them. Anymore."

"I can't believe you told Williams," Isaac moaned.

"Told me what?" Chief Williams was standing at the door. He moved inside, closing the distance with an easy gait. "Hey, fellas." When he got to Eddie he said, "May we talk, Eddie?"

"Talk," Eddie grunted.

"Can it be somewhere private?" the chief said, politely nodding to Isaac.

"Oh, he don't matter," Eddie said. "This is private enough."

Chief Williams looked at Isaac, then back to Eddie. "You sure?"

Eddie nodded.

"Does Isaac know?"

Eddie nodded again.

"Figures," the chief chuckled. He had such an amiable way about him, Isaac thought. "My wife tells me I'm always the last to know." He looked around the warehouse, taking it in. "Is Isaac here the only one?"

Eddie nodded.

The chief paused, then took a deep breath. "Okay," he launched in with some animation. "I couldn't quite figure out why a harmless old guy like you would turn himself in for something as crazy as these four vandalisms. It didn't make sense."

"I told you," Eddie said. He pretended to be irritated, but Isaac could tell that he was more tired than he was fed up. "I wanted a future. I wanted to come clean."

"Come clean for what? See, you didn't tell me that, which is why I was more than a little perplexed. I'm not a local. I don't know the past here." The chief was pacing a slow, winding circle. "But Mattie Thomson does," the chief continued. "I brought her some flowers this morning, some I picked from my own yard. And Mattie told me the most fantastical story. It's almost as fantastical as an old guy like you flooding the houses of nice people like Nathan Parramore. What did Parramore ever do to you?"

Eddie was silent.

"Mattie told me," Chief Williams said gently. "Mattie told me everything."

"Mattie's crazy," Eddie growled low.

"Yes," the chief nodded. "Some days more than others. But she told me the truth today, didn't she?"

Eddie didn't budge.

"Didn't she?"

Isaac couldn't hold back any more.

"Horace Abbey, John Gray, Donald Martin, Nathan Parramore, Ralph Jackson. They and more people in this town burned down Eddie's house," Isaac said. "They wanted to run Eddie's wife and baby out of town. They thought the house was empty, but it wasn't, and they burned it right to the ground."

"Why were they trying to run Eddie's wife and baby out of town?" the chief asked. He seemed to know the answer, Isaac thought.

"Didn't Mattie tell you?" Eddie asked.

"Mattie's crazy," the chief said. "You tell me."

Eddie was silent.

With trembling hands, Isaac handed the picture of Eddie's family to Williams. He was angry that Eddie was having to go through this, was angry that Eddie was going to jail. And it dawned on him suddenly that he was going to lose someone he cared about. Again.

"This is a black-and-white picture," Williams said without looking up from it. "Am I right to say that there's a black woman and a white man in this picture?"

Eddie sat looking at his shoes.

"Am I right to say this is you, Eddie?" The chief held the picture in front of Eddie. The chief was pointing.

"Yes," Isaac blurted out. "And that—," he said, pointing.

"—is Mrs. Patrick," the chief said. He still had not taken his eyes off of the picture.

"Her name," Isaac said quietly, "is Celestial Walker Patrick."

"Celeste," Eddie said, studying the concrete floor.

"And that," Isaac said, pointing again, "is Josephine."

Chief Reggie Williams looked up from the photograph and scanned the warehouse roof. "I see," he whispered. "I see."

Isaac followed the chief's gaze up. The cracks and dots of light diffused the dark between the rafters. Isaac blinked back the water from his eyes. He was so tired, so emotionally drained. And the picture made it all so real and so painful.

"They're bastards," Isaac said quietly to the chief. "They deserve this. They deserve so much more. Eddie didn't do anything wrong."

The chief raised his eyes and looked askance at Isaac.

"Yes, I did," Eddie mumbled.

"Who cares, Eddie?" Isaac asked.

"I do," Eddie said wearily. "And so do you."

"Come on, Eddie," Isaac said. "I don't want you to go to jail."

"Jail?" the chief interrupted. He wore a wry smile beneath arched eyebrows. "Who said anything about jail?" Williams handed the picture carefully to Eddie, who took it without looking the chief in the eyes.

But Isaac couldn't take his eyes off the chief. Isaac was desperately trying to read his face.

"No, I didn't say anything about jail," Williams mused. "Four vandalisms like this—you created a hell of a lot of water damage, that's for sure. I'm no judge, but four vandalisms like this, your age, no prior record, the circumstances of the crime all point to a few years of probation. But not jail. Not for you, anyway."

Eddie looked perplexed, but Isaac's heart was pounding up his windpipe at the thought that Eddie would be free, free to keep working at Chum's, free to keep living his life.

"Besides, charges may never actually be pressed."

"How you figure that?" Eddie growled, searching the chief's face. "Those people would like to see me under the jail."

"Well, Eddie, I suspect all they want is their soggy houses repaired and ruined carpets paid for, that's all. First of all, they'd have to find out who did this. And I can tell you, you're the furthest person from anybody's mind." The chief slipped his hands into his front pockets and continued his slow pacing. "If they, by a long shot, did find out, and if they pressed charges, that might be too taxing on them. See, I'd have to notify the newspaper that our villain—you, sir—had, at long last, been captured. They'd ask, why'd he do it, and I'd say . . . "

Isaac jumped in, speaking with his hands. "You'd say because these people were members of the Klan," Isaac said, triumphant. It had been a roller coaster of a morning. The whole summer had been a pressure cooker. "You'd say they were members of the Klan who burned down Eddie's house and murdered . . . "

Isaac stopped short. He was too happy about this sordid thing. "You'd say they murdered his family," he added quietly. Isaac heard far-away laughter coming from the store.

"Which is why," the chief added slowly, "they might not be eager to press charges. They might not want the world to know."

"The world already knows," Isaac said. "Everybody around here—all the old-timers, anyway—they know. Mattie Thomson knows. Hank Grady knows."

"I didn't know," the chief said. "None of the newcomers know." The chief paused and arched his eyebrows like the big M at McDonalds. "They don't know in Norfolk." A slight smile eased across his face.

"That's right!" Isaac spouted. "I could call the Virginian-Pilot!"

"You won't do any such thing," Eddie barked. "You're not getting this. You're missing the whole point."

"Yes, I would, Eddie. If they pressed charges I'd do it in a heartbeat. I'd call the *Pilot*," Isaac said earnestly. "And I do get it, Eddie. I have a conscience too, you know. I care about what's right and wrong."

"They don't know in Richmond," the chief continued aloud to no one. "They don't know in Baltimore. The FBI doesn't know."

"We could call Tennyson right now," Isaac said. The wheels of his mind were spinning like cartwheels. "We could get them on hate crimes, on murder."

"Stop it. To hell with them," Eddie said. "Telling the world isn't going to bring my wife and daughter back."

Pigeons outside were flitting beneath the eaves.

"We're not talking about getting your wife and child back, Mr. Patrick. Unfortunately, nothing can do that. And I'm sorry," the chief said. "Very, very sorry."

"But we are talking about justice," Isaac said. "We are talking about what's fair. And Eddie, there's no way that it's fair that you go to jail. That's not brave, or noble, or right."

Each molecule of dust floating in that shadowed air seemed burdened by light. The three of them were silent for a long moment.

"You know," the chief finally said, "Isaac here has provided good information. Should an arrest be made, someone needs to collect the reward from P.O.T.S. Five thousand dollars."

"I don't want the money," Isaac sputtered. "I won't do anything to hurt Eddie."

"Son, I could be very wrong, but if any of these families do find out and do decide, against my law enforcement advice, to press charges, the information you've already provided is probably enough to warrant the reward."

"I told you," Isaac insisted. "I don't want it. Give it to Mattie Thomson. Give it to the church. Not to me. I did want it, a lot. But there are a million things more important—like Eddie."

"Oh," Eddie sighed dramatically. "I'm getting sick."

"Let me finish," Williams intoned. He waited for Isaac to calm down. "All's I'm saying is that Eddie might not be averse to making lemonade with lemons. I'm guessing Eddie wouldn't mind one bit your relieving Hank Grady and the fine people of P.O.T.S. of five thousand of their dollars."

In the lumberyard a forklift was beeping as it backed up. They were probably getting ready to load a truck. Any minute Will might come in to ask for help.

"If somebody is going to get money, might as well be Isaac," Eddie allowed. If he was trying to cover up his grin, he wasn't succeeding. He stood up, testing his bum leg. "Look, all this chit-chat is real nice," he said, rolling his head around stiffly, stretching his neck. "Somebody should have made hot tea and muffins. But daylight's wastin'. Chief, arrest me now, or come get me after five o'clock. I've got a lot to do today, and I'd better get started."

Reggie Williams stood flat-footed looking at Eddie. He seemed pleased with himself. "Are you going to leave town, Mr. Patrick?"

"And where would I go?"

"Are you a danger to yourself or anyone else?"

Eddie rolled his eyes.

"Are you a danger to anyone's house?"

Isaac still had several house-sitting days at the Jacksons', the last house left.

"Well?" the chief asked.

"Never again," Eddie said to the floor.

The chief turned to go. "I know where to find you," he said. "And you both know where to find me. I'm here to serve and protect." Chief Williams turned to go. "See you, fellas," he said over his shoulder as he sauntered out into the lumberyard.

The warehouse was quiet. Some days Isaac thought that the place was like a tomb. This morning it was full of back-lit dust chasing wisps of air and muted light. It was like a sanctuary.

"Look, Eddie, I just want to say—"

"—You've said enough," Eddie said. "You talk more than any kid I've ever known. And there's nothin' left to say." Eddie looked at Isaac squarely. "Thanks," he whispered.

Isaac nodded. He felt like he'd just hit a double with two men on base. He realized in a flash how hungry he was to play baseball again, where all that mattered was knocking the cover off the ball, running bases, scoring points, trying not to lose a throw from the shortstop in the sun slanting low over third.

He inhaled to speak, but Eddie shot him a hawkish glance. He had been going to say, "You're welcome." Isaac picked at a hangnail on his thumb, then asked, "So the FBI man is buying your land?"

"Not all of it," Eddie said. "Just part of it. Just a couple of acres way back from the road. It's above the creek that leads out to Wampum Bay. A nice piece of land under the trees."

Isaac recognized that spot immediately as the place where Eddie's house had burned down. He remembered the foundation bricks that he and Kate had stumbled upon on their picnic. He remembered how beautiful and quiet it was there. Isaac tried to picture the house with a clothesline, with a porch swing, a long dirt driveway leading between rows and rows of Silver Queen corn.

Eddie spoke quietly. He was in a faraway place, explaining to no one that he had already given Agent Tennyson a key to his barn and his blessing to try to fix his old Farmall tractor that hadn't turned over in nearly twenty years. He explained that Tennyson had a family, a wife and two kids. It was time a family lived on that land again, time something was made of that farm.

Eddie looked at Isaac. "I told him that you'd help him."

"Okay," Isaac said. "I guess I could chip in."

But Eddie wasn't listening.

"Lots needs to be done," Eddie continued. "I told him you get off from here at five o'clock and you're free on weekends, seeing how you don't have a girlfriend anymore to distract you."

"Who says that won't change?"

"A girl liking you?" Eddie thought about that for a long couple of seconds. "If it happens, and I have serious doubts, you could bring her along to help. I hope she's strong." Eddie held his coffeepot full of water and stood close to Isaac. They both regarded the picture of Eddie's family taken half a century before.

"She was very beautiful," Isaac said.

"When she first saw the tenant house my parents expected us to live in, I thought she'd start to cry. Would want to go back to Richmond that minute. But she just walked around the place, sizing it up." He poured the water into the machine and set the pot on the burner. He clicked it on and sat down on the metal chair that leaned. He stared at the first drops of coffee gurgling into the pot. "It was summer and it was hot. But under those trees it was green and cool. We walked out back, up the rise, to that creek. 'Mercy,' she said. 'This land is beautiful, Edward.'"

Eddie studied the lines of his hands, the cracked nails, the signs of work and age and sun. "I'll never forget those words," Eddie whispered. "From that day forward, I've been calling that trickle of water out back of that house Mercy Creek." Eddie looked at Isaac and smiled. He gave one more long look out the warehouse door.

"We've got work to do," Eddie said, winding up with difficulty into his gruff mode. He walked to the workbench. Isaac noticed a slight limp. He must be sore from their marathon walk the night before.

"We've done a lot of work already," Isaac said, looking around the warehouse. But he wasn't thinking about the warehouse or the deliveries or the neat stacks of wood or the swept store.

Eddie roughly bumped into Isaac as he took a deep whiff over the steaming coffeepot. He took the picture from Isaac's careful grip and pinned it on the wall above the time clock.

"We had every intention of growing old together. Seems I grew old all by myself," Eddie said. "With people like you being a pain in my aching back."

"Get used to it," Isaac said, heading to the door. "Yes, sir, we've done a lot of work together this summer, and we have a lot left to do." He knelt down in the sunlight to tie his shoes. He spoke without looking up. "Hey, Eddie, I'll be off on vacation week after next, and you'll have to cover for me while I'm gone. My dad and I are going up to Chincoteague for the pony penning."

"That's the first I ever heard of this, boy."

"My dad hasn't heard, either," Isaac said, standing, limbering up his back, spreading his legs, stretching. "I didn't know myself until recently, until a few minutes ago, actually. Some things come on you quick, you know? Chum knew when he hired me that Dad and I were likely to be gone a week. He said that was fine. Anyway, I'm going to go home right now and see if Dad can join me at the Duck Blind for breakfast this morning. We've got to get the ball rolling right away, see if Mrs. Watson's place is still available, that sort of thing. I'll be back right after breakfast, Eddie. Two hours, max. I've been so busy with other things, lately. But this can't wait."

"Your father won't have time for you this morning, I don't think," Eddie said. "When I drove by your place just now there were two guys installing one of those new-fangled satellite TV dishes. It appeared your dad was supervising the whole affair out in the front yard."

Isaac was only halfway listening. He was walking through the pool of sun filling the lumberyard, making slow circles with his arms, loosening his shoulders. He was rolling his neck left and right.

"Who's going to straighten the store this morning?" Eddie called out. "Chum likes it done first thing."

Isaac was in the middle of the lumberyard, jogging backwards for the gate. Eddie leaned against the warehouse door, trying to look angry.

"You could do it for me, couldn't you, Eddie? I'll owe you one. But watch out for Hank Grady. He's a little on the agitated side this morning."

But Eddie couldn't hear because Isaac had turned and was running. He was heading out the chain link gate towards the sidewalk and the alley next to Mattie Thomson's house. He was picking up speed over the asphalt, over the crooked curbs and browning grass, over the root-buckled concrete driveways and flowerbeds and garden hoses, over all the sadnesses and treasons and heartaches. Eddie wasn't going to jail. The cowards who'd have to press charges would have to stick their precious necks out too far.

Isaac imagined he could hear summer crowds in the metal stands at Norman Field shouting to their Little Leaguers, "Batter, batter, swing!" He was flying now, colors blurring past. He could feel the cold water of Mercy Creek where he and Kate had played and could see his mother's melting warm smile.

For the first time in a long time he felt like he was right where he belonged, right where he was supposed to be.

"Batter! Batter! Batter!" they yelled, stomping in the stands, clapping, smiling.

"SWING, BATTER, SWING!"

HUB CITY
PRESS

Hub City Press is an independent press in Spartanburg, South Carolina, that publishes well-crafted, high-quality works by new and established authors, with an emphasis on the Southern experience. We are committed to high-caliber novels, short stories, poetry, plays, memoir, and works emphasizing regional culture and history. We are particularly interested in books with a strong sense of place.

Hub City Press is an imprint of the non-profit Hub City Writers Project, founded in 1995 to foster a sense of community through the literary arts. Our metaphor of organization purposely looks backward to the nineteenth century when Spartanburg was known as the "hub city," a place where railroads converged and departed.

HUB CITY PRESS FICTION

New Southern Harmonies • Rosa Shand, Scott Gould,
Deno Trakas, George Singleton

Inheritance • Janette Turner Hospital, editor

In Morgan's Shadow • A Hub City Murder Mystery

Comfort & Joy: Nine Stories for Christmas • Kirk Neely

Through the Pale Door • Brian Ray

Expecting Goodness & Other Stories • C. Michael Curtis, editor

My Only Sunshine • Lou Dischler